WITHDRAWN
WORN, SOILED, OBSOLETE

Also by Patrick Dacey

We've Already Gone This Far

THE OUTER CAPE

THE OUTER CAPE

A Novel

Patrick Dacey

Henry Holt and Company
New York

Henry Holt and Company
Publishers since 1866
175 Fifth Avenue
New York, New York 10010
www.henryholt.com

Henry Holt® and ®® are registered trademarks of Macmillan Publishing Group, LLC.

Copyright © 2017 by Patrick Dacey
All rights reserved.
Distributed in Canada by Raincoast Book Distribution Limited

Library of Congress Cataloging-in-Publication Data

Names: Dacey, Patrick, author.
Title: The outer cape : a novel / Patrick Dacey.
Description: First edition. | New York : Henry Holt and Company, 2017. | Includes bibliographical references.
Identifiers: LCCN 2016037299| ISBN 9781627794671 (hardback) | ISBN 9781627794688 (electronic book)
Subjects: LCSH: Domestic fiction. | BISAC: FICTION / Literary. | FICTION / Family Life.
Classification: LCC PS3604.A226 O98 2017 | DDC 813/.6—dc23
LC record available at https://lccn.loc.gov/2016037299

Our books may be purchased in bulk for promotional, educational, or business use. Please contact your local bookseller or the Macmillan Corporate and Premium Sales Department at (800) 221-7945, extension 5442, or by e-mail at MacmillanSpecialMarkets@macmillan.com.

First Edition 2017

Designed by Meryl Sussman Levavi

Printed in the United States of America

10 9 8 7 6 5 4 3 2 1

This is a work of fiction. All of the characters, organizations, and events portrayed in this novel either are products of the author's imagination or are used fictitiously.

This book is dedicated to the memory of my mother;
Her love, her goodness, her grace.

But there is the inevitable return, we are forever going out and coming in, joining and abandoning, alone and together.

—William Goyen, *The House of Breath*

THE OUTER CAPE

PART I

ROBERT AND IRENE

1990

ONE

Robert Kelly had constructed the argument to put his wife on the defensive. It worked, as he knew it would, which, in a way, was even worse than having done nothing at all. So after Irene stomps around the bedroom, gathering together the stray pieces of clothing for tomorrow's laundry, Robert grabs her arms and pulls her toward him. She beats against his chest, then succumbs to his lips and tongue pressing against her neck. He yanks the straps of her dress down her arms, pushes up and sucks on her breasts, pulling hard on her nipples with his teeth. "Ow," she says. "Don't. Don't stop." He grabs her delicate hands in his giant paw and locks them behind her back with his grip, then nudges her toward the bed with his knee against her crotch. "Keep quiet," he says. On his knees, he pushes aside her underwear and laps the juice from her pussy, reaching up to put his fingers in her mouth when she starts to moan. Her legs shudder. He grabs her up from the bed and holds her like an offering. With his thick, hardened quadriceps, he pushes open her legs and enters her, gently at first, then harder, working as though with every thrust he adds another brick to a wall he is about to destroy. The veins in his arms pulse as he presses his fists down into the mattress, and his calves burn as he maneuvers his pelvis to reach the spot that makes her body quake, feeling himself grow thicker as she shouts the first syllable of his name like a cheer—Ra-Ra-Ra.

But Robert Kelly is no longer a fighter, a ballplayer, a soldier. Now he runs and plays golf and sells three-bedroom homes near the ocean in Wequaquet, Massachusetts. He only competes against himself.

After he comes, he rolls onto his back, and Irene moves to his side, her leg across his. She wipes the sweat from his forehead, plays with his chest hair, and picks at the dry skin on his nose. He lies there with his eyes open, spent, waiting for Irene to fall asleep.

When had they last made love like that? It felt like it had been before the children were born, twelve years ago. Nathan, then Andrew. Neither of them planned or expected, simply inevitable, Robert thought, whether he wanted them or not. He was glad they were boys.

But since the children, there were no more restaurants, no more visits to the city or late nights walking the sidewalks in New York, buzzed and careless, talking about their lives before they met (all those stories had been told and retold by now), or uninterrupted lovemaking (now they usually did it on their sides, faceless, quick, and because she said it felt slimy between her legs, he came in his palm to avoid ruining the sheets). They are directed toward the children, by the children, who don't know how good it had been for their parents, would never know, as long as they lived, how free and happy they once were.

But today was different. Today he had come home to the house a mess, and Irene in the carriage house, sketching a bowl of fruit—plums, maybe—and the boys covered in mud, lying half-awake in the living room, with the television so loud his own shouts for them to get in the bath barely reached them.

"That's enough, Robert," Irene had said, yelling back at him as he began to threaten the boys with a smack.

"What do you do all day?" he said to her, his mind wild with an unmerited madness. The site of dirt, dust, and the occasional bug in the kitchen made his head buzz and boil. He felt it was a sign of disrespect. The kids didn't respect him. His wife didn't respect him. The bugs didn't respect him.

"*Me*? That's supposed to be a joke, right? You're gone day and night, and the one afternoon you come home unannounced and the house isn't cleaned to your liking, now I do nothing?"

"Look at yourself, anyway, dressed in . . . what do you even call this? A smock? What are you trying to be? Some kind of artist? Still?"

"I'm not *trying* to be anything, Robert."

Because that was long ago now, fifteen years at least, when she had been an artist, and he sat on the edge of their double bed in the apartment above the Cuban restaurant they first shared in New York, listening to the yipping dog next door combined with the blaring horns outside—peaceful, the noise, something you could get used to if you were sleeping with a beautiful woman—and she finally revealed her work to him, and he reluctantly expressed interest, may have said, "This one is intriguing," not because it wasn't, but because he didn't know if it was, and when she had asked him why, he grew red in the face and she kissed him on the mouth and neck, and bit at his ear and said, "I love you for not knowing why."

Full of love then, full of a kind of disgust now.

He said with a kind of cool indifference, "You're a phony, that's what you are."

He barely felt the blue and white porcelain creamer strike his forehead until later, after his brow took five stitches, and the lump throbbed with pain. But he remembered how quick Irene had been, to grab it from beside the coffeepot and fling it across the kitchen island. And just as quickly as he went down, she was there beside him with a wet cloth, helping him to his feet, to the car, to the emergency room. She had called to the older of their boys, Nathan, to take care of the house while they were gone.

Now, in bed, after the boys had fallen asleep, and Robert had taken advantage of Irene's repentant guise, exhausted from the sex, the arguing, the childish fear he had of emergency rooms, Irene crossed her leg over his, and he could smell the thick perfume of her after-sex, the taste of him on her breath as she spoke.

"Let's agree again never to fight like that, especially when the children are in the house."

He knew they had heard them from the bathtub, saw the blood on the hand that had covered the wound when he had thrust his finger out and shouted for them to stay in their rooms.

"We're so lucky, Robert. Aren't we?"

Weren't they? They didn't have to worry about money or their sons' health or civil unrest. They were sheltered in the best way.

"But maybe that's the problem," Robert said. "Maybe we need a spark."

"Those stitches weren't enough?" Irene said, and smiled.

"You know what I mean."

"I don't, Robert. I'm not happy. But I'm not unhappy."

To say something like that was worse than being a phony, Robert thought. It meant you didn't care what you were.

When his father's health had begun to fail two years ago, she had been the one to push Robert to take control of the family building business. She had been sure then that settling down on

Cape Cod would bring stability to their lives, order, and with stability and order, happiness.

For Robert, crossing over the Sagamore Bridge was like crossing from one world to another, and to return to the Cape was to deny every natural instinct in a body crying for him to stay on the other side.

Ever since he had graduated college in '74, Robert had been selling paper products for Mobile Corp. He used the same tools of salesmanship his father had taught him when he was a kid, the ones he had used to convince restaurant managers and hotel owners that they needed his supplies.

"Let's say you suddenly run out of tissue paper and towels," he'd proffer with a young and winsome smile. "Now you have everyone's germs on your tables and bar stools, infected food goods, sick workers, health code violations. . . . I could go on. Point is, your future could be full of glory or garbage. Really, I shouldn't have to convince you to keep clean. You look respectable to me."

He had made a decent living as a single guy in a studio apartment in Hell's Kitchen. But once married and with Nathan on the way, Jesus, decent wasn't good enough anymore. He took higher-paying sales jobs with Mobile Corp that allowed him to work from an office but meant they had to move from one uninteresting and depressing city to another. In Richmond, Virginia, they rented a house for nearly half what their apartment cost in New York, a brick rancher with a big yard and a carport. But it was summer, and the local stores had run out of air-conditioning units, and the fans only made them hotter. One day, while Robert was at work, Irene started on the laundry that had been piling up in the corner of their bedroom. After dropping the whites in the washing machine, twisting and pulling the knob, her clothes stuck to her bulging stomach and fattened breasts.

She pushed back the wet hairs that stuck to her forehead. She had the sensation of walking through the shallow end of a pool as she tried to make it to the freezer to cool down, and fainted just in time for her head to miss the edge of the counter. Robert found her on his lunch break and called for an ambulance. She woke in the hospital, panicked about the baby, was assured everything was fine, just heat exhaustion, happens all the time here in the South.

"Well, guess where I'm never living again?" she said to the doctor, while looking at Robert.

They moved to Dover, then Camden, then Hartford, and finally had spent most of the past year in Rochester, in an apartment not unlike the one in New York, only larger, and above a Laundromat. Irene had gone to the local Goodwill and asked to have the necessary pieces of furniture delivered to their new apartment; then, with careful planning, and three or four cans of paint, she built a space for bright colors to combat the stillness created by whoever had lived or died here last. She painted and repainted the walls, put up new wallpaper, changed the curtains. All of these changes had little effect on Robert. He recognized a new pattern, but the vibrancy of color was lost on him. He sensed Irene's unhappiness, her moving away from him into busying herself with never-ending projects. She'd begun to exclude him from plans with the kids. Saturday mornings she would be up early, the boys dressed, already at the door when he woke, saying, "We're going out to the lake for the day," and leaving him there to wonder if he should follow or stay put, if he was part of his own family or not.

Robert's future, what Irene would accept as a future, was as clear to him as a silver star at twilight: first the house, then furniture and kitchenware and linens, country club gatherings, clam bakes, college tuition payments, one week all-inclusive resort stays, life insurance, retirement, bird watching or some other type of bullshit hobby, a condo in Florida, and a grave beneath a flat stone. He shivered.

"They want me in Kansas City," he had told Irene.

"Missouri? Do I look like a woman who belongs in Missouri?"

"I don't know. Do you?"

"You know how they pronounce Missouri in Missouri? *Mis-ery*. Because that's what it is."

So it was settled. He could see it in her eyes. He had started this life with her and, up until now, hadn't been tested. Robert still remembered in New York after they had first met, how she could get a cab by standing off the curb and letting her elbows fly out behind her, like wings rising. In 1988, just before Independence Day, Robert had handed in his two-week notice at Mobile Corp.

The kids then were ten and eight. Andrew, the younger one, had his eyes closed as they crossed over the bridge. His older brother, Nathan, punched his arm.

"Quit being such a pussy," he said.

"Nathan!" Irene shouted. Then to Andrew, "Honey, look at the boats down there. Whoever counts the most wins a prize."

They sat up and watched the sails sink in and puff out, the flumes of white wash in the wake of churning motors.

"How many do you see?" Irene asked, and in his nervous excitement—at a prize, a treat—Nathan stretched his neck and scanned the water, shouting out, "Four, five, six." He knew Andrew wouldn't be able to see past him, while also trying to count the boats on his own side.

Irene passed back the last doughnut from the half dozen they had bought in Milford, a jelly cream. Nathan ate his prize with regret—he felt his father's eyes scan the bulge of his stomach in the rearview mirror. But also his brother knew he had cheated and that he was only trying to impress Mom and Dad. Nathan offered the last bite to Andrew, who took the piece, crushed it in his palm, and threw it out the window.

The Wagoneer was stacked so high with suitcases and bedding and small pieces of furniture, Robert had to use the side mirrors in order to see the cars to their left. As they descended onto the peninsula, there was a drumming underneath the hood, then the sharp tapping like a clunky washing machine as the Wagoneer picked up speed. To Robert, the noises of his old Wagoneer made it sound as though the bridge were collapsing behind them. Technically, the Cape is an island. Without the bridge, you would need a ferryboat to take you across to the mainland, where each village has its Main Street and Sea Street and old barns renovated into antique stores or pricey restaurants with stuffed quail on the menu. The farther out you go, the narrower the roads get, the closer the ocean, so that at night, when there are only one or two cars passing by, you can hear the sloshing of the fishing boats in Wequaquet Harbor, hear the waves roll and crash and draw back into the sea.

Irene rolled down her window and stuck her arm out, letting the wind push back on her hand. The smell of salt and hot sand swept through the car. She inhaled and exhaled, relieved. Then she looked back at the children, Andrew with his arms crossed and eyes closed, Nathan sucking the powder off his fingers.

The wood-paneled Wagoneer hit the dip at the end of the bridge, then whipped down the tree-lined highway, sand swirling in its wake.

Robert and Irene were at peace for a while, still in love, gracious and kind to each other. Then they grew angry and aggressive, urging each other toward bitterness. Now, though, what lingers is a stale emotion, a sense of love he recognizes in the way

Irene smells when she gets out of the shower, or, still, even with an extra thirty pounds, the careful way in which she dresses, slowly, so that none of the clothing bunches or wrinkles. Sometimes she kisses him just so, and he feels what it was like to kiss her, Irene Duffy, the girl he had met in her father's bar, when he welcomed uncertainty. Embraced it. And fell in love.

TWO

All the following week it rained. Robert took the week off to nurse his head, and he slept the best he had in years—he took two Nembutals before bed and said peace to the world. The boys were in and out of the house, making a mess Irene eventually let be. Her nerves had never been stretched so tight. She had felt the violence in her when she threw the creamer at Robert's head, and it gave her power.

When Robert finally decides to rejoin the family, it is Sunday, and again it is raining. There has been flooding near the shore but no reports of structural damage to houses or boats. Irene reads him yesterday's paper, as she has done the last four mornings after he had complained of headaches, even though the headaches had weakened and were met by a slow throbbing ping he welcomed over the noise of the kids and his wife's complaints about things needing to be done or things that hadn't been done when needed. Irene reads him the story of a tourist who had gone missing. His family was stuck in the Farley House Bed and Breakfast on Sea Street. But it turned out he hadn't been missing. He had jumped aboard a fishing boat leaving from the harbor two days ago. The captain, once aware of the man's identity, informed the authorities the man was safe. He had just needed a break.

"Can you imagine?" Irene says.

Robert knows better than to answer.

After breakfast, he drives to the Dunkin' Donuts on the other side of the Sagamore Bridge and sits with the *New York Post*, examining the point spreads for the NBA games. He's been on a monthlong losing streak. He feels he's due. When he finishes his coffee, he calls into Barney the bookie, an old curly-headed, cigar-smoking ancient who has been around since Robert's father was placing bets on the Irish. Then he drives along the canal, and into Sandwich, where much of the land is untouched. Ruthless zoning restrictions have been put in place to protect the habitats of plovers and terns. Birds, for Christ's sake, Robert thinks. What about people?

When Robert returns home, the boys have taken their mattresses off their beds and stacked one on top of the other, then placed their pillows in front of the mattresses. He notices the Magic Marker Xs on the cotton pillowcases, and they pause in their made-up game when he comes down the hall. His childlike curiosity allows them to proceed to hurl their old stuffed animals and action figures at the Xs. The boys soon begin pushing each other into the pillows until Nathan, who is big for being only twelve, gets too rough, and Andrew, two years younger, small and thin, smacks his head against the top mattress and falls to his knees.

"Dad?" he says, looking up at Robert through his fogged glasses.

"That's what you get," Robert says and walks outside.

Irene has lost her patience and is sitting on the back step smoking a joint, which Robert has asked her more than once to think about giving up, now that they are settled for good. He begins to say something, but having heard the door open, Irene throws up her free hand.

"Please, take these kids out of this house," she says. "I need a friggin' break."

"Where do you want me to take them?" Robert asks.

"I don't know. Somewhere. Anywhere. I'm losing my mind."

"Okay, calm down. I'll take them to the movies."

"Not some R-rated movie, either. Last time Andrew had nightmares."

"Well, I refuse to pay money to see a bunch of cartoons whacking each other off."

"It doesn't have to be a *cartoon*, Robert."

"I'll check what's playing."

The boys sit in the backseat during the ride to the theater, battling for head room in order to see the handheld video-game screen one or the other taps at furiously.

The two films playing at the Cape Cinema Double are *Ernest Goes to Camp*, which is about some yokel, a grown man who, as the title aptly states, goes to camp, and the other is *Full Metal Jacket*, which, according to the *Herald*, is supposedly one of the most accurate depictions of the Vietnam War. After reading that review three weeks ago, Robert has been eager to see the film, but Irene hates violent movies, especially war movies—she had vomited a quarter of the way through *Apocalypse Now*.

Not that Robert had been *in* the war.

Close enough, he tells himself.

One night, when he was seventeen years old, his father had given him a choice. He was standing in the hallway, in his grass-stained baseball uniform, with his sweaty ball cap under his arm. His father stood and turned and looked at him.

"Score?"

"Seven-two."

"Did you win?"

"No."

His father didn't care for baseball, said that if one of your greats of all time was a three-hundred-pound sack of fat who could barely run the bases without coughing up a lung, then you couldn't call yourself a sport.

"Get cleaned up," he had said. "We need to talk about your future."

Robert nodded and jogged upstairs.

In the shower, he got the water so hot it scorched his skin until he was numb all over. His younger brother, Brian, was out with friends, drinking cheap beer and flirting with girls. Red had no faith Brian would end up anything other than a cog. He didn't have brains, or discipline, or a sense of timing. "You got your mother's genes," he had said more than once, and Brian would grin, not understanding his father meant to insult him. Robert, on the other hand, wasn't allowed to leave the house unless his father said so, and always it was to play sports or help out at a job site.

Robert's sister, Maureen, was standing in the doorway of her room with a towel wrapped around her breasts and her hair bunched up under a shower cap. She'd been growing her hair for the past year, and when it was down, it went nearly to her thighs. She was tall and lithe and moved through the house like a force no one knew how to rein in. Robert envied her. The scented candles she had burning were unable to cover the ripe odor of weed sneaking into the hallway from behind her bedroom door.

"Leave any hot water for me?" she said.

"I can smell it in the hall," Robert said.

"You look like a lobster," she said and got closer and put her hands on him and gripped his arms. "I'm going to crack you open and eat you all up." She nibbled at his skin and grinned mischievously as he pushed her away. When the bathroom door shut and the lock was applied, he heard her start to sing something, something, how did it go, that song she was always singing back then?

"The way I see it," his father started as soon as Robert pulled the chair under him at the kitchen table. The two were separated by the corner at the table's head and side, which still had the scratches from the stray kitten Brian brought home a decade ago. He had found it in the woods one Sunday, lost, frightened, and had brought it home and kept it with him through the night. She had slept docilely, occasionally pawing behind her ear, and he had thought she'd be a welcome addition to the family. But after being fed, she clawed up the furniture and pooped on the rug and made her last stand there on the table's edge, hanging on as his father tried to wrench it loose. Then, frustrated by its pathetic cries, he had squeezed her stomach until her paws hung over the edge of the table, limp, like wet leaves from a tree branch. He had looked at the children and his wife and the mess on the floor and table and said, "Most strays get much worse." Then he took the kitten's body, yet unnamed, out in back to the brush pile, tossing her there like a sack of grass clippings. In the middle of the night, Robert had woken to use the bathroom and, through the hall window, saw his mother in the backyard, shovel in her hands, digging a hole.

"Look at me," his father said.

Robert moved his eyes from the scratches in the table and followed his father's sun-reddened neck to his thinning, gingery hair and back down the slope of his forehead to the tiny crease between his eyes, where he kept his gaze.

"The way I see it," his father continued, "is you have two choices. Either you get into Notre Dame or you sign up for the army. I won't pay for a school I don't respect and the army needs strong boys who can't find a place in traditional sport."

Robert had argued then about his shoes and equipment, the Pennsylvania basketball his father bought him that always lost air after a few dribbles, the cleat-less cleats he wore for baseball, and the holes in his socks that helped to breed a terrible foot fungus that he battled all through football season. After the Thanksgiving Day game that year, he spent a week lying on his bed with his feet propped in the air by the A–B and G–H entries of the encyclopedia set no one in the house had ever read. His mother rubbed liniment oil between his toes, letting the fungus cook like a frying steak until it was dry and peeling.

"Which would you prefer?" his father asked now.

"School," Robert said.

"You're not as stupid as you look, you know that?"

His father gave him the application and told him to fill it out and said he would mail it the following Monday.

"Make sure your handwriting is clean and your grammar's correct. The way those gooks are fighting us over there, you'll wind up dead if you don't get in."

College had been a fearless time, at first. He excelled in statistics, advanced calculus, and courses in pre-law and finance management. The language of his professors was exact. But he could not grasp the writings of Saint Augustine or the nineteenth-century impressionists. They spoke to him about a kind of love in something he had yet to comprehend, if he ever would at all. Sitting in his dorm room, with his roommate, Frank, writing in a notebook at his desk, Robert read, "What, then, is my God?

What, I ask, unless the Lord God? Who is Lord but the Lord? Or who is God but our God?" He flung the book across the room. Frank shot up out of his chair.

"For fuck's sake, man," Frank said.

"Exactly," Robert said.

In high school, he had trained himself to run and dive and hit. He needed to feel that aggression again. So he joined the rugby club, first as a lock, then as a fly-half. He bulldozed over the other players. His legs were cut and thighs bruised. That night, at the captain's house on the top of the hill near the lake, he stood in the loud cry of hairy beasts shouting "Oy!" and crushing beer cans against their foreheads, while girls slid topless down the hill toward the lake, and John Bonham beat the hell out of "Moby Dick," and sensed a kind of peace that never came with prayer or study.

He was part of a tribe, fearless and unaccountable.

In early November, during a game against Michigan, he broke his wrist on another player's kneecap during a scrum. His hand limp, he lost his balance and rolled over to protect his wrist. Then the player on the other team drove the metal spike on the sole of his shoe into Robert's leg. When the other player ripped his foot away, it tore the skin back like a thin peel of apple.

The following week, the team brought over girls from Saint Mary's. They gathered on the beach at St. Joseph's Lake drinking from kegs they'd rolled down hills and set up in the light from church candles. Robert made out with a tall, blond girl named Brittany. She played with the curls in his hair and let him put his fingers inside her. Someone finally got a stereo hooked up in the boat house. It was 1969—"Crystal Blue Persuasion," "Bad Moon Rising," "Get Back"—every song a dream or a warning. Even before his injury, Robert couldn't dance on two legs, let alone one. Brittany found someone who could. By the time he realized he was drunk and alone, the cops raided the party. Slowed by the pain in his leg, Robert was caught and brought up for dismissal for disorderly conduct unbecoming of a student of Catholic values.

He was disciplined with academic leave for the spring. But he wouldn't go home. He stayed in South Bend washing dishes at Corby's. Why be afraid? he thought. Fear of the draft was spurring crying jags from bull-necked boys, fights between men young and old, survivors of the last war and the soon-to-be-dead, protests through the pedestrian suburbs of South Bend.

On July 1, just as he tied the apron around his waist to start his shift, he heard the dates being called on the radio in the kitchen. Someone turned up the volume. Robert stood brave against the numbers. Everyone was trying to avoid Vietnam; he had decided to embrace the fuck show. "Call it," he said, catching from the corners of his eyes the turning heads at the bar. "Don't provoke the sons of bitches," someone said. But, by urging his number to be called, he felt the opposite had happened. He had shielded himself from the massacre with his own insanity. "Whatever," Robert said, and, as he turned to start on the dishes, he heard the announcer call his number. He paused in the kitchen doorway to catch his breath, then turned on the water and started washing the large plates first, then the smaller ones, then the beer mugs and glasses. Walking back to his room in snow on the other side of the lake, he passed two priests with their hands clasped in front of them, solemn in the eyes. He stopped by a bench, put his hand on the cold wood, and vomited.

In the morning he called home and explained to his father what had happened in South Bend and why he thought the army would be good for him.

The call was short.

"I can't say I'm surprised," his father said.

"When I return, I'll do better," Robert said.

"If you return," his father had said and hung up.

Vietnam was a death sentence. Robert knew it even then. If you made it home in one piece—or most of your pieces—the person you used to be was gone. Once back in the world, Jake Cunningham lingered near the football field and smoked cigarettes. He'd been two years ahead of Robert in high school, played linebacker, had a knockout for a girlfriend. He had gotten into dope over there and had a bullet graze his ear. Now he was part deaf. All his fame had disappeared. Then he disappeared.

Robert's injury had healed fully by the time his group finished basic training and was preparing to get their assignments overseas. He had already written his brother and sister and told them how he loved them and that he hoped they loved him, too, and that he didn't have any regrets (which was a lie). He did not say everything he wanted to say because there was still a part of him that believed he would not be killed—the same part that had embraced the show. He sealed the envelope and asked one of the sergeants to send it if something were to happen to him. The sergeant said that if something were to happen to him it would only be a result of not paying attention during training (which was also a lie).

Robert was easily the worst shot in his class, if he was even able to put together his rifle in time to get a shot off during marksmanship training. He often had his rifle in pieces like a sad child unable to fit together the pieces of a jigsaw puzzle. You needed a certain kind of grace and rhythm to assemble a weapon used to blow people apart. And when he finally did get the thing built, his shots missed left and right and high. His drill sergeant was keen to say that ammo was a much more important commodity than life, before ordering Robert to give him fifty push-ups, which he gave and gave, day in and day out. So many, that by the time basic was over, his chest was the size of an ape's and he'd added three inches of solid muscle to his biceps. Because of his size, Robert was a nightmare in a barroom brawl, though at that size, putting together his rifle had become near impossible.

The day Robert's troop was given their assignments, they took a knee in the barracks and waited with violent restraint. He remembered the sounds of heavy breathing, cracked knuckles, and a dripping faucet in the adjacent latrines. No one moved when their name was called and they were given their posts. Already Robert had begun to design a more complete kind of afterlife than the one he was taught in catechism school, one where he had his pick of beautiful women and there was plenty of beer and he could watch movies and play sports and never get old, which he thought was an advantage to dying young.

Then he heard the executive officer say, "Robert W. Kelly, Stuttgart, Germany," and with his giant hand, he covered his face and spread his fingers, as though donning a torn mask.

Later someone asked him if his head hurt from the bag of horseshoes he'd been hit with. Someone else took a dump in his footlocker. Not until many years later did Robert think about those young men, with whom he had gone through training. By then he couldn't remember most of their names or faces. But he remembered their eyes when they were told where they were going, and this is what truly scared him, not their lean, trembling bodies but the roomful of eyes.

In the pubs and dives and basement card rooms of Stuttgart, Germany, Robert felt free and unaccountable—one and the same in his mind—and he'd fight and fuck and stumble over the snow-covered cobblestones with bruised ribs, scraped knuckles, and a warm heat in his groin, making his way back to the garrison, slipping the guard five bucks, until the MPs were on to him for continuously violating curfew, and, because nobody wanted the job Robert had, the MPs gave him a few knocks in the ear and a demerit that would stay on a record he would later have pulled up for the first and only time, when he was on his way to prison, and this by the state's attorney, who, being a Vietnam veteran himself, used it against Robert's lawyer's plea for leniency.

Robert spent most of his days working behind a raised school desk, like Bob Cratchit, in an office the size of a Datsun, handing out six-month job notices to soldiers returning from Vietnam. One morning, a man named Reynolds came in and sat down in the chair across from him. His face shined with sweat, and his eyes bulged out of their sockets. Robert had seen others like him, men who needed something to erase the recent past. Robert only had janitor duty at the gymnasium left for this work cycle. Reynolds didn't look like a janitor. He was bullnecked, muscles strained tight in his white T-shirt, and a torso as strong and thick as a red oak. He looked like he was in the business of destroying things and not cleaning up afterward.

"You got something else for me, pal?" Reynolds said.

"I'm looking." Robert flipped through a file full of blank paper, an act he learned early on, followed by, "Don't see anything, unless you want my job," which no soldier did because, to them, what Robert did was a joke.

Reynolds lit a cigarette. He smoked a quarter of it in one long inhale and flicked the ash on the papers on Robert's desk.

"You think you're lucky, don't you?" he said, his gaze like a weapon.

"It's out of my control," Robert replied. This, he felt, was the only explanation he could give that wouldn't further the confrontation.

"You're unlucky," Reynolds shouted. "Hear me?"

Robert looked at the man. A long, snakelike vein ran from his forehead to his left eye.

"I killed everything. I killed frogs and gooks and birds and boars. You don't know how that feels, man. To walk across the earth with all this death around you and see the sky's just the same sky."

Reynolds stubbed the cigarette out on the sole of his boot. He took the card from Robert and then spit on his desk and walked out.

Outside the Cape Cinema Double, Robert lets his cigarette go down to his fingers and the slight burn against his nail causes him to flinch and drop the butt in a puddle. The boys are waiting for him to pay the lady at the ticket booth. They kill yellow and blue and red creatures every day, Robert begins to reason. What's the difference between killing something in a video game and seeing someone get killed in a movie?

The lobby is filled with children in wet boots chasing after each other, under and over the ropes, until one plump kid no more than six or seven catches his foot on the rope, smacks his face on the ground, and rolls around screaming until his father picks him up by the collar and drags him out of the lobby like a piece of dry cleaning. The madness stops as the rest of the children wait for the four-thirty showing of *Ernest Goes to Camp* while the fathers sit on benches under the awning outside and smoke. If Hollywood really wanted to know what hell was like, Robert thinks, they'd be in the Cape Cinema Double on a cold, rainy Sunday afternoon.

"Three for the camp movie," Robert says.

He pays the lady at the counter and takes the tickets and shuffles the boys over toward the restrooms.

"Now listen, we're not going to see that dopey movie, okay?"

The boys' eyes grow wide with delight and, possibly, fear. The word "dopey" has some magic effect on their brains, and even though they *do* want to see *Ernest Goes to Camp*, they're now entranced by Robert's secret plan.

"We're going to tell your mother we saw it, but we're really going to see this other one. It'll be a lot better, trust me. And there'll be a camp, too. A boot camp, which isn't the same, but in this camp you get to shoot guns and say bad words. Doesn't that sound better?"

The boys nod like puppets. They don't fully understand all that has gone into this open disregard for their mother's wishes. Not that they need to. They're *his boys*. If he wants to take them to a war movie, then for fuck's sake, that's what he's going to do.

The movie has already started and the theater packed with big, long bodies. The three of them have to hunker down in the very last seats in the front row, directly opposite the giant screen.

"It's like having the theater all to ourselves," Robert says, ushering the boys into their seats.

He takes the aisle seat and hunches down. This close, it's like the soldiers are firing their rifles right at them. The noise is so loud that at one point Robert turns and sees Andrew with his fingers in his ears.

"Put your hands in your lap," Robert whispers harshly.

"What?" Andrew says loudly.

Robert grabs his hands and presses them down onto Andrew's thighs.

"I have to go to the bathroom," Andrew says.

"It can wait."

"But I really have to go, Dad. I won't get lost. There's no missing where we are."

"Fine. But make sure you use a stall."

Nathan, transfixed, doesn't register his brother's exit. The drill sergeant is yelling at the soldiers, saying bad words Nathan knows but putting them together in ways he'd never heard before. Then a group of soldiers beat Private Pile with soap because they had to do extra push-ups. Robert shares some of his Junior Mints with Nathan and whispers that he had a drill sergeant just like this one, a real prick.

Is it over his son's head? Robert thinks. Some of it, sure. *"This is my rifle, this is my gun. This is for fighting, this is for fun!"* But when the audience laughs, Nathan laughs, and at least he's having a good time and will probably remember that line so he can use it in school to make friends. Robert knows it's cool when kids say they're allowed to see R-rated movies, and part of him would still rather be cool than loved.

Robert is so lost in thought that he doesn't catch on to what's happening in the latrines toward the end of the first half of the movie: Private Pile on the toilet, shouting at no one, those dead eyes and the rifle at his side. But he sees it now, as though the images of the film from beginning to now have caught up to him in one whole burst of light, and when Private Pile presents the gun barrel to his mouth and pulls down on the trigger, it's too late for Robert to cover Nathan's eyes before the blood and brains hit the wall. Nathan screams and bats his ears. The sound is worse than the gunshot. Both theaters can hear it. Robert tries to hold him still, but Nathan won't stop batting his head and even strikes Robert in the nose. Robert picks him up as he used to when Nathan was an infant. He holds the back of Nathan's head against his shoulder and looks toward the fuzzy theater wall half-jogging up the aisle and outside under the metal awning.

For a while, Nathan cries and snorts and rubs his chubby face on Robert's shoulder. Then Robert stands him up and swipes his thumb under Nathan's eyes. He's been crying so hard his face is red and puffy. Robert tries to apologize. He tells him what he saw isn't real, it's just a movie.

"But," Nathan says, "someone must've done that for it to be in a movie, or else someone thought it up in their head and isn't that real, too?"

Robert doesn't have an answer. Perhaps because the answer is too simple. A grown man can go to camp again just as a private in the army can blow his own brains out.

On the ride home, Nathan sits in the backseat staring out the window. Even when Andrew has topped his own high score on the Game Boy and tries to show his brother, Nathan doesn't react.

"You didn't come back to our seats," Robert says to Andrew.

Robert looks in Andrew's eyes in the rearview mirror sternly, and his son's face twitches. Well, shit, he thinks, not you, too.

"Go ahead," Robert says, "tell us what Ernest did when he went to camp. We need to get our stories straight."

Later that night, Nathan eats his food in silence, while Andrew architects brilliant, absurdist buildings out of the starches on his plate, then uses his spoon to knock them down.

After an episode of *Cheers*, Robert and Irene move about the house as though preparing it for another family who will be arriving in the morning. Irene tidies up the newspapers and magazines, and stuffs the Nintendo set and controllers behind the television. She is back to being a homemaker, which makes Robert feel even more guilt than the day before. He doesn't know what he wants her to be anymore.

After she empties the half-full glasses and puts them in the dishwasher, they smoke a last cigarette on the front step under starlight.

"This has felt like the longest day," Irene says, taking a drag.

"The rain finally stopped," Robert says.

"That's true."

In bed, Robert feels Irene's leg rub against him. Already her legs are prickly again. She says something. Then she says, "Kiss me, Robert."

But it isn't the same as last week: there's nothing at stake.

"Not tonight," he says.

"You're such a bore," she hisses, then turns over.

Robert spends the following morning in the trailer at the subdivision going over blueprints and piles of documents from council meetings.

There's a knock at the flimsy trailer door.

"It's open," Robert says.

Candice Dunning, the wife of his foreman, Mike, stands on the last wooden step, her head peeking inside. Robert sees the glow of her face in the rectangular light shining through the trailer windows. She's a pretty thing, but so are certain flowers and pop songs and moonscapes. Otherwise, she's Mike's wife, the hot blonde Mike brought to the company's first Memorial Day cookout. She's a married woman who up until recently Robert had maybe two or three conversations with in the last eighteen months he'd known the couple. She is soft and sweet, and a mother. She makes decent pasta salad and has an annoying cackle for a laugh. Her daughters look healthy. Robert is proud of that.

"I went to the model first," she says.

"Mike isn't here," Robert says.

"I know. I wasn't looking for Mike."

Robert realizes that now. She is inside the trailer. She has never been to the subdivision before.

"What can I do?"

"Be quick," she says, and he smells her cinnamon-flavored gum and something else, something distinct and overpowering, like boxes of ripe fruits stacked together at a farmer's market.

He stays seated, lifts up her dress, and pulls down her panties over her cross-thatched shoes. Then he breathes in as much of her as he can stand. It's that smell, rare and fleeting, he's trying to take home with him, because, as before, this, he tells himself, is the last time.

THREE

Irene remembers how when they first pulled down the pebbled drive of the house on Main, Minnie Rodgers, the real estate agent with whom she'd been speaking for weeks leading up to their move, met Robert and the kids and her on the wide front porch. Minnie had been holding, by the tip of her fingers, a silver cage with a blue canary inside. Her gray hair was cupped around her narrow head like two elephant ears.

"Oh, good, you made it!" she said with affected cheer. "Don't mind Annabelle here, I take her everywhere."

Minnie Rodgers guided them through the front door, separating Robert from Irene and the boys.

"So, this is what we call a classic Greek colonial. The house had been built by a sea captain named Nichols. He and his wife and their ten children lived here through three generations."

As they went through each room, Irene managed to ask and have answered every question she had jotted down on her little notepad. She was concerned with the upkeep of such a large home. She didn't want to waste her days sweeping the floors, vacuuming the bedrooms, and polishing the tables and countertops. In her mind, she was still a working artist. These last twelve years had just been a long interlude, a time to gather perspective. Settling down meant now she could paint again. Motherhood wasn't her intended life's work. You didn't get much credit for raising good kids, and all the blame when they turned out bad.

"The Nicholses had a housekeeper," Minnie Rodgers said. "In fact, they had two."

"Has no one lived here since?" Robert asked.

"Of course, of course. There was a pilot and his family here last. He died, sadly, in a car accident. I believe the widow said she was moving back to Ohio, or something. Before that, the house was a museum showcasing the Nichols family's antiques and artifacts, once the Nicholses had lived out their final days here and none of the three boys had any boys of their own. There was something in the deed, though, that made it so that if the museum did not turn a profit, then it could be put back on the market."

Robert had pointed to the chipped paint on the exterior, the large drum in back that meant the house was heated with oil, the split deck boards and rotting wood and single-paned windows.

But the history, the molding on the stairwell, the large open kitchen, the bay window in the dining room, which let in light from the early evening sun, and the two guest rooms for entertaining friends and family on long weekends—all of it was so overwhelmingly agreeable to Irene's sense of what a home should be that when they were back in the Wagoneer, on their way to Robert's father's house, she already felt like the captain's house on Main Street had been waiting for them all this time.

But now, large as their house is, Irene feels, with all the things they've collected in the past two years, that she can barely breathe. Panicked by a creeping claustrophobia, she spends most of the day in the carriage house out back, with just her stool and easel and a view of the dripping leaves on the trees outside the windows. She smokes a little grass in a metal pipe she keeps hidden in a broken floorboard, while looking at the sketch of the bowl full of nectarines she had begun weeks ago. She sits on her stool and blows the smoke up the flue, then tears the page from the sketchbook and burns it to mask any lingering odor. Just like the drawing of the woman lying on her side, and the outline of a man with his hand on his hip and his finger pointing down toward a child, and the falcon's nest she had seen on the pole at the bridge crossing over Oyster Bay, she cannot remember the story behind the beginning, the reason she had picked up her pencil and started in the first place. They are like bones to her now.

An ocean of pink colors the sky outside. "Oh," she says. Then she remembers she had better start dinner before Robert gets home.

In the kitchen, she heats up a frying pan of olive oil, pounds the chicken cutlets, rolls them in flour, and covers them in bread crumbs. Then she steams broccoli and carrots over a double boiler. She drinks a beer and listens to Neil Young's *Everybody Knows This Is Nowhere*. While the chicken is cooking, she goes to put back on her wedding ring but notices it is missing. Now she sees Andrew sauntering around the kitchen with one of her long scarves around his neck, showing off to an invisible gallery of jealous women the oversized pear-cut diamond engagement ring Robert had bought her on credit years ago.

"Oh my," he cries in their adoring voices. "He didn't! Oh, yes, he did."

Andrew has a hand on his hip and those glasses as big as ski goggles cocked sideways on his face.

"Sweetie, don't lose that," Irene says.

"This? Oh, this is nothing. *You should see ma au-to-mo-bile,*" he says, ramping up a Southern accent he could have only picked up from his recent addiction to Huckleberry Hound.

She smacks him on the butt.

"Get out of the kitchen," she says, laughing. "And give me back my ring."

She puts on *Surrealistic Pillow*, and turns up the volume.

"Feed your head," Grace Slick sings. What year was that? Irene thinks. 'Sixty-eight, 'Sixty-nine. *"Feed your head."* But at the age of thirty-eight, when the good drug years are behind her, when a little pot to relax and a dab of coke when she and Robert are on vacation is about all she can handle. It's hard to return to that place of openness she once had, when her head could be fed by the euphoria that surrounded her. Whatever was inside most people during those years has now spilled out, replaced with rational logistics, the fastest route from point A to point B, and her greatest fear is her greatest irony, that she is somewhat comforted by the fact that she is no different than most people.

Irene calls for Nathan and Andrew to set the table. Nathan plods down the stairs reluctantly, while Andrew holds the dishes across his puny forearms.

While the chicken is cooling, Irene mixes a drink of vodka and ice, wondering if she has forgotten anything. She lets her mind drift. She thinks of the bowl she had sketched and crumpled and burned. It was just a bowl. Who cares? She has meals to prepare, youth sports games to attend, school functions to organize; and the house, always the house needs to be restocked. On the recent pages of the drawing pad in the carriage house, she had taken inventory of the pantry and the refrigerator and the four bathrooms and the laundry room, as though they live in a shop that sells everything from asparagus to cotton swabs. She has not had an intelligent conversation about art, or artists, or anything really, in a long time.

The next day, Irene drives to an art supply store in town, having decided to try to paint again. The same childish excitement she had when she was young beats through her as she selects different oils, brushes, and colored charcoal and carries them to the register. Back then, she might be able to afford two tubes of paint, and the other colors she stuffed in her pockets and purse. Now she pays for everything in full, and the girl at the counter with her nose pierced through with a bull ring makes a print of her credit card and throws the tubes and brushes in a bag, looking at her briefly with a snarky smile, as if to say, "Expensive hobby." But just the same, lethargy takes over once she's in the carriage house and has set her paints on the wooden folding table beside her newly sanded easel. She looks at the canvas, her canvas, for a long while. She smokes three cigarettes in a row. When she hears the phone ring in the main house, she has reason to leave her work, even though she knows she will not get to the phone in time to receive the call. She crosses the wet grass in the backyard, takes off her sneakers midway, rolls her socks off, and feels the soggy earth against the palms of her feet. She checks in on Checkers, the bunny Andrew had begged for as a present for his birthday, and remembers explaining to him that there were bunnies everywhere, especially in the morning, eating up her flowers. But Andrew wanted one in a cage with a little water spout and feeder, and for a few weeks after his party, he fed the bunny diligently and stood by the cage making bunny faces, twisting his mouth and wiggling his nose. Somehow, caged, fat Checkers has acted as a deterrent to the other bunnies who were eating Irene's flowers earlier that spring.

She tosses her shoes and socks in the mudroom, then pours a glass of beer and pushes the message button on the answering machine, annoyed to hear the phone on the other end click.

She sits in the stiff, floral-printed chair beside the phone and waits. Then she picks up the phone and dials Robert at the office, but his secretary says he's just gone out to a job site.

Later, around two in the afternoon, she drives to the supermarket and buys a Bavarian cream pie and a carton of milk. At the kitchen table, she eats the pie and drinks two tall glasses of milk. She smokes a cigarette while looking at the empty container, her disgust assuaged by a mild sense of accomplishment. Once a week, around happy hour, when she was little, Irene's mother would drop her off at her grandmother's apartment in the spring-inspired senior living community set off Route 33 and go meet up with friends at a bar called Partners. Irene's grandmother was a thick, Swedish woman in wool skirts upon wool skirts, even in summer. She never preached or complained. She ordered and criticized. Irene's shorts were too short, her makeup made her look like a whore, Bs were okay but was that all she wanted to be in life? Okay? She fried steaks on an iron skillet and watched as Irene ate around the fatty gristle, then tapped her fork on the plate and said, "Finish." There was something to be said about a woman who could eat the gristle off a steak. Irene remembered that the grueling ordeal was worth it when it came time for dessert. She made chocolate chip brownies and lemon pound cake and braided bread dusted with cinnamon with an apple pie filling throughout the center. From a woman of God came her love of sweets.

She picks the crumbs of pie from the waxed paper, goes to the bathroom, and shoves her finger down her throat. The moment she feels the burn drive up her septum and wet the inside of her nose, she experiences a rush of adrenaline so pleasurable it's as if she's in full contact with every part of her physical self. She coughs, gags, and lets the sweet chunks of pie slip from her mouth. She feels her abdomen stretch, chest expand, lungs pump, mouth contract, and eyes water. She had started throwing up just after last Christmas, when Robert had said, "Is it me or is your rump getting a little big?" He had apologized, of course, and he wasn't unkind with his honesty. But she felt a great implication in his remarks, a threat that if she didn't lose weight, she would have to accept the consequences, the most important being that he would fuck other women. At first, she felt frightened by the act, that she could commit her body to such a violent reaction. But soon she had begun to enjoy the rush of it—the consumption, preparation, and expulsion. It was not unlike the first time she took a shot of tequila in Eddie Prince's basement when she was a sophomore in high school or that first line of coke when she had visited those friends from school who had all moved to Manhattan after graduating from college. She curls her upper lip and brushes her chocolate-stained teeth, then wipes the tears from under her eyelids and splashes water on her face. Afterward her body tightens, her bones are sore.

The doorbell rings. Irene doesn't answer. Then she hears a sharp knock on the door. What's wrong with you? she thinks. What if it's about the boys? She pushes up her hair and wipes her forehead with a washcloth. As she reaches for the doorknob, she notices the chocolate on her middle and index fingers and sucks it off before opening the door.

A large square package has been left on the step. The delivery driver is back in his truck. He's portly with a creepily thick mustache. He waves to Irene when he sees she has picked up the box. He will not do in tonight's dream scenario. She takes the package inside, slices the tape with scissors, and opens the cardboard flaps. Inside is a porcelain jug she had ordered from Christie's two weeks ago. She can't remember why she ordered it. Painted on the jug is a pattern of blue and white swivels. There's a tap at the bottom and perhaps she had an idea that this might be a fancy way to serve water or punch to guests during semi-casual dinner parties. She pulls off the bubble wrap and places the jug in the cabinet left of the refrigerator, where other items such as the power juicer and ice cream maker are stored and never used. As she's removing her hand from the cabinet, a spider crawls down from the inside of the cupboard door onto the back of her palm and up her arm. It moves so quickly that she doesn't scream as she normally would have, but instead giggles girlishly as its spindly legs move under her shirt and the spider falls between her breasts. She lifts her blouse and the spider drops to the floor and skitters toward the pantry. Suddenly she feels an overwhelming urge to have sex with her husband. She'll bite his chest when she comes, tear the flesh from his body. The violence of the other night is still with her.

Until the boys come home from school and throw their book bags in the mudroom and run up the stairs. She hears them banging around, probably tossing each other on their beds. Then there's a heavy thud on the carpet. Andrew crying. Nathan mimicking his brother's cries. Something breaks against the wall. Irene starts toward the stairs but then stops herself. For Christ's sake, let the two of them rip each other to pieces.

FOUR

THE FOLLOWING SATURDAY, ON MEMORIAL DAY WEEKEND, IRENE'S parents arrive without notice. They are spur-of-the-moment people.

"Why not enjoy being alive when you can't possibly know how good or bad it is to be dead?" her father had said to Irene once when she went through a brief period of teenage depression after breaking up with Eddie Prince.

While helping her parents unpack the gray Volvo sedan, Irene is compelled to say something about her father's baggy slacks and stained white shirt.

"Not to worry," her father says. "I brought my special jacket."

"That hideous plaid blazer you've had since 1955?" Irene says. "The one with the burn hole?"

"Am I embarrassing you already, honeybun?"

"Mom. Talk some sense into him."

Her mother had always dressed her father for when they went out but never complained if he didn't feel like wearing something he wasn't comfortable in, because that was the point, she believed, to feel comfortable.

"It was either this or his lucky lemon-colored trousers," her mother says.

Irene huffs up the stairs. She's not really embarrassed. She just wants her parents to show some respect for themselves. Then she remembers why she's so concerned about their outfits. "Dressing decently tells people you respect yourself and deserve their respect," she remembers Robert saying just after Andrew was born, and she didn't feel like wearing anything else but big sweaters. "I'll remember that the next time you decide to wear that plum-colored polo," she had said, even though, later that night, she threw the big sweaters into a garbage bag. The next day she donated them to the Salvation Army.

"I keep forgetting just how *big* this house is," her mother says once they're inside. She drops her bag of shoes by the door. "It must take you hours to dust."

"Not hours, Ma," Irene says.

"Please, dear, something to drink."

As Irene pours a glass of white zinfandel, her mother walks through the kitchen and into the dining room. She stands looking out the window, trapped in light.

Her father is transfixed by a painting on the wall of a cat licking up spilt milk.

"Did you do this, honey?" he asks.

"No," Irene says and smiles. She hates cats but not this one. "I wish."

"You wish you could paint cats?"

"Something like that."

What she wishes is that she had the patience or fortitude, or focus, to sit down at her easel and work one image from her head onto the canvas and into the world.

"Do you remember that thing you were supposed to draw for the school?" her mother says, taking the glass from the counter, amused.

On the wall in the hallway of the west wing of Norwalk

High School, Irene, a below-average student, who her teachers had described to her parents as a floater—someone who had no official group, a free spirit, a wanderer—had begun a mural of half the Manhattan skyline, a portion of the Brooklyn Bridge, the head of the Statue of Liberty, and what looked like a mass of people rising up from the streets, just the outlines of their faces, quotation marks above their heads, waiting for her to fill them in with whatever prophetic words were worthy enough to keep for each succeeding class, read and reread until finally they were like ancient etchings on the insides of cave walls, slowly disappearing with every ball toss or fistfight or key stroke along the wall, until, finally, the wall was knocked down.

She would look at the mural every day and wonder what on earth was going on in Midtown Manhattan at this moment. Or, was that the point at all? She began to work on one part or another, even going so far as to shade in Richard Nixon at the top of the Empire State Building, hundred-dollar bills falling like rain, dead bodies wrapped in flags floating on clouds above the skyline, the entire coterie of evil hunkered down in underground bunkers, praying for forgiveness. But how could someone possibly get all of that into one portion of space? As she worked, more ideas came to her and soon she was overwhelmed with the entire thing and packed up her paints and brushes and told her art teacher, Ms. Spang, she quit.

"Having too many ideas is never a bad thing," Ms. Spang said.

"I'm just not in it anymore," Irene said.

"Literally?"

"No, like, spiritually. I don't feel connected."

"Oh, okay. Whatever."

Gabe Walcott, a senior, with little to no talent, was given the task of reworking the mural and, in a matter of one week, painted over Irene's work and managed a faceless soldier holding up the peace sign. It was so poorly rendered and obviously trite that Irene had laughed when it was unveiled.

"What a fraud," she cried. Gabe, who came from a wealthy family, was on his way to Northwestern with no fear of being drafted.

Ms. Spang shushed her.

"Shush yourself," Irene said, and walked off to get stoned in her car.

The only thing left of that mural is a photograph, and even the photograph is missing.

"I saw a painting of two circles for sale in the gallery next to my office," her mother says. "Do you know how much they were asking? Six thousand dollars. Can you believe that? Not that I know the first thing about art, but it made me think, if all I need to do to make six thousand dollars is paint a couple circles, then I might as well quit my job today."

"It's not as easy as it looks," Irene says.

Her mother drinks down the rest of her first glass.

"Well, maybe not," she says, and taps her glass with her pink, painted fingernail. "Another. Please, dear."

As a girl, Irene had been foolish and beautiful. She never suffered. She couldn't recall one terrible thing having happened to her. Her parents were not strict like her friends' parents, never told her that she couldn't go on a date with so-and-so, and she couldn't remember them once asking her what she wanted to do with her life. This kind of freedom was cherished. She had no curfew, no bedtime, and no authority figure outside of school. Her parents had big parties with the neighbors, the upper middle class of Norwalk, the insurance agents and advertising salesmen and local merchants. Occasionally, the mayor was seen grab-assing with the young wives. There was a thick layer of smoke hanging above those beautifully dressed people, and Irene, eight or nine years old, in her nightgown, with her hair down below her shoulders, sat near the record player and listened to swing music. When she was asked to dance, she took the big, sweaty hand of a man wearing a lavender ascot. He twirled her effortlessly around the living-room floor and told her she was going to break a lot of hearts one day.

Her father had been the former police chief. He retired in his midforties and bought a bar on Post Road. She remembered him coming home the day he had put up the money for what he later called Duffy's Tavern. She was ten years old then, thin, with great, blue eyes. Her father had rented a red convertible and drove it around the cul-de-sac where they lived, honking the horn, calling for her mother to come out and take a ride with him. Her mother was wearing a yellow scarf, her curled hair bouncing beneath a wide-brimmed hat, between her fingers a cigarette in a long, blue filter, a glass of wine in her other hand. She gave the glass to Irene and ran out to the car, the hat flying off her head, though she didn't go back for it. Irene sniffed the wine and took a sip and spit it out. She picked up the hat and put it on her head. Her parents rode around the neighborhood, playing the radio as loud as they could, the neighbors out on their lawns, watching them as if they were part of a parade that had no purpose but life itself. Her parents had small ambitions. They were happy people, good people.

After high school, she rented an apartment in South Norwalk. During the day that summer, she worked on charcoal drawings in her room: faceless outlines, hands, breasts, vaginas, and feet. At night, she tended bar with her father. Her best friend since middle school, Susan Varney, modeled for her on Saturday afternoons. Afterward they got stoned and listened to Buffalo

Springfield and talked about movies and boys and someday moving to California or Florida, anywhere warm and wet.

In the fall of 1974, Susan met a boy and moved to Portland, Maine. And Irene, claiming her right to the future they had discussed, took a bus to Miami Beach. She made friends quickly—Deadheads, wanderers, seekers of an East Coast movement now that California was ruined with drug addicts and psychopaths. She stayed in a room at a boardinghouse two blocks from the beach and walked on the sand naked at night, sometimes alone, sometimes with other women, lovers, or strangers—it didn't matter; they were all naked. If someone wasn't naked, then he or she became the outcast, the weird one. Even a cop, flashing his light, his cock half-erect in those ridiculously tight shorts they were made to wear, calling out, "What are you dumb hippies doing? Beach is closed."

In Florida, she saw purple. Maybe it was the acid, the pot, the tequila—she painted in purple shades for nearly six months. First, in the boardinghouse, then, after attending a party at a bungalow in South Beach a couple of months later, and waking up next to the bungalow's owner, a tanned, bone-thin man with a tail of black hair, who made her breakfast and stared in her eyes longer than she was used to, and said his name was Adrian and she was one of the most beautiful things he'd ever seen, she continued to paint in purple shades, now with a better view of the ocean, and a partner who said he felt like he knew her insides by what she painted. Adrian paid for her brushes and oils and canvases. When she finished one piece, he would tap a nail into the wall and hang it, light a joint, and stare at her work until he was finished smoking. Adrian was receptive to the idea that at a certain time of day, the beach, palm trees, flowers, high-rises, and faces of people strolling along the sidewalks could hold a union of one color.

"Do you know what you're doing?" he asked.

"Am I supposed to know?"

When they made love, Adrian threw her legs up and pushed her knees in toward the side of her head, so that her body was tilted to the side. He whimpered when he came. Afterward, he took back the control he had lost in bed. He talked art and politics and revolution. He was condescending and abrasive. With each day that passed, he looked uglier to Irene.

One afternoon, just before Christmas, they woke up and walked to the Howard Johnson's a mile down on the beach. Irene had pancakes with whipped cream and buttered pecans. He ate a cantaloupe and drank a tall glass of grapefruit juice.

"You're going to get fat eating that way," Adrian said.

"It's the only thing I ever eat. How could that make me fat?"

"Not fat now, but later in life. You develop a habit and you can't break it without some sort of spiritual intervention. I don't see you as the type to be receptive to such an intervention."

Slowly, as though mimicking the anger pushing up inside her, she pushed the plate of pancakes toward the edge of the table, then flung the plate to the floor. The pancakes briefly flopped on the floor like fish; the whipped cream lay flat and still.

Adrian followed her lead, toppling over the water glasses, emptying the salt and pepper shakers, tossing the napkins from the metal holder up over their heads while other diners watched in horror. The manager grabbed Adrian by the collar and tried to shove him out the door, but Adrian pushed the manager so hard he fell backward over his heels and landed face-first into the pancakes. When he stood, his face dripped with whipped cream, a pancake piece stuck to his cheek. Nobody said a word as Adrian and Irene walked toward the entrance, Adrian holding his middle finger up over his head. Irene reached into her purse for a five-dollar bill, which she placed on the counter as she passed the nervous, outstretched hand of the purple-haired cashier tending the till.

Late that spring, on a rainy, thunderous morning, Adrian came back to the bungalow with his hair matted in blood, nose broken, and knuckles skinned. He wouldn't say what had happened. He sat on the bed with his head in his hands, dripping wet; dark red bulbs dropped from the ends of his hair. Then he laid back and curled up and fell asleep with his shoes on. Irene cared for him when he woke up later that afternoon. She helped him to the bath and shampooed his hair, and with a comb scraped away the chips of blood—some of his hair came out, too, but Adrian didn't stir. There was bruising along his side, but he refused to see a doctor.

"What if you have broken ribs?"

"I probably do. So what's the point?"

"They'll give you something for the pain."

"I like pain."

"You let this happen? I don't understand."

"How could you? You've never really felt pain in your entire life. That's what I've learned from being with you this short while, that things will be easy and I won't have to do much and life will be boring."

"I think you're doing too much coke."

"Probably. But that doesn't take away from the reality of what we are."

"What are we?"

Adrian stood in the tub, then leaned against the tiled wall.

"Animals," he said. "Do you know what they do when they can't find food, when they're starving?"

"What?"

"They eat their young. Do you know why?"

"Why are you telling me this?"

"Do you know why, Irene?"

"Because they're animals?"

Adrian laughed then, a hoarse, throaty laugh, followed by a bout of coughing.

"The reason they eat their young before anything else, even before they eat other animals, is to protect them. But the young can never know that's why. So it's sad, really, because these animals that eat their young, they die of depression once they're satiated. Eventually there is food for them to eat again, but they choose not to. They grow thin and docile, and lie down in the fields to die or be killed."

"Are you planning to eat me?"

"I hope I don't have to."

"I think you've officially lost your mind."

"Or found it."

He stepped out of the tub, wincing from the pain, and tried to put his arms around Irene.

"Don't come near me," she said. "You think I'm some helpless creature you're protecting by getting rid of me? That's a fine lie. At least be a man about it and tell me what's really going on."

"I'm going back to New York in a few days. I think that's best. I have some people there who'll let me stay with them while I figure out what I'm going to do."

She knew he wasn't asking her to come with him. She knew that to even bring it up would sound pathetic, make her appear more wounded than he was.

That night they made love with her on top, moving slowly, and his moans not only from the feeling of sex but from the hurt in his sides and chest. Irene dug her thumb into his side just as she was about to come. His body gripped from the pain, and his cock grew harder inside her.

Afterward, when Adrian had fallen asleep, Irene went out and sat on the beach and smoked. She sat there until the sun began to rise above the horizon of the darkened ocean, like a golden egg.

For the rest of July, she lived in the bungalow alone. She couldn't afford the rent. She still had a little money saved, but it felt like she'd be going backward if she returned to waiting tables. She had come here for something, she thought. There had to be something.

At the end of the month, she started getting sick, and, after seeing a doctor, discovered she was pregnant.

"What am I supposed to do with a baby?" Irene asked the nurse.

"You don't *have* to keep it," the nurse said casually. "You can go to one of those places. I can give you an address."

She took a bus to a clinic on Collins Ave, a small building that, from the outside, looked like a shelter for skid row drunks. Windows shuttered, above the door a red cross. She had pressed forward, given her name to one of the nurses there, but left as soon as the nurse had gone to the back. Irene walked down to the beachfront and, for a while, sat on the edge of the planked walkway, under a swaying palm tree, her toes in the hot sand, her palms planted on her stomach as if on the earth itself, urging what was inside her to grow, give proof of the life she knew existed beneath. Irene imagined another life, one with her child, possibly traveling to a town out west with cleaner air and work for mothers. She would raise Charlotte, Sam, Janis, Colin, Fiona—the names she had written on the notepad in her tiny motel room with the beetles bursting against the wall, nearby the hospital—there, waiting tables while her artist friends watched over her baby, and then, when she or he was old enough to go to school, she would begin painting again. She would create something that would make her known around the world as a true force of expression.

The nurse tapped her on the shoulder and said, "Vamos, poca niña."

After the baby had been sucked out of her, the pain in her stomach felt like her soul leaving. The nurse from before said a prayer in Spanish while Irene lay in the bed sweating, exhausted, emptied, as the doctor pounded the sides of the air conditioner in the window.

"Not only am I a doctor, but a plumber, electrician, groundskeeper, and accountant as well," he said, attempting humor.

Irene smiled.

She was doped up still, and she took his hands and turned them over and said, "Don't hurt these."

Such beautiful hands, she remembers now, standing in her living room as her father drones on about an "artist" friend of his, Herb Calderhead, who used to sculpt wood with a chain saw until he cut off his own foot.

"That's enough about Herb," her mother says. "Where are my babies?"

"Come and see," Irene says.

Nathan and Andrew are much more receptive to Irene's father than to Red. He's the kind of grandpa who makes farting noises with his armpit and clicks his tongue loud like a crack when he knocks their heads with his school ring. Her mother speaks in Swedish to tease them, and the boys try to mimic her, while Robert's mother can't bother to keep her cigarette smoke out of the children's faces.

When Robert returns that evening, later than usual, he shouts toward the sunroom for Irene, who is playing cards with her parents while having a nightcap.

"Didn't you see their car when you drove in?" she asks as he sits on a stool in the kitchen with a beer. "Why do you smell like a fishing boat?"

"I went for a swim."

"In this weather?"

"Is that so strange?"

"Honey, don't be rude. You know how much my father loves you."

"Is your mother sauced yet?"

"On her way."

"All right, then."

Robert and Cliff shake hands and hug like proper men, with an arm on the shoulder.

"Sylvia, I didn't even recognize you," Robert says, glancing at Irene, who sharpens her eyes at him as he embraces her mother gently and then playfully nips her behind, which makes her chuckle. Her mother slaps Robert's chest and blushes. When Robert opens a fresh box of cigars, even Sylvia has one. The four of them sit in the low light drinking and smoking.

Irene is silent while Robert commandeers the conversation. This is the only way he knows how to be. It's not that he needs the attention, so much as he invites it with his presence, and not just his size, his black hair and black eyes, but by the way he so easily crosses one leg over the other as though natural for a man of his masculinity, and the way his top lip curls, and how he snaps his fingers to put emphasis on sound, a bang, what he heard the other night outside, and saw in the morning it was a dead pigeon that had flown into the window and dropped to the ground.

"Oh, dear," her mother says, transfixed.

Robert veers into politics, boat licenses, and something about a coyote roaming around one of his subdivisions, how he hired someone to track it down, an ex-army sniper, a real badass. Her parents are fascinated and, by this time, quite drunk.

"What's that about a boat?" Irene asks.

Robert stops what he's saying about the sniper and looks at her.

"I missed something. You said a boat?"

"That's right. Didn't we talk about this? I said I was thinking about buying a boat, to take the kids out fishing, or waterskiing. I was telling Cliff about what a pain in the ass it is to get a license."

"It really sounds like a big pain in the ass," her father says and grins.

"Cliff," Sylvia says.

"What?"

"You're drunk."

"I am. That's true. And why not?"

"Good point," her mother says, and pours herself some more wine.

"When would we have time for a boat, Robert?" Irene says.

"Weekends. Holidays. I'll teach you how to sail."

"Oh, I can just picture it," her mother says, and chuckles.

"I think I'll check on the boys," Irene says. "We'll talk about this boat idea another time."

As Irene leaves the room and starts up the stairs, she hears her father say how he'd love to take a ride on that boat.

"You can't even swim," her mother shouts.

"Who cares?"

FIVE

THE NIGHT IRENE MET ROBERT, HE WAS WEARING A POWDER blue suit with a striped maroon tie. It was 1977, and pretty much anything went, but with his curly black hair, dark eyes, and freckled cheeks, she thought the suit was a joke.

"Is it that bad?" he had said.

"You really should burn it," she said.

Suddenly conscious of her blinking, she drew her hair across her face, flipped it back, and walked to the end of the bar to pour a shot of bourbon for the fat guy in suspenders who came in off the train every evening.

Irene had the following day off. She went into the city and spent hours looking at the work of the impressionists at the Museum of Modern Art. When she returned home, her father told her there was a tall, good-looking Irish man in the bar who'd asked about her and asked what she did and if he had owned the bar all his life and where they lived.

"We talked about the Mets," her father went on. "He asked about my tattoo. He was drafted. Did you know he was drafted? He seemed pretty interested in my naval career, and my time on the police force. I thought if all he wanted to do was get in my daughter's pants I would've told him to beat it, but here's the first boyfriend I've met of yours that isn't afraid to look me in the eye."

"He's not my boyfriend," Irene said. "I don't even know his name."

"His name is Kelly. That's his last name. I forget his first. That's how taken I was with the young man."

Irene's father remembered everybody's name and when they were born and where and what they did for a living. Only a trickster, a hypnotist, could cause him to forget.

"Anyway, he left his number. It's there behind the phone."

She took the number and looked at the terrible penmanship and knew he must've played sports or worked a job that was rough and unclean. She thought to throw the number away but instead kept it in her purse next to her cigarettes.

When he sat down at the bar the next night, Irene put a napkin with her number on the bar and poured his beer. Out of the corner of her eye she saw him studying it. Once he understood what it was, he smiled coyly, like a child caught in a white lie. Then she put the cold mug on top of the napkin and said, "You call me. I don't call you."

He lifted the mug, the wet ink now unreadable.

"Oops," she said playfully.

Robert reached over the bar and grabbed another napkin and put it down next to the wet one. He placed his mug on top of it and handed the wet one to Irene.

"I don't need this anymore," he said, and smiled. "I've already got the number memorized."

After he left, Irene said his name—Robert. Then the variations of his name—Rob, Bob, Bobby, Robby. She thought he was cute, and possibly teachable.

A week later, Robert picked Irene up at the tavern in his rusted red jalopy and took the FDR past 106th Street to 125th and into Harlem. He turned to her and smirked as if this was some kind of joke and he was going to turn around, which Irene would have preferred.

"You don't have anything to worry about," Robert said. "I get along well with the jigs."

He turned onto Lenox Ave and drove her to a club he considered to have the best steaks in the city.

Inside, there were men in fur coats and women in leopard print dresses. Smoke floated just beneath the ceiling. The booths curved along the walls creating a sort of coliseum-like feeling with the dance floor in the middle of the room. A band played funk music. Only on a first date with a man she didn't know would she ever again listen to such music or be caught dead in such a tacky restaurant, or love every minute of it.

When she looked up at Robert, he looked as though he could pluck her up and toss her into the sky with one hand. Here is a man, she thought. Despite herself, she wanted to feel his power, to have him inside her, to smell the salt and liquor and smoke on their bodies, to be animals.

After they finished eating (the steak was good, but not the best), a tall black man with long fingernails and a manicured mustache came up to their table and asked her to dance. She looked at Robert and Robert nodded. She was offended that he wasn't offended. She took the man's hand and let him lead her out across the floor.

Even in her wildest let-go moments in front of her bedroom mirror Irene had no idea how to dance to the type of music the band was playing. She tried to follow the other dancers shuffling their feet and kicking out their knees and throwing up their arms. She copied them so as not to look foolish. At one point, Irene caught Robert laughing when she almost toppled over, spring-boarding off the floor after a rising bass line that had everyone down to their knees. How the song kept going without any lyrics, Irene couldn't understand. She was folk music and rock 'n' roll; she liked to think the words mattered.

She was now sweating under her arms and between her legs. She feared Robert might be sickened if they made it in the back of his car later, which she had a feeling they might.

When the song ended, the man with the long fingernails delivered her to Robert, who was sitting with one leg casually crossed over the other, fitting a toothpick between his teeth.

"Your woman can't dance worth a shit," the man said and let go of her arm. As he was walking away, he put up both his arms to reveal the holster of a knife attached to his pants.

Robert took Irene's hand and said he'd already paid.

"Don't worry about these jigs," Robert said. "They all think they got something to prove."

"He's right," said Irene. She could still feel the bass line under her heels. "I'm really not much of a dancer. I can do the mashed potato, I can do the twist."

"You're funny."

"Then why aren't you laughing?"

"That's a good question."

She asked him for a cigarette. He lit one for her and watched her smoke while sitting on the edge of the seat, rubbing the sole of her foot with her hand.

After a few drags, she stubbed the cigarette out in the ashtray and walked ahead of Robert, through the throng of slickly dressed people, out into the sticky city air, thoughtless, unable to hear even the sounds of the cars speeding down Lenox Ave.

When she turned around, Robert was on top of the black man with the long fingernails, beating his face in with his fist. Another man rushed forward and kicked Robert in the stomach and he fell to the ground onto his back. The two men were on top of him now. The man with the long fingernails pulled out his knife and slashed Robert's side. When Irene screamed at the blood soaking his shirt, the men backed up under the club's awning.

"Call someone," she said.

The man with the long fingernails looked shocked by his own violence. He turned back and shouted for someone to call an ambulance.

Later, in the emergency room, she thought to herself, this man is crazy. Then she thought, you must be crazy, too. Why else would you want to spend the rest of your life with him?

SIX

MEMORIAL DAY. ROBERT PACKS THE WAGONEER WITH A COOLER and radio, and Irene fills a beach bag with towels, sunblock, and potato chips. Irene's parents play with the electric windows in the backseat. Nathan is sitting between them, rocking up and down as the smoke from Robert's cigarette blows out and back into his face. Andrew's in the way back, pulling at his scrotum through his swim trunks, something he's been doing a lot recently.

After they park and set up the chairs and beach towels and radio, the boys swim out to the wooden raft on floats held in place by a long rope knotted to the lifeguard's post. They quickly make friends with other children, playing games common and medieval—King of the Castle, Shark Bait, and Survival—all of which are slight variations of the same game. They splash water at each other's faces, push down on each other's heads, and race to the deep where their toes can no longer touch the bottom.

The radio is tuned to the classic rock station: the Stones, the Beatles, the Animals, the Monkees, the Police, the Jimi Hendrix Experience.

"Is there anything that could ruin such peace more than rock-and-roll music?" Irene's mother says. "Can't we just listen to the waves?"

"It's better than listening to Daddy," Irene says.

Cliff is snoring loudly, his white T-shirt bunched up under his head. He has a sloppily inked tattoo of an anchor on his forearm. His skin looks pieced together in different shades.

When the boys come in from the water, Irene hands them their towels and they dry off and lie on their backs on the warm sand, stretching their arms and legs as the pink and orange light spreads across the sky. A double-engine glider plane flies overhead. Andrew reaches his hand up and pretends to grab hold of its tail.

Irene wets her thumb and cleans the corners of the boys' mouths. They squirm and wrench their necks.

"Hold still," she says, pinching their noses once she has finished. "Okay, all done."

The boys run ahead toward the Wagoneer.

Cliff snorts and turns on his side.

"What a dream," he says.

"What dream?" Sylvia says.

"I was playing centerfield for the Mets."

"Oh, for crying out loud."

Robert carries the beach chairs under his arm and hoists the bag of towels, Frisbees and footballs, the radio and empty paper tubs of fried clams. Cliff walks in front with his hands clasped behind his back, singing "Meet the Mets, Meet the Mets." Irene puts on her large straw hat and her white framed sunglasses. Both she and her mother are wearing summer dresses, big and flowing.

At the dinner table that night, Nathan picks at a dried scab in his ear where his mother had missed with the sunscreen. Andrew pushes his spoon into his crotch, just to try it out.

Robert closes his eyes and blesses the food.

"Holy Moly," Cliff says.

"Dad," Irene hisses.

"What? I'm starving."

Andrew divides the food on his plate into a palette of bold solid colors. Nathan mixes his food together into a mash of carrots, potatoes, and chunks of grilled steak. They eat fast and drink their grape juice with such terrible impatience that when Andrew goes to fill his glass again, he spills the juice on the table. Nathan throws the nice linen napkin on top of the stain.

"Don't use that!" Irene shouts.

She picks up the napkin and shows it to Robert.

"Now I'll never get this out."

"It's just a napkin," Robert says.

"Forty dollars apiece," she says.

"Now that's something to shout about," Sylvia says.

"My bridge cost less than that set of napkins," Cliff says.

"You got a bridge?" Andrew asks.

Cliff shows his teeth and with his tongue pushes his upper tooth out and down, revealing the vacant space left below his gum line.

"Oh, Cliff. That's disgusting," Sylvia says, laughing. Cliff makes like he's putting his face back together and smiles, showing his full set of teeth.

"What are we going to do?" Irene asks.

"About what?" Robert says.

"The napkins."

"The what?"

"Forget it," she says, and tosses the stained napkin on top of her plate. "Why do I bother trying to make things nice anyway?"

Chairs are pushed away, crumbs stuck to the rug, a stain of dried milk on the table.

Robert sits on the back porch, smoking. Cliff, beside him, drinks beer from a glass. The sky is nearly flat on the horizon, purple above the scattered clouds. There is something crushing yet hopeful about a sky like this.

Later that night, Irene looks in on the boys. They have separate rooms—Nathan's windows face the street in front, and Andrew's into the backyard. Nathan's walls plastered with posters of athletes, and Andrew's with superheroes. Each has a chest full of toys to share and a bookcase where they stack their albums of baseball cards and action figures and comics. But at night, Andrew often sneaks into Nathan's room and sleeps on the floor beside Nathan's bed.

Irene kisses them both on the forehead, then sits on the floor on the other side of Nathan's bed. She can hear her father sharing some of his old navy stories, and her mother brings up a bit of news she has recently read in the *New York Times* about this being one of the best times in the nation's history to invest in real estate. Robert speaks to them as if they're the most important people on earth. He is capable of making himself believe they are, just as he is with Irene and the boys and the slow kid who bags their groceries at the A&P.

SEVEN

THE NEXT DAY, ONCE HER PARENTS HAVE LEFT, IRENE CAN'T shake the nervous anticipation that comes from being alone. She makes cucumber and cream cheese sandwiches and cuts them up into squares and wraps the plate of squares in plastic and puts the plate in the refrigerator for when the boys come home from school. She sits on a stool at the kitchen island and lights a cigarette. It's half past ten in the morning. She sweeps the floors and puts a load of laundry in the washer, then makes the boys' beds. She finds a wad of tissues between Nathan's mattress and box spring. She puts away the dishes and pours a cup of coffee. Now it's almost noon. She turns on the television. *Rat a tat tat tat! Rat a tat tat tat!* Soldiers firing machine guns at a stone building. The picture is grainy. Another war. Or another movie. She shuts off the TV. Strands of blond hair fall across her eyes.

Irene feels as though she's floating from room to room. One moment she's in the kitchen, then the bathroom, then the living room, then in bed. How did she get to all of these places without walking on her own two feet? The rooms are different sizes and shapes and colors. They are past rooms where she has lived. They crumble and fall away once she leaves them.

It's as though she has lived inside a different person every five years. And each of them looks worse and worse. How pointless it is to live so long in order to look so terrible. You don't win anything by surviving. If only she could be remembered as sixteen forever, with an unknown life ahead of her, looking back at everyone looking at her, guessing, wondering, who is *she*, where did *she* come from, what will she *be*? Like Vermeer's *Het meisje met de parel*. She would never be more than a question, a fascination, a girl.

There is one beer left in the refrigerator. She takes down a glass from the cherrywood cabinet and pours in half the can. She sips the beer and lets out a little burp. The mail, she thinks. She puts on a pair of sneakers. She puts on her fur. Why not? At the mailbox, she tries to forget the empty feeling in her stomach, her stomach contracting, the burn in her throat. She wishes she'd brought her beer.

The nausea passes. Cars whip by. People eager to get home to their husbands and wives and children and dogs and cats and television sets and soft couches and private bathrooms. She misses that feeling of going home. She hasn't been anywhere other than home in years.

Irene touches the arms of her coat. Fox fur. And the pearls around her neck. How Robert years ago had led her through the lobby of the Plaza toward the elevators past the long row of brass-tinted pay phones. They made love in a suite overlooking Central Park during the Thanksgiving holiday when they went to Connecticut to visit her family, and then to New York so the boys could see the Macy's Day Parade. They had snorted coke with Michael Douglas in a marble-tiled bathroom at the Oak Room. Men held their hand to her side longer than they should have. Women talked behind her back. And in the village of Wequaquet, she was still a marvel, an outsider, a woman to behold—because she was not from here, never dropped an *r* when she was speaking, looked radiant in mink or wool, wore her hair up, down, curly, and straight. She had two boys, a hard-working husband, and a name that went back before the town's, a name that made her mother to them all—the schoolteachers and shop clerks and housewives alike.

She reaches inside the mailbox for the circulars, the bills, the invitations to this party or that gala. The mailbox is full of future responsibilities. It's a trap, really. Why did she come out here in the first place?

But Robert in his powder blue suit, sitting on a stool in her father's bar, watching the tiny television set above the bottles of good liquor, struggling with the matches that went out each time he brought them to the end of his cigarette under the twirling fans above. And she laughed at him, at his suit, at his inability to light his own cigarette, at his striped maroon tie, which he took off and rolled up like a long tongue and stuffed in his pocket. There was nothing yet but her laugh and the boyish look over his shoulder and her long fingers curled over her mouth and his embarrassed smile and her name and his name and the match that finally sparked the end of his cigarette and her silent applause and the surface of each other, the animal attraction of smells, of skin and hair and bone, and how, without knowing anything else about the other, without ever having to speak another word, they had become intimate partners.

She holds the mail in her hand and walks along the hedgerow between the sidewalk and the front yard, where the boys play football and Wiffle ball and badminton, and when the weather turns, they collect acorns and bring them to the back of the house and leave them for the squirrels in front of the large oak tree. In winter, the Christmas parade goes right by the house, and Santa will wave to the boys.

The hedges need to be trimmed. Loose branches shoot out at

odd angles. She pulls a few that have died. Between the hedge and the side of the house the ground is always damp from little light, the cause of so much dirt on her kitchen floor from the boys forgetting to take off their shoes in the mudroom. The oil drum is rusted and should be replaced. Leaves and pine needles are scattered along the mangled crabgrass in the backyard. The split leaves she remembered pulling open and sticking to the bridge of her nose to amuse the boys when they were young.

She brings the mail in and places it neatly, in order of necessity, on the counter. She guesses she can make a shopping list. Or she can go out and see what's on sale at Filene's. Maybe she'll get an idea. Maybe she'll have a reason to return to her sketch pad in the carriage house later this afternoon, or tomorrow morning, after the boys leave for school.

EIGHT

You could say that the town of Wequaquet, Massachusetts, was built by the Kellys, though no one ever said such a thing. Still, Robert Kelly, son of William "Red" Kelly and Florence Zappa, holds a sort of quiet pride in seeing his family's name emblazoned on the signs in front of the new Meadowbrook subdivision.

When he was a boy, Robert listened to his father deal the future to potential home buyers like a deck of cards full of kings and queens.

"The future," Robert's father had said, "is what everyone fears most."

But forty years of political gamesmanship, endless paperwork, and petty conversations have begun to take their toll on Red. He is nearing seventy. He takes long naps during the day and has trouble hearing people over the phone. He's exhausted. He has trouble urinating. The doctors say it doesn't look good.

"Something in my gut," he had told Robert over the phone, not more than a week after Robert had decided to move back to the Cape.

"What something?" Robert had asked.

"A blockage. I forget what they called it. A big word for what's probably a little nothing."

In those first few months home, Robert had set up in Red's office in the renovated library on Sea Street. He spent the day decoding the old man's medieval system of numbers, names, and dates, written down on scraps of paper and filed away in folders carelessly stacked wherever there had been space. A part of him believed his father had purposefully challenged Robert to a maddening quest, and that by organizing all this paperwork, restoring the files to order, Robert would come to know the town, the names and occupations of its people, if they had children or were just starting out or had planned to retire.

After work, wound up on coffee or liquor or coke, and the voices of so many people he had met that day or had taken calls from, he had no place left in his head for what Irene was saying about the boys or plans for that weekend. Irene made sure the house was clean and the TV guide was set beside the remote control in the living room, and there was a plate in the oven. His head hurt. He drank a glass of water and then another. After dinner he sat still and quiet on the front steps and smoked a cigarette and listened to the faraway howl of dogs at night, and once the dogs were brought in, he could hear the ocean in the distance, the roaring force of what was wild and unconquerable. He remembered diving into the waves and feeling them pull him away from shore, at first trying to fight against them with his cycling arms, but then letting the waves take him out until he was past the ropes and could barely see the beach. From the front door, Robert would call to Irene to tell her he was going out for a while, then drive the Wagoneer through the neighborhoods his father had built, the houses neat and uniform, simple ranchers for simple people, he thought. You had to build hundreds of these boxes to make the kind of money his father had, and by that time you were too old and bitter to enjoy it. The real money was on the shore, along Southbay Drive, and Robert drove along the one-lane street up toward the Wequaquet Country Club, the Wagoneer's motor churning like a thick winding chain. He studied the shoreline for empty lots. He'd have his secretary draw up a proposal later that week. But nothing would come of it. Regardless of how many homes the Kellys had built, they were still seen as a lesser company, suited more for the workingman than the super-wealthy vacationer who would spend a month a year in a three-million-dollar house on the water. Already feeling like an imposter, Robert searched up and down the coast for any parcel of land along the beach. No matter how many wheels he greased, he could never get a lot on the water. The Kellys were known for building a house quickly and under cost; sturdy houses without many flourishes—the Quahog, the Yarmouth, the Conestoga: three different models with the same square footage, but priced based on east-facing corner, central, or west-facing. Robert took the head of the zoning board to lunch at the Wequaquet Country Club, played golf with each of the seven town councilmen, picked up the tab at the Lobster Claw for the building inspector, who had curiously mentioned, while cleaning the guts out of a lobster tail with his fork, how lucrative it had been working for his father, Red, over the years. He had to become a trusted man, separate from his father in style and substance, but just as ruthless.

The Saturday following the visit from his in-laws, Robert quietly removes himself from bed without waking Irene and goes into each of his sons' rooms, squeezing their big toes until their eyes open.

"Get dressed and downstairs in five minutes," he says.

Robert smokes impatiently in the front seat of his 1979 Jeep

Wagoneer. Even though he can now afford a Porsche—and, more important, can think about how he can afford a Porsche—Robert has sat in those sport cars with his knees in his stomach, the steady hum of the engine like the consistent buzz of a mosquito, a reminder that this class of car belongs to a certain class of people. Every morning he kicks the starter, and the engine groans and finally turns over, and a feeling of security catches him briefly in his depressed reverie, like someone patting him on the back and gripping his shoulder and telling him he's doing pretty damn well.

The boys run out and hop in the backseat. Robert drives to the Dunkin' Donuts on Route 132 and buys a large, black coffee and a bag of glazed munchkins. He hands the bag of munchkins back to Nathan.

"Share," he says.

"Anything to drink?" Andrew says.

"No."

Robert passes the high school. His legendary story as a defensive end for the Wequaquet Red Raiders grows each time he has the boys join him for a weekend drive. Now he's telling them about a "big jig" who threw an uppercut at him and broke his jaw after Robert had "cleaned his clock" all game long. He points to a spot on his chin. The boys try to get a good look, and even though there's no scar there, Robert trusts they believe him, the same as when he drives along the shore and says, "There, right out there, I was almost bit once by a shark. You know what your father did? He punched the shark in the head. *Bap*." He gives a whack to the dash. "And it swam off like just another fish."

Even if the story isn't true, Robert wants his sons to know that being afraid is part of being alive. Andrew's nearly eleven, and already Robert sees a weakness in him, an inability to keep up with the other boys on the ball fields or up the hills to go sledding or when swimming laps in the pool at the Y.

Robert will occasionally grab the boxing gloves from the mudroom and take Andrew and Nathan out in the backyard to teach them how to fight. The jab was the most important punch you could throw. The jab stunned your opponent and could make his eyes water if you hit him correctly; then, in that momentary blindness, you could throw a cross or an uppercut and knock him flat on his back. If he was bigger, if you knew you were outmatched from the get-go, you lowered your head so that when he took a swing, he sprained his wrist or broke his hand.

The first time they boxed, while living in Rochester, when Nathan was six and Andrew four, Robert brought the gloves in and held Nathan on his lap while he fitted the big spongy mitts over his little hands. He gave Andrew a bell he could hit with a serving spoon and then announced that it was round one. Robert got on his knees and put his gloves up to show Nathan how to protect his face. Nathan could barely hold the weight of the gloves above his elbows, and Robert touched him in the chin, just strong enough to let Nathan know he needed to react. Then Nathan swung his arm out and the momentum sent his gloved hand square into Robert's face. By instinct or accident, Robert swung back and knocked out Nathan's front tooth. His mouth was bloody, the serrated enamel making tiny cuts in his tongue. Andrew hit the bell over and over again until Irene came into the bedroom and picked Nathan up and took him to the hospital. He has a fake tooth there now, the size of a chicklet, stained behind the molding under the crack, which makes Nathan, only a few months away from being a teenager, look slightly unstable.

Neither of the boys have best friends, but they have some friends, because all of the children live close to each other, go to the same schools, and play on the same teams. In the same way, Robert wouldn't call the fathers of these other boys friends, but they share pride and desperation and envy. They are connected by the strange arena of peewee sports. Robert is conscious of the fact that everyone, including the kids—if, say, one mentions Mommy and Daddy are getting a divorce—are potential leads. So he never gets too close or too distant; he hovers, offers to pick up the tab after games, when, along with the other fathers, Robert drives the boys to the Happy Panda for Chinese or Jack's Pub for pizza, and the boys and men alike trash-talk the other team and report on different parts of the game. Always a hero is announced, someone who had the biggest hit in football or the game-winning shot in basketball or the longest home run in baseball. Taller and thicker than most of the other boys his own age, Nathan is usually the hero, often enough that after a while the boys grow jealous and hateful, and tell their fathers Nathan hogs the ball or doesn't play fair, and the fathers suggest to Robert that his son play with the older boys. Last fall, Nathan had to play football with the freshman high school squad, and at practice and in games he got crushed. The boys were faster and stronger, and Nathan still hadn't learned all the rules of the game and had to think about which way to block on offense and which gaps to fill on defense. He isn't as productive when he has to think.

As he drives across the Wequaquet River Bridge, Robert is reminded of, and reminds his boys of, how he and his friends used to jump off the bridge when they were kids, and the time a bunch of guys from Falmouth, their rival, were on the beach and they started messing around with his sister. Closing in on her, pulling the straps down on her bathing suit, pinching her thighs, so that her only escape was the water. Robert and his friends whipped those boys like horses, and they ran as fast, too.

Robert pulls over at the end of the wooden bridge. He checks the side-view mirror for oncoming cars and then tells the boys it's okay to get out now. They follow behind him, single file, down the dirt slope to the moss-covered rocks, where the river water comes up and laps at the toes of their shoes.

Andrew slips at the bottom and falls on his side. He rolls over and stands up. His glasses are fogged and he takes them off and rubs them with his dirty shirt. Now they're dirty and he takes them off again and hands them to Robert.

"Can you get these clean for me, Dad?" he asks.

Robert wets his thumb and rubs the dirt off, huffs on each eyeglass, fogging up the lenses, then wipes them clear with the cuff of his shirt.

They sit under the bridge with their backs against a slab of sloped stone. It's cold, still spring, and Andrew shivers with his knees pressed up against his chest. Nathan squats by the mouth of the river, looking like a hunchback, flicking broken bits of gravel into the water. Robert smokes and the smoke drifts over the river like a fog.

"What're we doing down here?" Andrew asks.

"Taking some time," Robert says. "When do I get the two of you to myself for longer than ten minutes?"

"I don't know."

"Nathan, come over here. Sit beside your brother."

Nathan lumbers over, caveman-like, and leans back against the stone. In a few years he'll be as tall as Robert, maybe taller. He'll have to get used to dipping his head down in public places.

"I have something I want to say to the two of you."

"What is it, Dad?" Andrew asks.

"It's a delicate issue."

"Delicate?"

"Like your mother's glassware, except in a different way. Nathan, are you listening?"

"Yes."

"Look at me. I'm talking about love. I want to tell you boys that I love you. I love you more than anything in this world and it's important for me that you know I do. Do you know I do?"

Andrew straightens up. Nathan grips his knees with his large hands.

"Do you love your father?"

"Sure, Dad," Nathan says.

"Andrew? Do you love your father?"

"I guess so," Andrew says.

"Why do you have to guess?"

"I don't know," Andrew says and bows his head.

"Okay. That's okay."

The boys look at each other, communicating in silence the awkwardness of this moment, and Robert knows, as well, that if he and Brian were down here with Red, they might have already leapt into the river. Of course, their father had never told them he loved them, never like this, anyway, and Robert doesn't know if this is the best way to tell them or if, given another shot in the future, it will scare them just the same to hear his voice, soft but firm, talking about love.

"Can we go now, Dad?" Andrew says. "It's freezing down here."

"In a minute."

They sit in silence for a while. Robert smokes and looks at the river. Andrew rubs his hands up and down his arms. Nathan bites his fingernails.

"All right," Robert says. "We can go now."

They walk back up to the top and stand at the bridge railing and look at the river. Robert wonders if he was convincing enough, if his sons believe that he loves them as much as he says he does. Every rushed hug, every kiss on the corner of the lips, an awkward exchange, not a show of love, really, as much as proof that men shouldn't engage in soft, physical contact for more than a few seconds. In one quick motion, Robert moves behind Andrew and picks him up and hangs him over the wooden rails so that his feet dangle in the air.

Andrew screams not to drop him.

"Don't look down," Robert says.

But as soon as he says this, Andrew looks down at the muddy water and marsh grass and sharp rocks below.

"Dad, what are you doing?" Nathan shouts.

"Pull me back," Andrew pleads.

"I've got you, Bud," Robert says. "There's no reason to be frightened."

Robert tightens his grip, his fingers pressing against the muscles between Andrew's ribs.

Andrew's body goes limp.

"Dad!" Nathan shouts, moving closer.

Finally, Robert pulls Andrew up over the railing. He and Nathan run to the car. Robert stays by the railing a moment longer. He smells the foulness of the marsh, tastes the salt in the air.

Once back in the Wagoneer, he looks at the boys sitting in the rearview. Nathan has his arm around Andrew, who has been crying. Robert starts the car.

"Let's get some candy," he says.

After the boys choose their assorted candies from the wicker baskets along the shelf in the red penny candy store on Main, Robert drives through the Meadowbrook subdivision with the windows down, at peace in the smell of the dry dirt in piles, the yellow glaze of sawed trees, the foundations spread in the dug holes. Money is bulldozed land, poured concrete, railroad ties and two-by-fours, Sheetrock, posts and beams, brick, shingles, sod, shrubs, and doors waiting to be fitted into their hinges.

Inside the model home, Robert brews a pot of coffee so the house will smell like morning, like home. He spreads out the housing guides and the daily papers: the *Globe*, the *Wall Street Journal*, and the *Boston Herald*. He places a tray of raspberry and cheese Danishes by the coffee and eats one while looking out the back window to where a cardinal used to perch on a limb of an oak tree the previous spring when he'd just gotten the permits to start leveling the land. Now, the cardinal is gone.

High on candy buttons and Pixy Stix, Nathan and Andrew run through the half-framed houses and down into the dug holes where the foundations are to be built. The two of them, he knows all too well, are priceless advertisements—healthy, good-looking, happy, and white.

His inquirers today are mostly boat shoe– and cloth belt–wearing men and women in their early thirties, looking to settle down, to subject ambition and passion to memory.

"I wouldn't think of raising my sons anywhere else," Robert tells the Wheatons, a couple he met two weeks earlier. Sharon, the wife, is two months pregnant. Robert leads her to the plush blue couch in the living room. The husband, a young advertising executive named Jim, follows behind, then steps in front of Robert and turns toward the bay window, rubbing his chin and looking out at the stumps from the leveled trees.

"I love how open this room is," Sharon says. She said the same thing last time.

Jim looks at his wife wearily. Then his eyes shift to the side, to no exact point; though, Robert knows, Jim has most likely felt that sudden, abrupt end to his past life.

The elation Robert has always felt after making a sale is kin to power and a sense of being untouchable. His mood, though, is quickly depressed by the fact that his sons have no idea what he does for work, and Irene only seems to care about the money, or else she might say something stupid, like, "When you're happy, I'm happy."

What does being happy have to do with anything? he thinks, driving back to the house, the boys half-asleep in the backseat, a check for five grand folded neatly in his pocket. It's not about being happy. Successful people aren't happy. Sure, they have moments of remembering what it was like to be happy, but otherwise, they are action seekers. The more the terms are complicated, the more risk involved, the more alive they feel. It's an addiction. They are sources of power looking to plug in.

This is how his new relationship with Candice Dunning becomes useful. Around three o'clock in afternoon, as during most afternoons over the past month—when the open house for the model home finally closes—Robert drops the boys off and drives back to the subdivision and calls over to the Dunnings', asking Mike to look at a piece of land off-Cape.

Robert waits a half hour, then calls the Dunning house again and tells Candice to come by the trailer.

"Naughty boy," she says.

"Bring lunch," he says.

They are always so hungry afterward.

They like having to be quick. It makes what they are doing easier to forget. Her hair is blond and curly and wild, like the hair of a lioness's collar. She undresses, then flattens and folds and hangs her clothes over two separate chairs. Dust leaps into the light and floats there. They are tall, athletic people. They don't make love; they fuck. Standing up, he behind her, a leg wrapped effortlessly around his calf. He grabs hold of her hair and smacks her ass. She commands him to do it harder. She calls him "Daddy." She says, "Harder, Daddy." When they are through, her skin is blotchy and loose. She dresses, then brushes her hair. Robert holds his come in his hand. There's a towel under his desk.

Afterward, they eat turkey sandwiches and pickles, and neither of them talk about the sex. Robert is past the point of caring about his performance. Even if the sex is strange and violent, and not at all very good, they enjoy the secret of the act, which is the driving force of his seeing her in the first place—the childish hush-hush reexperienced, looking away from each other once it's over, unable to fully process what has happened, sensing the lingering consequences.

Candice leaves easily, kissing Robert's neck, his lips, poking his nose with the tip of her finger. Her smell is on his fingertips. He pushes open the windows of the trailer, grabs a can of lavender scent from his desk drawer, and sprays it in all four corners of the boxed-in room. In the model home, he washes his face and brushes his teeth. Later, he will go to the gym, steam and shower, return home a different man. He will sit at the dinner table with Irene and the kids and try to listen intently as each of them takes turns convincing Robert of the difference between a necessity and a desire, and the afternoon affair with Candice Dunning slips back into the small box of regrets that sits alongside the box of justifications.

NINE

THE DAY ROBERT HAD RETURNED HOME FROM HIS POST IN Germany, he'd found his mother sitting in the dark smoking cigarettes and drinking rose-scented wine.

"Where's Dad?" he'd asked.

"Your father, well . . . ," she swirled the wine around in her crystal glass, ". . . he went belly-up. I think that's the phrase he used, or belly-down? I'm not sure either makes much sense, the way you die, floating on water or facedown in mud. Anyway, we're broke, honey, end times, Nixon, Ford, the whole country's a mess, pack your bags, I'll come back for you . . . those are the sorts of things he was saying on his way out the door. That was two weeks ago."

Robert sat and, for a moment, felt the calm of a house without his father's presence. But it wasn't right. The sharp truth of the matter was that without his father he had no reason to fight against the many versions of him he had encountered in his thoughts and dreams. Sometimes Red was kinder than he had remembered. He kissed Robert's forehead and said good luck and pinched his ear. Robert looked forward to spending time with that man.

"Do you have any idea where he might be?" he asked his mother.

"My guess? He's in that awful apartment of his in Boston. The one he thinks I don't know about. I'll get you the address."

Robert's Boston had consisted at that time of ideas instigated by his father's dinnertime sermons. There was the Garden and not much else. Streets like the tentacles of a sea creature, flanging out toward the cars on their way to more peaceful destinations, pulling them back to the heart of the Common where preservation was more important than innovation, and the creature laughed at any proposed change, unless of course you were proposing a new rule or amending an old one. Robert remembered his father hoisting him up on his shoulders in the rafters of the Garden, smoke curling around his head, the giants like dwarves on the hardwood court below, K. C. Jones, John Havlicek, Bill Russell, the black and white and green, dancing in balletic arcs across the floor, and the red-faced, beer-swilling onlookers, yelling at the top of their lungs to pass the damn ball, get it into the post, let that sweet-toothed nigger slam it home. Driving the old Buick back to Wequaquet after a game, his father often said, maybe to himself, "It's such a simple idea. Put a ball in a hole and get a point."

Robert had realized even then that the old man believed he had been born too late, that all the simple ideas in this world had been thought of and the only real way to make it was to complicate them so the future would not look so redundant.

The door to his father's apartment had been left partially open. Robert pushed it forward with his forearm, fearing the worst: the back of his father's head blown out. But the three rooms in the apartment were empty, and the cabinets bare and the bed neatly made. Only the stale smell of cigar smoke told him Red had been here recently. In the fridge was a block of cheese, a half gallon of milk, and two bottles of beer. Where the carpet met the kitchen floor, Robert saw a sparkling diamond earring. He picked it up and placed it on the counter next to a chewed-down pencil and a two-day-old copy of the *Herald*.

Outside, a heavy snow had begun, small prisms of light glimmered around him. He buttoned up his coat, bowed his head, and forged down the street.

There was a bar at the corner of every block. What would he say to the bartender? Have you seen a man who looks like me but shorter, aged thirty years with thinning hair and a crackly Boston accent? Wasn't that man sitting at the end of every bar with quarter drafts from here to Brighton? After a shallow search he went back to his car and ran the heater and swept the snow off his windshield. The rich white flakes kept the day alive and suddenly the city seemed small and easy to navigate.

He'd searched the North End, the Leather District, even a few cheap dives in Chinatown, before turning onto Tremont Street, driving slowly past the prostitutes in their colored leggings and fake fur coats, shouting at him as he passed, "Warm me up, Sweetie!" Then to the South End, with the boarded-up duplexes and bums frozen in a tuck. He drove back up toward Boylston, where he remembered the old man outside a place one night after a Celtics game, a bar called the Tam, in the Combat Zone, his father flushed red and raging, pulling a man outside by the collar and hooking his head in his arm until the man handed over an envelope. Robert liked to believe his father had connections to the mob. He was in off the boat and had both a notorious temper and a spirited kindness to those he considered friends. But, looking at the bar now, the hookers in their heels slipping out the front door, men in long coats smoking by the curb, naval cadets with big mouths and not much money, he knew the mob, Irish or not, wouldn't be caught dead around here. His father was a gambler, he'd won, and he didn't want to have to drive up to Boston the next day even if the rule was to wait until the following morning.

The thought that his father would be inside was too obvious to ignore. But where else would a drunk go when everything around him was on fire? Hulk-like and straight-faced, Robert navigated through the crowded dive. He described his father to the bartender.

"Might as well be asking me to point a finger in the crowd," the bartender said.

In the piss-stained men's room, Robert patted his cheeks and neck with cool water. Then he searched his coat for a cigarette but had none. From the hall leading back into the barroom, he guessed it would take him a half hour or more to get through the crowd, and instead he turned back and left through the door to the alley. A few busboys squatted near the dumpster, smoking. A bum moaned softly each time they flicked a bottle cap at his head. The pavement was slick underfoot. Robert slid forward, trying to stop himself from colliding with the bum, but tripped over the body and landed on his forearms, tearing the cheap fabric of his coat. The busboys laughed, said something to each other in Spanish. Robert turned over. He recognized his father's jacket: a brown wool overcoat with cashmere inlay. The coat was thrown over the body like a blanket. The left side of his father's face pressed into the snow.

"Dad," Robert said.

Robert rolled his father over on his back, then stood behind him and bent down as though about to move a piece of furniture, shoving his arms up under Red's armpits and getting him to his feet. Either Robert had gotten a hundred times stronger since being overseas, or Red's body had degenerated that much faster with the booze and bankruptcy.

"Red."

"That's what they call me."

"You're as light as a woman," Robert said.

"I'm not no broad," his father said, his words degenerated with drink.

"I didn't say you were. I said you felt like one."

"Plenty of big, potato-eating broads in this city."

Robert sat his father down in the passenger seat and put the coat over his hunched body. His father's head bobbled as they drove over chunks of freezing snow toward the apartment.

That night Robert lay on the couch under the lone extra sheet he'd found in Red's closet. He hadn't been able to sleep. The sheet smelled like his father's aftershave. He heard a knock on the door, a key rustling in the lock on the other side, a woman's voice, "Shit, shit, shit, shit," the keys falling to the floor, heels clicking down the hall.

In the morning, Robert went into his father's bedroom, where Red was fast asleep, a slight smile across his lips. Robert put his hand to his father's forehead. He felt warm. He pulled up the plain, wooden chair and sat beside him for a while. He guessed your dreams didn't care where you slept, in a king-size mattress with Egyptian cotton sheets or on a twin bed under a stiff wool blanket.

When Robert knocks on the door to Red's house, the old man's second wife, Blanca, answers, slightly annoyed, it seems, that there is no servant to do it for her. Blanca is a big Swede with silver hair, pasty white skin, and too much makeup. She wears sunglasses and smokes long cigarettes, and he can't recall her ever once smiling in the fifteen years since she's been married to his father.

"Your papa's in ze tub," Blanca says apathetically.

"Is someone watching him?" he asks, though not as defiantly as it came to him in his mind, as he's still trying to process the foreign yet welcoming touch of Blanca referring to his father as "Papa."

"He won't let ze nurse in," Blanca says calmly. "He claims she giggle at him."

"He could drown, Blanca. Don't you have any sense?"

Robert's parents had divorced when he was in his mid-twenties. No one cared about it but him. He was too old for sympathy by then.

Robert moves past Blanca with a childlike huff and knocks on the bathroom door.

"What is it, honey?" his father says. He calls anything he loves honey, man or woman or animal.

"It's Bobby."

He can smell the old man's cigar.

"Are you smoking?"

"It's fine. The doctor says to indulge once in a while."

"There's nothing fine about it."

"What?"

"I said there's nothing fine about it."

"Why don't you come in already? My peace has been permanently disturbed anyhow."

His father comes from a time and place where men were constantly pressed up against one another, where nothing was private and they worked and ate and bathed in the same stinking rooms. Women were not allowed. All boys of that time knew the male body much better than the female. They still had the capacity for falling in love at first sight. "I fell in love with your mother at first sight," Red had told Robert soon after his divorce was final. "That's how little I'd actually seen."

There's a tray attached to the sides of the tub that holds an ashtray and a cup of tea. Shaving cream foam spots Red's face and neck. He has missed the hairs high up on his cheeks. His once thick, squat legs are now bony and bluish. His chest heaves as he exhales a dark cloud of smoke, the hair between his sagging skin like spun sugar, and the hair left on his head the remnants of a bird's nest loosened and swept away in the wind. To get this close to his father feels to Robert like moving toward a giant projector screen; where at first he believes he might see the character much clearer, the face begins to blur and becomes unrecognizable.

Robert is the only one in the immediate family still close enough to witness Red's day-by-day descent. His younger brother, Brian, lives off-Cape in the western part of the state. His sister had gone to Amsterdam when she was twenty-two and never returned to the States. She's married to an unsuccessful Norwegian artist named Frederick. Robert rarely speaks to either of them anymore. Sometimes he wonders if it's better that he remembers them alive and healthy, than how they might be now, how they might end up later.

"Dad, you need a mirror," Robert says, unfolding the razor.

"I know my face," the old man says.

Robert nicks the hairs beneath the bones under his eyes. He wipes the blade with a washcloth and presses the flat back of his hand under his father's chin and runs the blade up his neck.

"The neck is the hardest part," his father says softly. "My hand shakes."

"It's not easy with these old razors. You know they put out a much better product nowadays."

"Oh, yes. Yes, I'm sure they do."

Robert makes clean, even strokes up to the chin, the foam peeling away like a pear skin.

His father grabs Robert's wrist with a sudden, unaccountable force. He wants to say something. Spit gathers at the corners of his lips. His eyes begin to water. His body clenches. He lets go of Robert's wrist and relaxes back into the tub.

Robert hesitates with the razor and looks at his father's clouded eyes and the thin, wet lather on his face, then continues scraping the last hairs under Red's chin. The tobacco in the cigar crackles. Robert flinches and nicks his father. The small cut bleeds wickedly, but his father has his eyes closed now, doesn't appear to have felt a thing. Robert dampens a towel and puts it to his father's neck, then takes Red's hand and guides it to the towel to hold it there.

"All done," he says.

His father plucks the cigar from the ashtray and sticks it between his stained false teeth.

"How do I look?" he asks.

"Like a million bucks," Robert says.

TEN

ANDREW FUSSES AS HIS MOTHER STRAIGHTENS HIS COLLAR AND pulls down the sleeves of his jacket with a quick snap.

"Why do I have to wear this stupid suit?" he says.

"Because this is what you wear to someone's funeral, out of respect."

"I think Grandpa would want us to be comfortable."

"You're probably right. But that's not what we think."

"Why'd he have to die anyway?"

"You can't anticipate when people will die, honey," Irene says. "Just like you can't anticipate when someone will be born."

"Yes, you can," Andrew says. "Nine months, give or take a week, unless the water breaks early, then the doctor has to factor in the baby's weight and the development of its lungs and so forth. Some don't make it, which is sad. Some don't turn out right mentally. That's sad, too. But at least they get to live. That's what I figured happened to Nathan."

"Who told you that?"

"No one. I just was wondering."

"He was born perfectly normal. That was the best day of my life."

"And when I was born? Was that the second best?"

"No, I mean, I didn't mean it that way. I had two best days. That was the first, and you were the second. You get three in a lifetime. I imagine when one of you marries and has a grandchild, then that will be the third."

"What if we have more than one child?"

"Then I guess whoever came up with the idea of only having three best days was wrong."

"But you were the one who came up with it."

Irene stands and parts Andrew's hair with three quick strokes of her finned hand. He's smart. Perhaps too smart.

"Go get your brother," she says.

As Robert pulls up to the funeral home, so, too, does a black town car, just behind his Wagoneer. The back doors open and the boys jump out, chasing each other around the front lawn. Robert helps Irene out of the passenger seat, then calls for the boys to wait by the front door, where a man in a green jacket is standing peacefully with his hands crossed in front of him.

The short, paunchy driver of the town car tips his hat to Robert before racing around the back and opening the rear passenger door, from where Blanca emerges, slumped over, heaving holy gasps on the crosswalk. The pearls dangling from her neck knock against her breasts.

"Oh, Jesus," Robert says.

The poor driver does his best to console her, placing his arm around her waist, as she crosses her arm around his shoulder, her giant left boob seemingly suffocating him.

"Irene," Blanca cries over the driver's head.

Irene and Blanca exchange quick hugs. For some reason, Robert feels compelled to shake the driver's hand and does so. Then he half-hugs Blanca, like someone might a sick person they're afraid of catching the flu from. Together, the three join the boys at the top of the stairs and greet the greeter in the green jacket, whose pleasant, nonthreatening, boyish face is enough to ease them in toward the dead.

At the wake, the boys stand before the body and scratch at the pant legs of their stiff suits. They look at their grandpa's frozen face. His shoulders pressed back and his chest perfectly still. Robert instructs them to kneel in front of the casket and put their hands together.

"Pray," Robert says.

When they are finished, Nathan asks if he can go to the bathroom. Robert goes with him. Any chance to get away from this room and the smell of aftershave and heavy, floral perfume is welcome.

As they wash their hands at the bathroom sink, Red's eldest brother, Walt, shuffles by and pats Nathan's head, then drops his pants at the urinal, showing his small, wrinkled buttocks.

"That's Uncle Walt," Robert says.

Walt lets out a wounded moan, then farts.

He leans his head to the side and says, "It's either this or the other."

Robert moves about the funeral home receiving hugs, handshakes, and slaps on the back. What is this rude, intrusive ritual? he thinks. They look at you when you're born and they look at you when you're dead. In between, they can't stand to look at you.

Robert heads down the hallway and out the side door beside the funeral director's office and lights a cigarette. Mourners keep filing into the funeral parlor. Some he recognizes, former contractors, not retired, so much as hunched, arthritic, broken.

Robert remembers how when he was a kid, sitting in his father's office on Friday afternoons, he'd watch the same men make this kind of slow walk into the room, heads down, silent, as his father sat there expressionless, a set of checks in front of him, already written and signed. Then there are the locals, the lawyers, the members of the town council, all of whom had once viewed his father as something of a malevolent colonizer, destroying unspoiled land for homes, paved roads, and signage. Like good puritans, they are here to forgive.

Nathan sidles up beside Robert, his shoelace untied.

"It's funny," Robert says. "All these people and not one of them knew what a prick your grandpa was."

"Why is that funny?"

"Not ha-ha funny, funny like ironic."

Nathan looks at him.

"I can't explain everything, Nathan."

"Okay."

Robert puts his hand on Nathan's shoulder.

"When does he get buried?" Nathan asks.

"Tomorrow."

"Where?"

"Beachwood, by the Seven-Eleven."

"It's nice there."

"I don't know if any of them care how nice it is."

Nathan laughs.

"That's ha-ha funny," he says.

"Tie your shoelace," Robert says, clutching the keys in his pocket.

ELEVEN

Conditions must be right for mass destruction to take place. When a tornado forms, the only thing one can do is get the hell out of its path. And when Robert Kelly wakes up that Monday after burying his father, he feels in his gut the end that's coming.

Becky at the Dunkin' Donuts drive-through had been fired for stealing out of the register, and so a new kid, some Brazilian girl in braces, hands him his large coffee but forgets the Sweet'N Low. Minor, but telling.

At the office, Mike calls to say he's just met with Charlie from paving and Charlie from excavation, and Charlie's saying he won't finish the roads in the subdivision until they get paid and the other Charlie's threatening to fill in the hole they spent a week digging for the man-made pond.

"Haven't we paid them?" Mike asks.

We? Robert thinks.

"Tell Charlie I'll settle up with him in the morning. Mention my father. They used to work together."

"And what about the other Charlie?"

"What other Charlie?"

"From excavation."

"That's the one," Robert says and hangs up.

The Prestons and the Shedlocks have yet to sign the paperwork for the sale of the first two homes in the subdivision, so Robert makes copies of their contracts and signs for them, takes the contracts to the bank, and levies another two hundred grand against the sales, which should keep his head above water until his father's estate is settled.

That afternoon, in the office of Luscious Betterent Esq., Blanca, via speakerphone, says she plans to sell the house, move back to Sweden, and give 60 percent of Red's estate over to the animal humane society.

"Animals!" Robert shouts into the receiver. "You dopey cunt!"

"Thees is why I don come to office," Blanca says.

"This, you mean. This! This is why."

"Oh, you stupid English language."

Betterent picks up the phone and handles Blanca with the kind of graceful, unwavering tone that makes Robert envious. Robert stands up and paces around the office. He looks at the diploma Betterent had received from Harvard Law. Then he smashes the frame with his fist.

"Oh, for crying out loud, Bobby," Betterent says.

Robert holds up his bloody hand.

"No, one second, Mrs. Kelly." Betterent tosses Robert a handkerchief from the drawer where he keeps his nail file, comb, and hand lotion.

"Okay, Mrs. Kelly, I understand. Okay, I will handle it," Betterent says, and quickly hangs up the phone. "Sit down, you goddamn maniac."

With his hand wrapped in the handkerchief, already splotched with blood, Robert fumes and fusses like a boy who's done bad and wants to do worse.

"I don't have many options," Betterent says. "Your old man felt you needed to work for your own."

"Let me be honest with you, Luscious. I'm stretched tight. Everyone's scared the housing market is about to go bust. No one's buying."

This is the first time Robert has confessed his insecurities aloud.

"You're in a tough racket," Betterent says. "You have savings, right? You've put money aside for the kids, I hope?"

"I was expecting this money. I just had a hole dug for a pond in my subdivision. We're going to fill it with perch."

"Junk fish."

"No one's going to eat them. Listen. You can't imagine how much money I got wrapped up in this place."

On his desk, there's a photograph of Betterent holding up a giant bass, a cigar between his lips, his big white belly hanging over his soaked bathing trunks.

"I'll tell you what I'll do," Betterent says. "I'll charge the widow, have my secretary write it into my after-hours fee."

Betterent stands, meeting over.

"The carpet cleaning, the hanky, the frame, don't worry about it," he says. "Have that hand checked out. You don't want to get an infection."

As he walks to the trailer at the end of the road in the half-finished subdivision, Robert feels the ground underfoot is slightly tilted. He putzes around for a while, crumpling up bills from contractors he can't pay, tossing them into the trash can in the corner. He calls a few banks in Florida and Nevada, banks that extend credit to even the most destitute cases. But with a third mortgage and a Jeep Wagoneer worth next to nothing, Robert has no collateral to put up against a loan. He looks at the Rolex his father had given him the week before. Funny, he thinks. The old man probably knew Robert would have to sell it, and sell it soon. He examines the stainless steel minute hand, watching it click past the sixth diamond. It's already half past eleven. Candice will be by any minute. He watches the minutes and waits.

When Candice finally arrives a half hour later, he puts his arms around her for some level of support or comfort. He feels her back tighten. She shifts to the right as he tries to kiss her neck on the left.

"Don't," she says.

"Don't what?"

"That."

She has become more desirable than ever before.

"I'm going to visit my family in Chicago next week. This place gets so depressing when all the people leave."

"What does that have to do with us?"

But as he says this, Robert realizes this was just a summer fling, something he hasn't been part of since his days working construction for his father, when the Irish girls on working visas he'd make out with on the beach flew back home, and the boarding school girls took buses back west to the mountains, ivy, and castles where they belonged. There was one named Bethany who he thought he loved. She was from Belfast. They had planned on moving there at summer's end. He was sixteen. She was twenty-two. She had wide, wild eyes, hair as black as a crow's feathers. He had saved $167 for a plane ticket, and when he went to retrieve his money from under his mattress, it was gone. His father had flown to Vegas that week for the opening of the college football season. His cash was in the hands of a bookmaker, his Irish princess walking along the black sand of Giant's Causeway Beach, where they were to marry.

"I'm sure Mike won't miss any work," Candice says. "Sometimes it's hard to look at him."

"He doesn't suspect anything, does he?"

"Does it matter at this point?"

Robert had imagined a similar conversation during the nights when he felt the guilt of not feeling that guilty over the affair, in bed next to Irene. Now it just seems pathetic to even try to tell her that he had been with someone else.

"Anyway, I thought I'd let you know I won't be coming by for a while," she says swiftly, and with great indifference.

After Candice leaves, Robert stands outside the trailer and takes in a long breath, then lights a cigarette. He sits on the trailer step, thinking about his father, if the old man was ever ashamed of the things he'd done in his life, the drinking and the women. Then he's struck with the image of Bethany's shimmering green necklace bouncing against her pale chest, between her small breasts and pink nipples, when they made love. She was so small, he was afraid to hurt her. They drank beer and laughed and listened to music on the radio in the small bedroom of a beach cottage she shared with three other girls. That was something, Robert thinks.

On the drive home, Robert tells himself to stay positive. Then he sees a dead and gutted deer on the side of the road. He tells himself, his world is over, not yours. Then, a split second later, a vulture flies straight into the windshield, thumping off the glass like a hard fist. Robert slams on the brakes, and the rear wheels spin out. He's planing toward the Wequaquet River Bridge. He muscles the wheel left, then lets it fly right, through his fingers, and grips the wheel as hard as he can, slamming the gas and regaining control of the Wagoneer in time to get across the bridge and pull over, making sure he's alive. His insides feel as though they're screaming, clawing, knocking at the wall of his skin to get out. He presses his head against the steering wheel, against a shard of glass stuck in the wheel, and not until his heart rate slows does he see the piece sticking from his forehead, just a moon sliver of glass in a dot of blood, strange but laughable. The head, the hand, the heart. Something, he tells himself, is coming for you.

That evening, Robert sits with his family at the dinner table, wishing for quiet. But Nathan has been sent home early from school, and that needs to be addressed, Irene says, as she passes around the glazed carrots. Robert tries to keep his father's tone out of his voice when he speaks to his boys, especially now, when he's conscious that the more he fights against being like his father, the more he finds he can't escape the transition.

He eats hurriedly, cramming a fork with a potato and vegetable, along with an oversized portion of baked chicken, and somehow fitting it all into his mouth, grinding the food down and swallowing while collecting another round on his fork, finishing his meal in half the time it takes the rest of the family to eat. Then he sits for a while watching the boys, soon instructing Nathan and Andrew to keep their elbows off the table and not to make sandwiches with their rolls.

Finally, he's had enough, folds his napkin, and places it on the table.

"What happened to you at school?" he asks Nathan.

Andrew cracks his toes. Nathan looks to Irene, who has her face down, staring at her plate as if it's holy.

"I hit Kevin Gaffney," Nathan says.

"I know you hit him. The whole town knows you hit him. But why did you hit him so many times? Who taught you how to fight like that?"

Robert glances at Irene, silent and apprehensive, as though she feels bad for their son, as though some wickedness he can't control is in him and it's Robert's fault.

"Did I teach you to fight like that?" he asks.

"No. I guess not."

"You guess not?"

"Some of the stories you tell us about how it was for you growing up, and how it was in Vietnam—"

"I was never in Vietnam."

"I thought you was."

"Were," Irene says. "Were."

"I was in Germany. I told you that. I was lucky. We had trouble on occasion. There's always trouble somewhere."

"Kevin was picking on him," Nathan says.

"And? Your brother can defend himself, can't he? I taught both of you the same way, didn't I?"

"You did knock Nathan's tooth out that time," Irene says.

"Eat the rest of your dinner," Robert says.

"Don't talk to me like I'm a child."

"Then stop butting in unless you have something constructive to say."

"Let him tell us what happened so we know his side of things, Robert, please."

"Okay, all right. Go on then."

"We were all outside after school, waiting for the buses, and Kevin comes by and shoves Andrew right into one of those handicap signs, and I went and helped Andrew up and he was bleeding from the mouth and then Kevin said, 'Now both the

Kellys are retards.' And when the buses came around the corner, I ran out and grabbed Kevin and tossed him into the side of one and hit him."

"Did he fight back?"

"I don't know. I think so."

"Did he?" Robert asks Andrew.

Andrew shrugs. His lip is swollen.

"He was in the parking lot. He couldn't see."

"My question is when did you know to stop hitting him?"

"I didn't," Nathan says. "Ms. Vech pulled me off him."

"And so you punched her, too?"

"She grabbed my butt."

Andrew giggles.

"Shh," Irene says.

"So you didn't really know what you were doing then? Is that what you're saying?"

"I think that's what I'm saying."

"How can you think you're saying something?"

"What?"

"Kevin Gaffney's in the hospital. He's got fractured bones in his face and his mouth is sewn shut. He's going to need reconstructive surgery, plus some new teeth. Do you know how serious a matter this is? How much it's going to cost me?"

"Please, not the money, Robert," Irene breaks in. "It's not about money."

"Of course it is. I have to pay for it. Not only that, but the dent in the school bus."

He looks at his son, and the way Nathan is looking back, with complete disregard for consequence, it doesn't enrage Robert the way he thinks it should. Instead, he's sort of glad, that in this town of so many pussy kids raised by their pussy parents, a boy like his exists to keep everyone honest.

"You don't know how strong you are, Nathaniel. I mean, it's good, good for the field. But these other boys, they're not as tough as you, they don't have the same insides as you do. Understand?"

Nathan nods.

"You're going to be out of school until after the winter break. You're going to help pay for what you did to that boy by going to work for me. Do whatever we ask you to do. No complaining. You think you're tough? We'll see just how tough you are."

"What about his schoolwork?" Irene says, having only now heard of this plan.

"He's going to keep up with the class. I'm having the dean fax over all his teachers' lesson plans for the rest of the year. When he gets home, he'll shower and eat, and go into his room and do his schoolwork. Maybe it'll help him focus. I mean, who fails sixth grade science?"

"Oh, don't be such a prick," Irene says.

Andrew giggles again. Then Nathan giggles.

Robert feels his face contract. He can't hold still. He starts to laugh along with the boys, all three of them breathless.

"This is serious," Irene says, trying to stifle a laugh. "Isn't it serious?"

"Yes," Robert says, howling now. "It's very serious."

As she washes out the mugs and coffeepot in the sink, Irene dreams of Florence. Why had she and Robert gone from Paris to Rome and back on their vacation last year? Robert had said he knew someone who had claimed that Florence wasn't worth the money. And maybe she hadn't missed anything. Maybe the smell in the Accademia where David stands is just the smell of sweaty tour groups surrounding what Michelangelo saw, not seeing, but snapping photographs, so that twice removed were they from actually seeing, and even farther away once the guide gave his opinions, mixed them with what their perception was, to see him under the dome of light, having fought or going to fight—now they had an answer. But it was better to see it alone, to let yourself be there, because you knew what the room looked like and you had studied the statue in a book of Michelangelo's work, and you had pictured it there in front of you, surrounded by no one, not even you, looking at every fine detail, the vein down the right side of his arm, the tips of his fingers, the slight curve that reveals the muscle in his leg, and all of it is for you, that night, that month, until you had to return the book, and then you knew it better than you would having seen it once, in person, and you wouldn't be swayed to think of it differently with the tourists (and you a tourist) knocking into your shoulder as they raise their cameras and click until this kind of music of whispers and clicks and footsteps removes the silence.

Robert's voice sweeps through that city of asters and stars. The browning grass and shedding trees outside the kitchen window.

She flinches when his hand touches her side.

"What were you thinking about?"

"Oh, nothing."

"Nothing? No one thinks of nothing."

Irene feels an urge to plunge her thumbs into Robert's eyeballs. Instead, she slaps his ears, and keeps slapping them, wild, furious, unhinged.

"What is the matter with you?" Robert says, grabbing hold of Irene's wrists and pinning her against the kitchen island.

Her breath slows and Robert feels the tension in her wrists release.

"I'm exhausted," she says. "So fucking exhausted."

TWELVE

BY OCTOBER 1992, NOT EVEN THE MOST ISOLATED BUILDERS IN the country can ignore the doomsday projections. The papers are calling for a housing recession by as early as winter. Still, Robert keeps his contractors working through the rest of autumn, on borrowed loans, having convinced the banks he has enough equity to pay them back. The country is at war, small businesses are folding up, and commercial real estate is at an unaffordable premium only recession-proof companies can take on, sensing like wolves the need people will have for video rentals and microwaveable hamburgers and honey-cured ham from God knows where. But Robert isn't going to be stifled by the banks' suggestions that he stay put for a year or two, let the market work its way back to level. His ego impresses even himself. He'll beat the market. He's a salesman, after all, and what good is a salesman if he can't even sell himself on the future.

Then, in a moment of destiny or irony or hallelujah, Robert's college roommate, Frank, rings him up at his house on a Sunday afternoon, while Robert is taking a drubbing on the NFL, asking if he might be interested in selling land in Tennessee.

"What do I know about Tennessee?" Robert says.

"Right. What does anybody know about Tennessee?"

Frank explains.

The proposed town is called Indian Trees Lake. Some lake, somewhere outside of Nashville. It's a scam—a smart one. You sell land, pocket the money, build a house or two, sell more land, until there's no land left to sell, and then you ask for more money, complain about costs, flooding, corrupt building inspectors, etcetera.

But Robert has ethics. Doesn't he?

Don't I? he thinks. He thinks about the summer when he was eleven years old and had the idea to open his own ice-cream stand. He needed someone to stake him first. His father said no, ice cream melts, dummy. His mother was asleep at the kitchen table. Robert took three bucks from his mother's purse and went to the A&P and picked up three gallons of ice cream and a bag of ice. The trick now was to say the ice cream was homemade. Even if he was selling it cheap, some people might pass by his stand to the parlor on Main because they made their ice cream right there in the back, charging a dime for your regular flavors and fifteen cents for, say, your banana or cantaloupe. He made up a sign that read YOUR FAVORITE HOMEMADE ICE CREAMS. Maybe he remembered his father telling him how the only way to really sell anything in America is to make them believe they already have what you're selling. He set up his stand near the stop sign up the road. He figured he could get a nickel a scoop, two-fifty a gallon, take in a total of four dollars, fifteen cents, after the bag of ice. Then, depending on demand, he could reinvest, buy six gallons, ten, twenty, hire the Sturgis kid next door, Brian's friend, to run ice for him, have a line of cars all honking their horns for the guy in front to make up his mind on what flavor he wanted. He saw a shop, with that same old sign above the door, people around the corner, people sighing loudly when he called out they had no more chocolate left. Then he'd open up another shop in Hyannis, and another in Buzzard's Bay, really playing to the tourist crowd—Famous Cape Cod Ice Creams—and soon he'd have shops up and down the East Coast, and a deal to box and freeze the gallons and sell them in every A&P across the country. It did cross his mind that what he was doing wasn't exactly on the up-and-up, but, after seeing his twenty-year plan, he didn't mind a kid trying to make it on his own. And when he sold his first cone, he taped the dollar to the front of his stand, and it stayed there for about fifteen minutes, until his father came by with a bat and demolished the desk and cooler and sign, then took the dollar and plugged it in his pocket.

"You owe your mother three dollars, plus interest. Two points every day until it's paid." He was steaming. That was the first time Robert really understood why they called his father Red. "I'm not going to have a thief for a son. My boys have ethics. We don't steal. We don't cheat. Understood."

Robert nodded his head.

He nods his head now as Frank says his name into the receiver.

"You there, Bob?"

"I'm here."

"So, what do you think?"

"Oh, fuck your ethics, Bob."

Later, watching his kids run around the backyard pegging each other with acorns, Robert says to himself, Why the hell not? With the housing market going from bad to worse, he calls Frank back the following morning.

"I'll send you out the prospectus today," Frank says.

Robert knows there are so many dupes out there and the prospectus Frank has developed looks promising: seventy-five lots with lake views, private docks, a community center with tennis courts and a fitness room, and a free membership to the local country club.

Paradise Is Closer Than You Think is written on the cover in soft blue letters, above the heads of two believable-looking retirees, folks who have never been beautiful or rich but have at last found a way to be happy.

Even Robert, who is no dupe, believes a town like Indian Trees Lake still seems possible. He sees it as a place of comfort and freedom, the small-scale America that people work so hard for, the end of dreams.

The first rule of any good salesman is being able to sell to yourself before anyone else.

An initial investment of five thousand dollars is all that's required to lock up one of the last remaining lots. The money is pooled in with other retired citizens' money, and all of Indian Trees Lake will become a shared community with shops and corner stores, fine restaurants, and planned weekend activities. Even if you don't intend on living there full-time or at all, or you're nearly on your way to that paradise in the sky, what a once-in-a-lifetime investment for your children, for your grandchildren.

Robert spends his weekends calling strangers from a sheet culled by David Bess, a hopeless alcoholic he and Frank knew from the old days, who now works in the real estate market down in Boynton Beach, Florida. He has a knack for extortion, it turns out. On a three-way call with Robert and Frank, he had explained how.

"You get middle-income folks who've been told all their lives they should invest in real estate, but were skeptical, and with everyone raking it in around them, the stock market in a tailspin, and their days running out, they'll think your call is a God sign."

On the phone, Robert promises recently retired Midwesterners naturalistic beauty, good weather, and fine, southern hospitality. For every five nos, there's a maybe, and for every three maybes, there's a sure-why-not.

Promptly, at 5:45 in the evening, he rings Jim and Sharon Estes, who shout over each other while sharing the phone, asking, "Who is this? What do you want? Indian Trees? What the hell is an Indian Tree? Go milk a goat!"

Next, he dials the number for Lee and Ruth Hodges, and when a woman answers, he asks if she's interested in living out the rest of her days in a place so peaceful, she'll think she's already died and gone to heaven.

"I'm out of lemons," Ruth Hodges says.

"Lemons?"

"Can you pick some up for me at the store?"

"Sure, I can do that."

"I drink my water with a little lemon, that's the secret."

"The secret to what?"

"What?"

"The secret to what?"

There's silence on the other end.

"You know," Ruth Hodges says, "I can't remember."

By seven o'clock at night he's been told to fuck off, suck corn, and sit on an Indian Tree; two couples agree to see a prospectus, and two more agree to send a check for five thousand dollars, after Robert amps up his pitch, claiming there are only two lots left, and one he's already promised to a famous actor with the initials P.N.

Frank, David, and Robert split 75 percent of the cash from each initial investment. The next investment is ten thousand dollars to start building. If investors don't want to move there in the next year or so, they can rent the house and Charity Investments, the company name Bess has come up with, will handle the paperwork and collections for a small fee. Bess, Frank, and Robert send investors stock photos of a lake with boats nestled up to wooden docks and kids running along a sliver of beach, with a note:

The only thing missing here is YOU!

By his estimate, in just under two months, Robert has raked in nearly five hundred grand. But once every lot has been sold, Bess urges him to keep selling.

"It's nearly Christmas," he says. "People are looking to spend money on a grand scale."

Robert has an inclination to get out, the same as when he saw the subdivision start to fail, but his pride trumps his panic, and even if he loses all, he thinks, at least he fought for more.

Then one of the investors, a former police chief from some town in Kentucky, drives to the Lakes, sees there are no lakes, and starts making calls.

On a snowy morning in mid-December, the FBI knocks on the trailer door, where Robert has been making his calls to Bess and Frank, who aren't picking up the phone. The subdivision is clouded in windswept flakes. Robert wonders if Candice has come back, and as he's about to open the door, it swings forward and knocks him in the head.

"You knocked him in the head," one of the agents says.

"He'll be fine," another says.

"He's bleeding. Jesus, Matt, he's not a gangster."

Robert touches his head, sees the blood on his fingers, looks at the two figures before him, blurring in and out of focus.

"We'll stitch you up, pal," the first agent says.

"And you're under arrest," the other says.

THIRTEEN

Early Christmas morning, two weeks before he's set to go to trial for his role in the Indian Trees Lake scam, Robert sits at the kitchen table and cries. He is finally broke. The federal government has seized his assets, the boys' college funds have been drained, and the cars and jewelry and furs pawned. Robert still has the Wagoneer, which, he knows now, is worth more in parts than in whole. He has his family, too. When the boys bound down the stairs, he wipes his eyes and hugs them and pats their butts on the way into the living room.

Standing next to the glittering tree—which he and the boys had driven up to Plymouth to chop down—is the NordicTrack Classic Pro Skier assembled by Robert in the carriage house two nights before and tied with a thick ribbon and bow.

"It's a brand-new invention," Robert says, having seen endless commercials of unnaturally fit and big-breasted women with tight abs and tighter asses, cross-country skiing, and, having noticed one morning as Irene was half-dressed, folding laundry in the bedroom, just underneath her panties the dimpled mass of flesh that meant the end of strong, feminine legs, and the beginning of aging, cheesy thighs. The gift, then, is a half-hearted attempt to get Irene to start exercising. All new things were like nothing you'd ever seen, until you saw it and then it was just another thing taking up space. But these new inventions gave him hope that if he was persistent and kept his ears and eyes open, he would be there on the ground floor for one of them someday. He was young still. He had nerve enough to fight.

He has already made the coffee and started a fire in the fireplace. Now he sits on the couch looking at the NordicTrack Classic Pro Skier, the bow tied around the straps of the skis, spread open and ready for use. The boys' presents have already been stacked in the order that Irene felt they should be opened. The boys swing their stockings in front of them, sit beside each other in front of the fire, and tip over the stockings, emptying out the candy and baseball cards and lotto tickets onto the floor.

"Merry Christmas," Irene calls from the kitchen, and Robert hears himself say, "Merry Christmas," but the sound of his voice feels very far away.

He watches the boys scratch the lotto tickets with pennies they have found under the couch cushions. Neither wins a prize, but the winning doesn't seem to matter as much as the possibility of winning, and they quickly discard the losing tickets in the fire.

Irene stands by the fire, holding a tray of butter cookies filled with jam she has prepared every Christmas morning since the children were born. She puts the tray down and sits, and the boys hug her and she kisses them gently and sweetly before they run to their presents and shake the boxes, deducing by weight and size the general contents of what's inside.

Then the boys turn their attention to the NordicTrack Classic Pro Skier with an exalted curiosity, pulling the straps over their knees, skiing backward, pretending the cord is a horsetail.

"Go ahead and open your presents now," Irene says to the boys, avoiding Robert's eyes.

"It doesn't even have to be a gift for you but for all of us," Robert explains. "You should see the results on these people after just a month."

"I understand," Irene says coolly, then covers her legs with a blanket.

Robert lights a cigarette and walks over to the machine, plugs it in, and hits a few buttons to make sure the boys haven't broken anything. He puts his feet in the straps and starts skiing. A breath of cigarette ash plumes out onto the face of the electronic pad.

"There's even a cable you can hook to the TV, so you can watch your soaps," Robert says between puffs on the cigarette. But the rest of the family ignores him.

Once the boys have finished opening their presents, Irene shoves a wrapped envelope into his hand. With his fingernail, he slits open the wrapping paper and pulls from the envelope two tickets for the Rolling Stones at the Boston Garden in February.

He looks at the tickets and then at the NordicTrack Classic Pro Skier. He knows he was wrong to buy her this for Christmas. Maybe as an out-of-the-blue present, but not Christmas, and he'll have to apologize, but to force him to apologize with a gift like this, tickets to the Stones, a gift he has essentially paid for, and now can't afford, is criminal.

According to the tickets, the seats are just right of the stage, a few rows back so that they can sit during the slower numbers.

"Good seats. We'll probably need earplugs, though," Robert says.

"Earplugs," Nathan says. "Don't be a homo, Dad."

Andrew starts to giggle, then looks at his father and quiets instantly.

"What was that?" Robert says, and then, in an effort to

make up the ground he has lost, he drops this little number on his son:

"You know, Nathan, you could stand to use that machine a few hours a day, too. You're quite the fatso."

The word feels so antiquated, so old and histrionic, Andrew is now giggling uncontrollably. Tears form in Nathan's eyes, his head bowed, shoulders slumped. Irene throws up her hands.

"I'm done with this Christmas," she says, and for the next few minutes, all three of them stay still as she hurriedly collects the wrapping paper into a black trash bag, finally carrying the bag into the kitchen and climbing the stairs to the master bedroom.

Those wild movements have scared them into the present, as though whatever had just been said was already a memory waiting to be dredged up years later.

Robert lights another cigarette and sips his coffee. Luckily the boys have other toys to entertain them: plastic monkeys with curled arms they can connect and let swing from a plastic ladder, a tape recorder to use when they perform their mock radio show *Nate and Andy's Fart Time Fun Hour,* a remote-controlled car (the third Robert has bought this year, which he knows will be broken by the next day and is the reason he has kept the receipt).

"Go on," Robert says, "play."

The boys are content; it doesn't take much. Maybe he was the same when he was a boy, Robert thinks, hiding these acts of violence away and with great focus and determination redirecting his attention to the pleasures in front of him.

There are two presents left under the tree, both for him. One is from the boys, a small box hastily wrapped in newspaper comics. Inside the box is a money clip with his initials engraved on the back. Elegant, useful, and inexpensive. The other is from

Irene, and by the size and shape of the box, he knows it can only be one thing: the snakeskin boots he had seen in a shop window in Manhattan years ago. Irene had walked ahead of him but came back to where he was standing, and he said how he had wanted to be a cowboy when he was a kid, and she had said, "Who says you still can't?" When he daydreamed he often did so thinking of big sky country, cattle trains, sleek brown horses, saloons and spittoons, silver-plated pistols, and fires whining in the cool, desert twilight. The previous spring, he had looked into taking a trip to a cattle range, where they let you play the part of a cowboy for two weeks, but it seemed superficial and overpriced; if he was to be a cowboy then he'd have to be one for life and that was not the life he was given. He'd need a horse, and the boots, and money, too. There was danger. He did not have to wrangle over prices with big-powered Texans. He took the money and the guns and the women.

The snakeskin boots are a start; they make the outlaw dream real, the scales freshly polished and with two loops on the ends to pull them up his calf. Maybe Irene has an inclination that he will run. Maybe she wants him to after all.

He sits on the couch and pulls on the boots, then stands and begins to walk. He nearly falls over and has to grab hold of the tree, shaking loose a flurry of pine needles. His heels clack on the hardwood floor as he walks to the full-size mirror in the bathroom, where Robert is overcome with how ridiculous it all looks: his leg up on the sink in his New England home, the snow outside, the snakeskin boots he can't even walk in. He sits on top of the toilet seat and pulls off the boots, smells the leathery insides. A brief sting of joy hits his throat. Then guilt. Then confusion.

He's no outlaw. He's no family man.

He doesn't know who he is.

FOURTEEN

In an effort to save money, Irene decides not to have the oil drum filled and so, at night, has the boys in sweaters, under heavy comforters. They sleep longer than usual in that warmth. So long, that on the first day back from winter break, they miss the bus and Irene has to drop them off. Robert has been out of the house for three weeks now—Christmas was the last straw—and has only called once to tell the boys he loves them and to tell Irene he's sorry. She refused to accept his apology and hung up the phone, her hand trembling. As she drives back toward the house, she thinks, fuck it, and gets on the highway toward Boston. She still has Robert's credit cards, and whether or not he can pay them off anymore is of no concern to her.

She parks in a lot near Newbury Street and, in her cheap wool coat, walks the crowded sidewalks full of vibrant, healthy-looking people. She has been on the Cape all through winter and so hasn't been around more than a dozen people at one time. Even the children who run to catch up to their parents, or sit impatiently on the benches while their mothers gather together their shopping bags, appear to have sweet, harmless faces and neatly combed hair.

Yes, she has put on weight. The purging has had the opposite effect than she had hoped. And she's been smoking more than usual, and in the unnatural light of the designer boutiques, she notices creases in the skin around her eyes and mouth. At Serenella, she tries on a number of cardigan sweaters, moving up in size, so that they hang down over her hips. Buy big, she thinks, because when you lose the weight, it will be that much more noticeable.

At the cash register, the Amex is declined, and the MasterCard and the Cape Bank check card.

"Seems your man has some explaining to do," the sleekly dressed, long-armed woman at the register says. The tips of her turquoise colored fingernails on her right hand hold the cards as though in a bird's claw.

Irene smiles, embarrassed.

The other women in line look at her as though she's an abandoned puppy, their greatest fear to be left wanting.

What does one do without money?

Irene feels like a fraud. Shopping is a habit, a way to fight boredom or gruesome thoughts of what if. This isn't me, she tells herself. She has been coasting through the days. But she believes it's important to struggle, that in never being challenged she had become soulless.

"I'll put these back," the saleswoman says and refolds the items on the counter. "But I need to cut up the cards."

The long winter shows in the blackened, crusted snow pushed to the curbs and corners along the street.

Irene drops her wallet in her purse and walks out of the store not too quickly. Outside she tips over her purse and pours out the contents on ground. She takes her wallet and picks up the change—pennies and nickels and dimes—and her lipstick and car keys, then kicks the purse into the parking lot. She walks to the pharmacy and buys a candy bar and sits on a bench in the park nearby where the boys used to play when they had first moved to town. She tears off the wrapper and bites into the hunk of chocolate, exhaling like someone who has just come up from being underwater too long.

Past the swing set, monkey bars, and spring horses, there are trails leading into the woods. She decides on the one with the fewest footprints—though there are doe prints, or are they the paw prints of a lost dog?—and walks, looking up at the trees, wondering, what am I supposed to think of these trees? What are their names? Why can't I remember something so simple, and vital? Still looking up, she misses a large root bulging up through the dirt, across the path, trips forward, and hits her head on the ground. A pratfall, it feels like. She laughs, outside herself, and brought back to the recent past, watching herself fall, flail, like a child without the experience to know yet how to break a fall (with your elbows, dummy, not your noggin). She comes to, rolls over. The tree branches are a blur, swollen, crooked arms made of the wood of the trees she cannot name. She closes her eyes, squeezes them; soft, hot tears bead at the corners. Then a voice, voices.

"Are you okay?" a man asks. "Is she okay?" talking to someone else.

"Don't touch her," a woman hollers. "We need to call someone."

"Oh, sure, let me just shout into this can on a string."

"Sarcasm, Alan. Remember your homework from the therapist? Work on controlling your sarcasm?"

"Sure. And you work on controlling trying to control everything."

"This is not a good example of that."

Irene realizes now that they must be husband and wife.

"Miss?" the man says. "Can you hear me? Miss?"

Irene opens her eyes. No trees. Just two, homely faces, pale, red-cheeked, necks covered with matching red and green plaid scarves.

"I tripped," she says, her voice shallow at first, then coming back to her, "then I thought I'd lie here for a while."

"It's pretty darn cold out."

"So help her up, Alan," the wife says.

"I'm going to, Rose, Jesus. I'm just trying to get some information first."

"Sorry, Doctor. I didn't know we were in the ER. I must've mistaken you for George Clooney."

"And I'm the one who's accused of being sarcastic?"

As they continue to bicker, Irene gets up and brushes the snow off her pants and jacket.

"Really, I'm okay," she says.

"See," Alan says.

"We can help you back to your car," Rose says. "I think we just go out this way, right, Alan?"

Alan looks unsure.

"We came in from that side," he says, pointing behind him, "didn't we?"

"Magellan over here," Rose says.

"Again with the sarcasm."

"Okay, well, why don't you start taking control then? Yes, you control and I'll be sarcastic. A role reversal, a game. This should be fun, actually. Tell us, chief, this way or that way?"

Alan rubs his eyebrows, raising up uncut hairs, then shuts his eyes and begins to tap his forehead with his index and middle fingers as though playing the first two keys on a piano. He opens his eyes and looks at Irene, then at his wife.

"Perhaps this woman has the right idea," he says, and sinks

down, bracing himself on one arm, until he has lowered his body to the ground, where he spreads out like a mass.

Rose looks at Irene as if to say, *Can you believe him?* or, *Can you believe all men?*

"Oh, for crying out loud, Alan," she says. Then, she says, "Why the hell not?" and kneels on the ground and unfurls at his side.

At least they're trying, Irene thinks, Rose and Alan. Maybe that's all a marriage really is, trying, failing, trying again, until one or the other gives up.

Irene walks the path back to the park. Still feeling a bit dizzy, she sits down on the bench again, until her eyes are able to focus. Dirty and wet and left behind or forgotten or blown away to here, against the leg of the bench, is a faded pink baseball cap with a print of an orange-yellow sun, and the directive, the call, in purple letters: VISIT PLUM ISLAND, MA.

"Why the hell not?" Irene says aloud.

Irene goes back to the house and, in her bedroom, shuffles through her underwear drawer. When they had money, Robert used to give her cash at the start of the week, a kind of allowance. She spent it on things—accent furniture, dinnerware, stereo equipment—to fill the house, things they didn't really need, but looked needed, looked like they belonged once they were set in the empty spaces she found for them. Whatever money was left, she hid in her underwear drawer, as though subconsciously expecting she might need it at some point. She has eighty dollars left, and the first twenty is spent filling up the gas tank.

She takes Route 1 to Scotland Road, listening to a tape of Van Morrison's *Astral Weeks*, singing the words she knows beneath his voice, smoking and flicking the ash from her cigarette out the window. She's much younger like this, and she doesn't look at her face in the rearview mirror.

Few shops are open along the main road on the island. She passes shanty homes and mansions and a small harbor, parks in the lot across from the beach. The wind blows her back a bit as she takes the wooden walkway to the beach and sits on the steps and stares out at the sea. The chill in the wind pushes tears from her eyes, and she turns her head to see a kaleidoscope image of clouds and sun and sea grass along the dunes.

Late in the afternoon, she asks to use the phone at the only inn on the island and calls her neighbor, Francine, a widow in her midsixties who has taken pity on Irene since Robert left, declaring that whenever Irene needs some grown-up time, she'll be happy to watch the boys for her. But Irene has been reluctant to let anyone near the boys, unsure if they'd lash out in her absence, if some secret violence waits in them, ready to be used on an unsuspecting subject.

"I'd be delighted to help," Francine says, in a way that sounds condescending, as though Irene is interrupting something important, something that will require her to do a favor for Francine in the imminent future.

Irene waits for Francine to jot down the number of the inn, then gives instructions as to what the boys can and can't eat, and then Francine says, "Don't worry, go enjoy yourself."

But how can she enjoy herself? Who is she without her boys? Panic sets in. She shouldn't be here. There are no such things as signs. The hat was just a hat. Plum Island is just a place. You are just a mother, and not a very good one, leaving your boys with this woman you barely even know. You're a bad neighbor, too.

She's on her way to her car when, in the sinking orange light, a hand clamps down on her fatty triceps and pulls her back from a large pothole just off the curb. The woman is dressed as a gypsy, cartoonish, with a red scarf wrapped around her head and long peacock-like earrings, and a red sash across a knee-high black dress. But she has radical leather boots, double knotted hair, and a hard, tanned face. Irene thinks this makes her look trustworthy. A face like hers means she has seen certain things and has suffered, and is unafraid of sacrifice.

"I saved your life," she says in a deep, Eastern European accent, which sounds very near to the cartoon vampire her children used to watch on television every Saturday morning.

"Well," Irene starts, then looks back at the pothole, then to the woman, amused by her dress and brazenness. "I wouldn't go that far."

"You could have tripped, fallen awkwardly, and broken your neck. Maybe you fall and hit your head and suffer bleeding in your brain. Or maybe you twist your ankle and tomorrow, or the next day, you try to get down the stairs and fall again, break your neck or hit your head, and suffer bleeding in your brain. Are these not possibilities?"

Irene nods, says, "Thank you," and steps over the pothole. But as she's about to cross the street, the woman calls to her in a different voice, an accent familiar to Irene, hypernasal, using the *aw* sound for *a* when she says, "Please, dear, come talk with me awhile."

Her name is Sybil, and she's originally from Long Island. She used to live on the Lower East Side during her twenties, then in San Diego, Seattle, and Chicago, before marrying a man who owned a boat and had it docked in Plum Island.

"He's long dead now. He had lots of money, you see."

She tells Irene how she got into the business of reading people's futures. She felt the gift when she was young, when she had predicted her mother's suicide.

"In a flash, I saw her body lying in our claw-footed tub, half-filled with a deep red. I remember running into her bedroom and waking her up from one of her naps. She smiled at me. I thought, ignorantly, she must be happy. Then, three weeks later . . ."

"How horrible," Irene says. She thinks maybe Sybil knows something she will never know, or maybe she's just a macabre person, filled with the sinister stuff of life. She walks with Sybil down the sidewalk as if they are old friends, until finally they reach the front door to what Irene assumes must be her place of business, a basic storefront window with curtains closed and letters in red displaying her name in an arc: SYBIL. Below the letters a pair of hands seem to appear from behind a cloak and surround the prosaic crystal ball.

"Trust me, I understand your reservations. You seem like an intelligent woman. But people play into this shit, you see. If it means someone's more likely to pay to hear their future, why the heck not?"

"Looks like a scam to me."

"That's the attraction, though, get it? Most people think it's a scam, so I play it up and they come in and want to expose me as a fraud. Those are the easiest people to read. Most of the time I have them in tears in minutes."

"I've cried all I care to in the last three months."

"Yet, here you are."

Sybil unlocks the door to her shop and turns on a light standing on a small table in the center of what serves as her waiting room, with four chairs along the wall and a red cloth pinned to the side of the door, which leads to the larger room where she performs.

Irene follows Sybil into the room and waits while Sybil turns on a low light, then another.

"Would you like some water or tea?"

"No, thank you. I don't think I'm in the mood for something like this. My kids are waiting for me back home."

"I imagine you called a sitter," Sybil says.

"How would you know . . . oh, the man at the inn. I see. I understand now."

"What do you see? Don't give me that much credit, darling. Sure, most of this is a disguise, but not the cards, and not the third thing that hangs in the air between us and the world. You don't really believe I can read futures, do you? My mother didn't die in a tub. But I had that image. Instead she died slowly, day by day, in a boring, lifeless marriage to my deadbeat father. Now she lives in a trailer in Hollywood, Florida. You said you had kids, it's late, you don't strike me as someone who would leave them unattended. Pretty easy guess. But, that's not what I do with the bright ones. What I do with the bright ones is slow everything inside us and outside us down just enough to let in the power of a spirit guide. The guide can instruct us about the purpose of our lives. Please, sit."

Irene sits. The chair is soft and comforting, like a warm bath.

"Close your eyes," Sybil says.

Irene does as instructed.

"Relax. Breathe. Listen."

They sit across from each other without speaking. Perhaps ten minutes go by, perhaps an hour, but in that space of questionable time, Irene feels that for the first time, without drugs, the relaxing sensation of abandoning herself to some greater being.

She opens her eyes for a moment and sees that Sybil's eyes are still closed, her legs crossed, and her face placid and smooth, when before it had looked so rough and hardened. And when Sybil takes hold of Irene's hands, she stands and nearly loses her balance. They hug, and Irene thanks Sybil, and as she drives back through the city and over the bridge to the Cape, finally arriving at the house on Main in Wequaquet, she feels she is entering into a second life, where nothing appears the same as it once did, because, here are her children, in the glow of the television screen, and the kitchen is clean and the old furniture has been rearranged, and the house smells of Francine's floral perfume, and that large, looming threat of Robert returning is finally gone, which changes everything.

FIFTEEN

When Robert first arrives in Las Vegas, he rents a room at the Fly-by-Night Motel near McCarran International Airport and hangs around the casinos along the strip. The action, the lights and sounds of the machines, the smell of smoke and freshly cleaned carpet, the pretty women and barrel-bellied men laughing in their cocktail glasses gives him a spark, keeps his mind stimulated. He drinks a lot of grapefruit juice. He washes his hands ceremoniously in the ornate restrooms. He tries to focus his mind away from his boys, from what he has left behind.

But he's running out of money fast. He won't work for anyone, not as a regular employee; he's already been that man once before, and once is enough. He sits in the coffee shop at the Palace Station Hotel and Casino and searches the classifieds for opportunities, chance, a stake to get him started. Meanwhile, he still believes in luck. Every day he puts five bucks in the giant slot machine with a jackpot for a million dollars at the front entrance of the casino floor. Every day he loses five bucks.

Then, one morning at a coffee shop, he sees an ad in the back of the *Las Vegas Sun*:

The Art of Professional Gambling
Serious Inquiries Only
This is NOT a Game

He calls the number on the ad and an automated message instructs him to call another number. He calls that number and a man answers and says, impatiently, his name is Simon, professional handicapper and money manager. Robert starts to inquire. Simon interrupts, says to meet him at the Jack in the Box on Sahara in ten minutes.

Still not used to the layout of the city, Robert shows up ten minutes late and the parking lot is empty save for a black Lincoln town car with tinted windows. Out steps a squat-shouldered figure with a potbelly, wearing an unassuming color combination of tan on tan—coat zipped up and stretched down over the waist of his khakis.

"Simon?" Robert says.

"That's right."

Robert holds out his hand, but Simon keeps his hands in his coat pockets.

"You're in good shape," he says, and Robert can tell by the direct and unwavering attention in his eyes that Simon takes his work very seriously.

"I run."

"Well if you ran here on time, you wouldn't be losing so much money from the get."

"I didn't know we'd made a deal already."

"Why else would you be here? Come on, buy me a taco, we'll call it even."

As they eat, Simon explains how he's not allowed on casino floors anymore. He's been flagged as one of the few people in the world who can beat the house.

"I learned from my father—they called him the Ghost—he could break a roll just by looking at you, your soul, stealing your luck like a spirit thief. He ended up a cooler for the casinos. He was struck by lightning."

"Metaphorically?"

"Literally. That's how he died. Anyway, I learned how to count cards from him when I was young. He wasn't really a ghost—he couldn't steal your luck—he just knew more than you did about table games. I've never been married and don't have kids. I made a lot of money counting cards. I wore a suit, and, later, when I was flagged, certain disguises. Then I got kicked out for good, put on a blacklist, you might say. I can't be on a casino floor, can't place a bet. So I teach. The fact that I won in this life is enough. Everyone loses in the end, but few are allowed to win or to beat death so long they are made to quit.

"What does this mean for you?" Simon asks rhetorically. "You're already betting on a winner."

Robert is so engrossed, he misses the sales pitch, misses everything that could go wrong entrusting the minimal amount of cash he has to a stranger, someone who posts ads in the back of the *Sun*.

Simon gives Robert a key to a room at Caesars, along with a bankroll of five hundred dollars.

"You pay interest on that," he says, taco grease glimmering in the corners of his lips. "Two points a day."

The next morning, a breakfast of oatmeal, fruit, and two hard-boiled eggs arrives at Robert's door. A half hour later, Simon enters the room while Robert's in the shower. He pulls the curtain aside, tells him to dry off and get dressed. His clothes are already laid out for him: a plain striped polo shirt and a pair of jeans.

"You want to look like any other dipshit tourist in the casino," Simon says. "But today you watch. You learn."

First, though, a lesson in stupidity. On the casino floor, they stand just outside the ring of players by the roulette table, watching a dozen or so turns, people losing hundreds betting favorite numbers, trying to guess red or black, throwing chips on the double zero.

"Outside of the slots, which is just feeding the animals, roulette is the biggest con ever invented," Simon says. "Watch their eyes, the hope and desperation, understand what it means to be dedicated to a losing cause, brainwashed into believing you can win what you were never supposed to win in the first place. Internalizing that understanding is power."

Robert watches the silver ball fall into the numbered slot—23 Black. A subtle smile appears on the face of a man sitting at the table. It's the face of someone who has lost nearly everything, including hope, and just when the gods are about to put him out of his misery, mercy comes in the form of a weight and a wheel.

"Blackjack has the best odds in the house," Simon is saying, "but those odds don't take into account the dopes playing next to you. And casinos are smart to card counters. They got six, eight, sometimes ten decks. And sure, a few masterminds slip through, but again, here, the play is so fast, and that means more losers, so even if they get taken for a few million, they're still making money, just not making as much, which is why the mathematician mopes get their legs broke every once in a while. The game we're playing, Kelly, is craps."

Back in the hotel room, Simon unrolls and spreads a felt on the nightstand between the two queen beds, then picks four dice from his pocket and rolls them up against the wall.

"Now, every hour, there's one good roll. If you figure there are seven to ten rolls an hour, and you catch one good one, you can sprinkle your money the rest of the time by betting with the house."

"Won't that make me look bad?" Robert asks.

"You want to look bad? Lose all your money and play nickel slots down at Circus Circus in your shitty underpants," Simon says.

On the floor, Robert watches the slick-looking businessmen. "Phonies," Simon calls them. "Act like they know the game 'cause they smoke a cigar at the table." He sees them roll and lose, roll and lose. He catches the good roll at the end of the first hour, a meek, perspiring, fat man with stains on his shirt, but with a supple flip of the wrist, gracefully tossing the dice up against the bank, hitting seven twice before making the point, hitting the point three times in a row, a hard four, a hard eight, the point again, then crapping out, eight grand to the good.

That night Robert falls into the chair in his hotel room. He remembers his boys asleep in the wan glow of the nightlights in their rooms, their lips moving slightly, legs shifting beneath their sheets. The memory lifts his heart a little.

In the morning he eats breakfast with Simon and listens to him tell a story about a man he saw throw himself from the top of the Sands Hotel.

Robert makes a grand the first day. He makes six grand the next. He loses three the following. He returns each night to his room at Caesars Palace with the bankroll, which Simon takes a piece of, slipping the bills from underneath. No women, no shows, no television. The gambler's life is not unlike the life of any enterprising man whose objective is the enterprise itself.

A month goes by like this, until one morning Robert slips two one-hundred-dollar chips on a hard four—a bet a tourist might make, someone who crosses his fingers behind his back, a man who has a cocktail waitress blow on his dice. The hard four hits—paying 7 to 1—and two five-hundred-dollar chips, and four one-hundred-dollar chips are pushed his way. The eruption around the table jolts his brain, the same as a line of coke once did. But he doesn't press his luck. He plays the point, then runs with the house until the table clears. He is alone, trading glances with the surly pit boss and the overweight dealer. He remembers the story of Simon's father, wonders if this is what Simon had done, taken a chance, shown himself from the shadows, a ghost reborn? He flips the dealer two one-hundred-dollar chips, the same he had begun the day with. Tokens, he thinks, to balance the scales of luck.

On his way back up to the room, he thinks of how America loves, envies, despises, emulates, and resents its winners. The same can be said for its losers. Elgin Baylor, Pete Rose, Mike Tyson come to mind. But the steady hand, the long-game player, who, in middle age, has achieved a level of peace, comfort, and stability that most people wish for but will never have, America feels nothing for them, making sure that when those lucky few die, they go unremembered.

Whether or not Robert can articulate such grandiose ideas doesn't matter so much as feeling that truth in his heart.

The next day, he plays recklessly, placing bets on the pass line, tossing chips in the field, and, once he's up, he goes for more, throwing a thousand bucks on a yo-eleven that comes up a soft six. Later, he tells Simon that he felt lucky.

"Luck has nothing to do with it!" Simon shouts.

But Robert is primed for the action on the floor, urged on by the mere emotion of the win, or, he realizes later, sitting up in his bed staring at the blank television screen, the loss. Regardless of what he walks away with from the table, he feels the same sting of guilt, like a child standing at the exit of a county fair, looking back at all the opportunities for pleasure he might have (must have!) missed.

Finally, after three months, Simon has to cut Robert off. Beneath the painted sky above the Forum Shops, Simon hands Robert a one-hundred-dollar bill, like a cheap parting gift, and follows with a firm handshake. He says he can't fault Robert for his lack of restraint, but he can't support it either.

"Trust me, I know, the life of a gambler is one of extreme tedium and detachment from human nature. I haven't had a woman since 1982," he says.

Robert moves into a daily-weekly on Tropicana, where he begins searching the classifieds for any kind of start-up available. He wakes to the nightshift employees playing Metallica or Iron Maiden on their stereos, and jogs in the cool desert morning, just before dawn, imagining himself at some future time in the gated luxury of Spanish Trail, sipping coffee on his patio, looking out at the large palms surrounding the second tee of the private golf course. He runs toward the Strip, where old hotels and casinos have been imploded and the guts are being driven out.

This is how things start, he thinks, at the very bottom.

In a hole.

SIXTEEN

ON THE FIRST DAY OF SPRING, MARCH 21, 1993, THREE MONTHS after Robert has left her, Irene Kelly hosts the inaugural meeting of the Single Mothers Club of Wequaquet, Massachusetts. She has invited ladies she's befriended at the A&P and at her boys' basketball games. She knows the eyes of sleepless nights, no sex, and maybe too much liquor. She knows how their heads ache from the relentless and inane questions their children ask—"Where are my socks?" "In the fucking sock drawer!"—and the redundant battles they fight with their children to pick up after themselves, help out around the house, give Mom a break, "Can't you see I'm all you got?"

Betty, Stella, and Gwen. Among them, only Gwen has a daughter—from a previous marriage. Irene suspects she's here just for the wine. Betty and Stella have five boys between them. "I can't believe how bad they smell," Betty jokes, though her laugh is tempered by the reality of how beautiful all of the women's children once were, how sweet they smelled, the powdery scent of their heads, the dampened sounds of their little breaths as they slept in their arms.

Irene serves Swedish meatballs and guacamole and tiny quiches with ham and spinach and onion, along with several decadent desserts from the Portuguese bakery in Orleans. The women wait to see who will be the first to pick up a dish. They consume the appetizers and desserts like knowing alcoholics, at first dainty and discreet, and then, a few glasses in, without abandon, not even bothering to use a napkin. Irene wonders if they purge, too. She serves wine and plays Tom Waits on the stereo. Stella takes a sandwich bag of pot from her purse. "My son's," she says.

Stella had a date last week. The guy was a lawyer. He wanted her to put a finger in his ass.

"Did you do it?" Gwen asks.

"Of course she did," Betty says.

"Fuck you, whore," Stella says, then smiles. "Of course I did."

"I've done it," Betty says. "I think all men are secretly homosexuals."

"Oh, Lord," Irene says and cleans the platters of appetizers and desserts from the table.

Gwen takes three books from the bookshelf. She promises to return them, then tells a funny, though somewhat depressing, story about her five-year-old daughter, Samantha, finding her vibrator and using it to brush the dog's teeth.

Irene can't let this club only be used for gossiping. She has faith in the power of women together, and so she breaks the circuit of naughty stories by dimming the lights and striking a match, holding it to the candle at the center of the table.

"What is this?" Gwen asks.

"Are we going to cut our fingers and drink each other's blood?" Stella says.

Irene rolls her eyes.

"Please," she says. "Have an open mind. I'd like to try to bring us together for something bigger than appetizers and sex talk."

Still, the women feel compelled to trust each other, to try, because they have not tried anything new in so long.

They sit in the low light of the candle flame and hold hands. There is a kind of giddy church silence, a quietude that cannot be contained among stoned girls. Someone's stomach gurgles. Another quiets a burp, and the others laugh. Irene tries to stay true to what Sybil had taught her about slowing down everything inside and out. It has worked for her. She has seen, in practice, certain images she cannot relate to a specific genesis—running water buffaloes, a young couple singing opera in an alleyway in Florence, a room decorated to look like a tropical garden with flowers made of small, corrugated cardboard pieces.

"I think our dear Irene is becoming unhinged," Irene overhears Betty saying to Gwen later that night while she's filling the dishwasher.

Hearing this, Irene feels as if she's about to snap, that she has been woven into human form by invisible strings that have begun to loosen and break, and where one is connected from her elbow to her ear, now she can no longer move as fast or hear as well.

But she has to believe in something. She has to believe that when, over the next few years, the Bettys and Gwens and Stellas of her world have finally been snatched up by middle-aged men with big cars and small dicks, she will have her faith in something larger than herself.

SEVENTEEN

The next morning, after she sees the boys onto the bus, Irene drives to the town hall and asks about any job openings.

"You want to work here?" the secretary replies, surprised.

The town hall, built in 1899, is three levels with high ceilings and poor ventilation, which gives the inside the look and feel of a mortuary. Any monies allocated by the town council go to repairing the brick facade and copper tile roof, or the flower garden, which many aging, homeless vets use as a toilet.

The jobs available to Irene—given her lack of schooling, training, and work history—are Wequaquet Elementary custodial services or property tax appraiser.

"One, a monkey can do," the secretary says. "The other, not even a monkey would do."

But spending more time around kids when she doesn't have to sounds like torture, so she accepts the position as a property tax appraiser for the town. The work is menial but necessary. She lists, from the map of the town on the side wall of the office she shares with Bill Houseman, the street names that have yet to be marked, and where any number of houses need to be appraised and recorded in the town's database.

The trouble with her job is that someone needs to be home

in order for her to walk the property. Usually, when there isn't a car in the driveway, it means the owners are at work or out, and she makes a note to come back to the house when she has a similar route planned the following month. These notes and plans are time-consuming and her second attempts are usually the same as her first. She doesn't like to disturb people during dinner. She has already had a number of doors slammed in her face.

But by the end of her second week, she has covered most of the west end of Wequaquet and is prepared to move on toward the many homes along the beach in Southbay.

"You need to take your time," Bill Houseman says the following Monday morning. "This is government, Irene. We don't do things fast. That's why it works." Then he puts his hand on her shoulder. The hand feels foreign but not intrusive, like a bird has perched there and she doesn't necessarily want it to fly away.

"I like having something to take my mind off of things," she says.

"Well, you know," Bill says, and his hand moves down to her chest, where Irene is sure it will end up on her left tit. Is she supposed to flinch, or smack his hand away? She has time, because he makes time, moving so slowly. Once his hand is covering her breast, she lets him leave it there, wrist bent back, pinky finger twitching, and looks at his childlike face—red, puffy, and stupid. He squeezes once, for good measure, then pulls his fingers away and shoves his hands in his pockets. Irene feels sad. Bill is perspiring on his forehead and under his arms. Last week he ate bad Chinese food and was on the toilet for most of the afternoon.

"Let's not do that again," Irene says, and grabs a stack of folders and pushes them into her briefcase.

At the diner on Westerly, she buys a small coffee and a

doughnut, then drives to the beach and watches the seagulls fly against the blue and white light of morning. "Like a Rolling Stone" is playing on the classic rock station. She doesn't feel as old as the song. And yet.

Boys in the lake with their swimsuits on their heads; the robin banging its clipped wing against the sidewalk in pain; her mother with her hair in rollers chasing after Sukie, their dog, who'd eaten through her favorite evening gown.

She remembers fear, lying awake at night after running from Eddie Prince's car during a showing of *The Exorcist* at the drive-in in Danbury. Eddie had found her sitting behind the concession stand, her head moist with perspiration. "It's only a movie," he had said. But the way that girl's head spun and the green goop that flew out of her . . . who thought of these things? Where did they come from?

"Eddie," Irene says, but she is trying to talk to the Eddie then, not the Eddie now. She had heard he was married with four children, all girls, and had recently moved from the city back to Norwalk to open his own real estate company.

"People make mistakes," her mother had said soon after Robert left, "some bigger than others."

But Irene won't look at her missed opportunity with Eddie Prince as a mistake. Without that mistake, she wouldn't have Nathan and Andrew.

"He brought you home and I saw you two kiss and the way he held you and his face turned red under the light over the front step," her mother had said, still talking about Irene and Eddie, circa 1973. "You'd been so scared and he didn't mind leaving and missing the rest of the movie. He even called you when he got home, but you were already asleep and I answered and we talked for nearly an hour about films and movie stars and his family and where he was thinking about going to college. I invested a lot of time in that boy, too, you know? What a shame."

She parks at the end of Southbay on the curved road that looks as though it heads straight into the ocean and eats her doughnut and drinks her coffee. Once she has finished, she gets out and heads toward the first house on her list, a modest but priceless nineteenth-century two-story cottage across from the beach. A red Volvo is parked in the driveway. She rings the doorbell and waits several seconds. When the door opens, she sees Linda Blair in the entrance, wrapped in a pink robe, her hair a mess. Irene can't control herself. In shock, in horror, she shouts and shuts her eyes, the same as when she saw the young Linda Blair's head twist around on her neck in *The Exorcist*.

Linda Blair reaches out and takes Irene's hand.

"I'm so embarrassed," Irene says, cowering slightly, her free hand over her mouth and nose.

"Don't be," Linda Blair says. "I look a sight in the morning."

Irene follows her inside and sits down on the couch while Linda Blair fetches her a glass of water. She had heard Linda Blair kept a place on the Cape but didn't know in which town and guessed she was a private person, like most local legends—not that Irene would have mustered the nerve to seek her out on her own. She goes through her purse and finds her glasses and puts them on. The house is typical of the old cottages in Wequaquet—fine crafted mantelpiece, narrow stairway, hardwood floors of thick, wide pine. There are no photographs of old movie sets or any memorabilia suggesting she's a movie star.

Linda Blair hands Irene the water and sits beside her on the couch.

"I'm truly sorry," Irene says, flustered still. "You don't understand how scared I was. I didn't even stay for the whole thing. And Eddie . . ."

"Who's Eddie?" Linda Blair asks.

"Oh," Irene says.

She drinks her water, then tells a brief version of the story. She feels stupid because millions of people had seen this woman's head twist around and they all had their stories. But Linda Blair seems intrigued, or acts as much. She crosses her legs and puts her elbow on her knee and cups her chin in her small hand, like an actress would.

"You know I never even saw the film," she says, once Irene has finished the story.

"Really?"

She nods.

"I didn't even want to be in it, but I was pushed and I knew it was going to really scare people and I had never enjoyed being scared myself. And now my entire career, actually my entire life, is defined by something I've never witnessed. Life is like that, though, isn't it? You're part of the scene but you never see the scene once it's finished."

Linda Blair stands and rolls her shoulders back.

"Now," she says. "You have some work to do, yes? And I have to get ready for a luncheon."

"Of course," Irene says with mild disappointment. A luncheon.

At the door, they shake hands like Hollywood acquaintances, or how Irene imagines Hollywood acquaintances might shake hands—lightly, just around the fingers.

Irene walks down the step to the end of the drive. She looks at the number on the house and the red Volvo in the pebbled driveway. She gets in her car and lights a cigarette and sits there until her heart stops pounding.

EIGHTEEN

In the weeks following his failed run as a professional gambler, Robert's old life with Irene and the kids keeps him awake at night, the life he has left for the desert and the palm trees and the lights, an entire life that seems more and more as if it had been lived by someone else, some other, still there in the captain's house on Main, two miles from the beach, where he'd gone as a kid, running on the sand at dusk, destined to be an athlete, a soldier, a millionaire. And he had been all three. But now? Now he is another.

He calls one night to talk to Irene, to lie to her, or perhaps tell the truth. He misses her. He misses part of how she was when they first met. Her laugh, especially. And her body. But not the weak will she had toward her art, the thing he had loved about her because painting was so foreign to him, and in that way, Irene became a place he had never been to before, open and exotic. He misses the toughness of her now, the way her voice changes just slightly, almost like a coo, when she speaks to the children. And her cooking. But not her sagging breasts, or the egg on her breath, and not the derisiveness in her voice, that he is nothing. If he takes the best of her and the worst of her, then here is his greatest love and his greatest enemy.

It's Nathan who picks up the phone.

"Yo," he says.

"Hey buddy," Robert says, speaking to his son as though he's three years old, and not thirteen.

"Dad," Nathan says. "Is that you?" And then Robert hears a crackling sound, like paper being crumpled against the receiver.

"Nathan, is your mother there?"

"I'm having trouble hearing you, Dad. There's a bad storm here. A tornado. We might have to take shelter in the basement."

"Please, Nathan. These calls aren't cheap."

"What's that?"

"I said put your mother on the phone."

"Dad, I can't hear you," and the crumpled paper sound again, then the faucet being turned on and off, and laughter—Andrew is beside him—and one or the other starts banging a pan against the floor.

Robert is angry, but a part of him is glad his boys are doing well enough to clown around, even at his expense. There's a kind of motivation in hearing them laugh, that even when things are bad, they aren't all bad.

Robert has recently begun selling a car maintenance package for Imperial Transmission, a string of auto service centers west of the city. If he knows anything, he knows how to make a sale, and there's a welcoming feeling in returning to an early time in his life when what he sold required him to go to the customer and not the other way around.

He knows nothing about cars. He wears a white-collared shirt with the American flag stitched on the left sleeve so that when someone answers the door they'll think it's the postman. In his side pocket, a tire gauge, pen, and a socket wrench. He only knows what kind of hell it's like to be in Vegas without one. You have to imagine what a young mother would do if her car overheated on the highway, or how a slick, tattooed dope with a car worth more than his apartment would look in front of his girl if and when the engine quit.

The pitch goes something like this: Ask them how often they have their oil changed. Once, twice a year? How much does that cost, having your oil changed twice a year? Let them think about it. Seventy bucks? Eighty bucks? This here costs $59.99, two oil changes, plus Imperial will rotate your tires, replace all your fluids, check the transmission, lube the chassis (what the hell does that do?). Look it over. "No." Comment on their lawn, their furniture, their upkeep of the place. People like to know they're doing a good job no matter what they're doing. Are they wearing a hat? Become a fan of whatever team logo is on the front of their hat. Be their friend. Be an actor. Take a look in the house. They keep things they want others to see up front: a photo, a vase, a painting. Is that your son? Yes. He's a marine? Yes. My brother's a marine. Really? Where's he stationed? San Diego. Beautiful there, but I prefer the desert. Who doesn't? Has he been deployed? Soon. He just finished basic training. He's young. I pray for them every day. Me, too. Are you religious? Sometimes. Good answer. I don't usually do this, but, I think we can knock ten dollars off the price here. Military discount. I guess I can have a look. That's one way.

Now, if it's a man, he'll think he knows everything about his car. He'll ask questions too difficult for a novice to answer, but more often than not, they're questions he doesn't know the answer to himself. He'll talk about his brother or uncle or cousin who's a mechanic. He'll pop the hood of his car, ask, "What's this belt here?" Call his bluff. Make it up. We call that thing the "Snake" at the shop. It runs smooth until it hits a crag. What about this? That's the pressure valve. Everything's got a pressure valve. And this? That's for your windshield wiper fluid.

Make sure to know the answers to easy questions. Everyone thinks they're a trickster. They might be tempted once the test is passed, but then they refuse. "No." Wait. My wife and I decide these kinds of purchases. Too easy. Your wife? That's right—his voice like a whisper. Ask him, "Do you have to check with your wife when you go to work?" Well, no. "Then why do you have to check with her when you want to buy something for yourself?" They could get pissed, but they won't. They'll justify it. Let them. She works, too. And how much does she spend on shampoo, nail polish, face cream? A shitload. And all you want to do is keep your car running smoothly, so you can afford to keep her looking good, right?

If it's a woman, she'll put it on her husband. He makes all the decisions. So, I should come back when he gets off of work? It implies she doesn't work, but she does. She wants to prove it. We have two kids, the young one's a handful. My wife's pregnant, I can only imagine. You'll see. Now, she knows what diapers, baby food, and doctor visits cost. But, it's still a "No." Ask, "Do you always have to ask your husband for permission?" She'll be stunned. She's thought about it before, her husband spends Friday night at the casino and Saturday morning at the golf course. Let's take a look. Five nos and a sale. You said ten bucks off, right? Working mother discount? Right. Check, cash, or credit?

After covering his printing costs, Robert takes home 95 percent of however many packages he sells. His average to date is ten a day, enough to afford him an office on the back end of the Strip and, because he knows he can sell more, he hires a new employee, Benny Torondo.

He found Benny when Benny found Robert and tried to pitch him one of his own booklets, one he must've dropped outside the office. He was a fast talker with enough energy to put him on a twelve-hour shift. He needed some grooming, especially the hair around his ears and sprouting out of his nostrils. Robert didn't mind the dirt in his fingernails or the black and gray stubble on his face and neck; made him look like a mechanic, a real grease monkey. Benny had been sleeping on the planks of various billboards—"The best penthouse in the city," he'd say—starting with the Jubilee, descending the ladder when workers had come to put up an ad for a new show. During the day, he looked for work, but no one was hiring known felons—"Three years for auto theft," he'd said, "and it wasn't even a car worth stealing." The day they met, Benny had been awakened at six in the morning by a kick to the stomach while sleeping on the ledge beneath the perfect triangle of a set of legs on an exotic dancer posted to the billboard. He'd found the booklet on his way to the Gold Coast Casino, then spotted Robert smoking outside the small office on Industrial, and approached him for a cigarette, before starting his pitch. Benny was no bum. He'd received a scholarship to Northwestern for electrical engineering, used to own a farm in Wisconsin, had a job researching alternative energy sources sixty miles north in the middle of the desert, where something went wrong. They were not so different, Robert thought. They were in a stage of readjustment, having lived other lives.

"Commissions only," Robert had explained, and he gave Benny an Imperial Transmission shirt and a bar of soap.

Each morning, they map out the routes they'll cover throughout the city, unafraid to enter any complex, knowing full well that even the rich appreciate a discount, their frugality being what made them so wealthy. They jump walls and run from security like children crossing freshly mown fairways with that same intense pleasure at the idea of getting caught, at the relief and accomplishment when once they are out of sight, together, gearing up for the next rush.

Word gets out. Other workers eventually follow, mostly men, tattooed or toothless, generally unkempt and undesirable to potential employers. They flock to the office and try on the shirts while listening to Robert's morning sales pitch. He gives each of them a pack of discount books, a city map, and a small wrench and tire gauge to keep in their shirt pockets. They are ex-cons, junkies, indigent divorcés. Robert is knowledge, hope, and promise. He gives them a rousing pep talk each morning, lays out an urn of coffee and two dozen doughnuts, marks the meeting spot for lunch (a fast-food restaurant with air-conditioning), and rides them out to the complexes. They scale the walls and coerce the gate operators and bargain with the stay-at-home moms who don't mind living out the fantasy of a muscular, rough-looking walleyed crook in their home. And, most important, they make sales. Robert takes 70 percent commission, and he splits with Benny, who was with him at first, when they had no idea how big the business could get, and as Vegas spreads out across the desert, so does the crew, eventually taking road trips to Phoenix and L.A., conning, acting a neighbor in the community, a family-owned auto shop, rare these days.

"Give them my name," they say. "They'll take good care of you."

When their shifts end, the men stand outside the office, smoking cigarettes and drinking the night's first beer out of tall silver cans. If they have made a half-dozen sales or more each, there's a joyous atmosphere, talk of which bar has cheap shots and waitresses with big tits. If they have done poorly, they hang on to their two or three book stubs quietly, pacing back and forth, thinking of a way to turn fifty dollars into one hundred. The casino domes shine like beacons of salvation over the maze of office buildings, and though they all know the suffering associated with those beacons, they are still drawn to them and in them they pray.

Robert feels he knows these men, feels he is one of them. He has succeeded. He has failed. Perhaps these men had families, too, and are in a bad way. Together, he thinks, they can get out. He, along with these men, are a community of second chances.

The men cling to Robert's morning speeches, and the fellowship of their after-work meetings at the Iron Horse Café, and their weekly outings to the movies or strip clubs, where Robert gives top sellers cash to spread among the rest of the crew, kickbacks shared and appreciated and fought for by discovering new developments, which seem to pop up every week, sometimes taking a bus thirty minutes north just to make a sale. And whether they return or not, more keep coming, until Robert has a solid fleet working for him.

In late spring, he moves into a two-bedroom apartment on Rainbow Boulevard and is able to have the kids fly out and see Vegas. He takes them to the casinos and shopping malls, shows them the fake lava spewing from the volcano in front of the Mirage, the forum as it would first be seen and known to them on Las Vegas Boulevard, the top of the stratosphere, the pyramids of the Luxor, giving them a vision of how limitless the West really is, the reason why he has traveled so far from them.

The children are too big to sleep in the same bed. Robert sets up the pull-out couch and Nathan stretches across it, complaining about the beam that's practically up his ass. They eat pizza and watch television, and when the kids fall asleep, Robert looks at them in the disconnected way one might look at a neighbor's house scattered with pieces of clothing—coats and socks—thrown lazily about. Something is not right, he thinks. We are not supposed to be here together.

Twice the office is broken into. The police claim break-ins are standard practice for thieves in these small complexes off of Industrial, where a block away is the Gold Coast, the Tally-Ho Strip Club, Discount Liquors. A box of booklets goes missing. A week later Robert realizes it's one of the men who works for him. He's out on bail or getting hammered by his woman or needing a fix. It doesn't matter; he knows all their excuses and learns early on not to follow their logic, that it's best to loan them a hundred bucks so they keep their minds sharp, focus their energy on the next sale, and the next and the next.

The second time the office is broken into, a framed photograph that hangs on the wall in the hallway of a blonde in a red, white, and blue bikini is taken. After the first break-in, Robert no longer keeps money or booklets or checks in the office. Instead, he puts them in a safe and carries the safe to the van and puts the safe in his closet. He and Benny have a good laugh imagining the confusion that must have set in when the alarm went off and the thief found nothing there, nothing in the main hall or where the men met in the morning, except maybe a few leftover doughnuts, which were eaten, and then he must have looked up at Brandi, the nymph of Venice Beach, holding every American dream in the coned cup she made by pushing her two breasts together with the bottoms of her elbows. Her eyes glancing over the tops of her sunglasses, asking the thief if he's man enough to take her. Does she not belong to him? This dream?

The break-ins are just the beginning of what Robert will later visualize as an implosion of his entire, fragile career out west. The concrete frames and steel beams rise from the desert like machine-made flora. Yet there is no one inside them. The bulldozers and wrecking balls are in a lot somewhere waiting. That summer, Stevie, the three-fingered ex-con and practicing white supremacist who has been working for Robert the last two weeks, gets drunk and climbs into an apartment and fondles a little girl; Toothless Ron, old and diabetic, falls dead from exhaustion after having scored six sales; and Billy Lang, a former state wrestling champ and degenerate horseplayer who has a long scar from the tip of his right ear to the bottom of the left side of his chin from being knifed for failure to pay one of his bookies, has run up to Canada in the company van.

The remainder of the crew disappears over the course of the summer, taking with them their phony postal uniforms, tire gauges, useless discount books they try to sell for a stay in a motel room. In the end, Robert has nothing to play with anymore.

Then Benny leaves. He says he's going back to Appleton, Wisconsin. He has family there. Robert gives him what little money he has for a bus ticket. They shake hands. Half hug. Two men used to parting ways.

One night, not long after Benny is gone, Robert drives through the desert to the Red Rocks and stands under the moon smoking a cigarette, listening to the wind surge through the canyons, forming a kind of mass that pushes him back off his feet.

A day and a night of driving east, and he's finally back in South Bend, Indiana. Initially, he had wanted to experience an old joy—to smell the cut grass in the quad, watch the early risers jog along St. Joseph's Lake, maybe even light a candle for his father in the Grotto—but it's cloudy and cold, and he is tired. He passes by campus and into town, where he finds a motel. The woman at the front desk gives him a key, along with an ice bucket and an ashtray. The television gets three channels, the carpet stinks of wet garbage, and there are a dozen or so dead flies in the tub.

That afternoon, lying on the stiff mattress, listening to a farm league baseball game on the radio, someone knocks on his door. He turns down the volume on the radio and opens the door as far as the chain lock will allow. A young woman with a fresh cut on her brow stands at the threshold, taking short, quick breaths, as though she has just been chased through the parking lot.

Robert releases the lock but blocks her from coming in, looking over her shoulder to see if anyone is following her.

"Motherfucker, I've been sliced. Let me in," she says, pushing past him.

"I don't want trouble."

"You got it. I picked you. Open the door."

Robert closes and locks the door.

"Get me a wet towel, please."

He goes to the bathroom and wets a washcloth under the faucet. She's sitting with her legs crossed, biting her thumbnail. Robert hands her the towel and she puts the cloth to her face and looks around the room.

"These places are little hells," she says.

Robert nods.

"I just need to rest awhile and then I'll go get this stitched up." She takes the washcloth from her face. "Do you think it needs stitches?"

The cut is about two inches long but not deep. It could have been made by a sharp fingernail.

"Wouldn't hurt to see a doctor," Robert says.

"Not about the cut, though, right?"

"I don't want to get involved."

"You have a cigarette?"

Robert hands her the pack. She takes it and puts a cigarette between her lips and widens her eyes.

"Light?" she says.

He lights her cigarette and she lies back on the bed and clutches her stomach. Then she weeps.

"Want to talk about it?" Robert offers.

"It's all so crazy," she says. "You know what I mean? I'm thirty years old and look at me. It's you. It's all men. They make women this way. When they get sense, it's too late. Then they're relying on men and they got this sense and no way to get out of what they've gotten themselves into, and, shit. Shit. Look."

A shadow appears in the stained window curtain.

"Be quiet," she says.

Robert tries not to move, but his body responds to the shadow, to the girl, to the drive and the country. He can feel his muscles relax, preparing for violence.

"Sophie, you in there?" the voice from behind the curtain calls.

The woman puts a straight finger to her lips.

"Sophie," the man shouts, and knocks on the door. "I just heard you. I swear I heard you. Is someone else in there with you?"

"Yeah!" she shouts back. "And he's big and nasty!"

"Oh, Jesus," Robert says.

The man beats on the door as though it's a paper drum. Such desperation, Robert knows, mean this man will keep knocking all night, until, at some point, the knocking will seem like a generous offer, a sign that he won't quit on her.

"I'm opening the door," Robert says.

"No, don't," Sophie says. "He'll kill you. I know it. I just know it."

Robert pushes aside the curtain and sees the man standing there. He isn't all that big but looks scrappy, the type of man Robert never liked to fight with in college; they could get at you fast, stun you with quick jabs, never giving you a chance to coil up for a haymaker. The man has on a plaid shirt and jeans and leather boots. Not as nice as Robert's snakeskin boots but more genuine, or real, because they've been lived in.

"I'm opening the door now," Robert says. "I don't want trouble."

"Stop saying that," Sophie says, annoyed.

Robert opens the door to where the chain hits.

"I was just sitting here listening to the radio," Robert says through the crack in the door.

"I understand," the man says.

Robert slides off the chain and slowly opens the door. The man stands just off to the right, still outside, short, scrappy, with fading blond curls and big ears and sunburned lips.

"I'm Sherman Young," he says, and holds out his hand.

"Robert."

They shake hands.

"You mind if I come in?"

"Why not."

Sherman Young steps inside the room. Robert notices a scar on the back of Sherman's head. The hair has grown around it.

"Listen, now," Sherman Young says, "I didn't do that to her. I hope you refrained from calling the police."

Robert glances at Sophie, then turns back to Sherman.

"Okay? We don't want to waste any more of your time."

Sophie is precariously quiet. She looks at Sherman, lips curled, eyes lowered coquettishly.

"How she got that scrape was we were messing around and she fell. That's all."

"It happens," Robert says.

"Sure does. I feel terrible and I tried to tell her that, but you see how unreasonable a woman gets when she's agitated and she's had a little too much to drink. Come now, baby. Come and let's let Robert get some rest."

"I'm not going anywhere with you."

"That is not what I was hoping to hear, baby."

"Well, that's what's happening. Me and Bobby. I think we got like some kind of connection. Don't we, Bobby?"

"Like I said. I don't want to be involved in this. I'm leaving in the morning."

Sherman Young presses his palms together.

"Look," he says, "it might be too much to ask, but will you give the two of us a second together? I promise we won't mess up your room here. I just need to talk to her, and then we'll be on our way."

Sophie flings the two fingers holding her cigarette at Robert, as though shooing him away.

"Five minutes," Sherman Young says.

Robert grabs his wallet and cigarettes and walks to the lobby. He pours himself a cup of coffee and sits in a chair by the door and reads a golfing magazine. The woman at the front desk is whispering into the phone. There's a half-eaten drumstick and some yellow rice on a Styrofoam plate in front of her. The coffeepot groans.

When fifteen minutes have passed, and Robert has learned how to correct a slice, he walks back to his room. The door is open and Sherman Young is sitting on the bed, bent over, holding his chin. His eyes are watery, as though he's been whacked in the nose.

"You see. She's nuts. You've never met someone so insane in all your life. My wife died a while back. She was nuts, too, but not like this one."

Robert hears the sound of screeching brakes. He and Sherman both go to the window. Sophie's inside a white Buick with a blue top, lying on the horn.

"I think she's taking off," Robert says.

Sherman opens the door and jumps out onto the walkway.

"Eat shit, faggots!" Sophie shouts.

The tires squeal as she speeds off out of the parking lot.

Robert walks with Sherman back to his room and sees his clothes and toiletries and a few spy novels piled on the bed. Sherman sits on the bed and checks his bag.

"She didn't steal anything," he says. "Well, except for the car."

"I'm sorry," Robert says, because, by now, what else is there to say?

"Don't be. I mean, I'm fifty-one, the things she could do in the sack."

Of course, Robert has been with crazy women. Not Irene, though sometimes she had an energy that bordered on it. He's thinking of Candice, of a few quiet girls from St. Mary's when he was in college, who had forever been told what to do, and the daughter of McRainy, a man who sold sinks to fast-food restaurants and vacationed in Wequaquet every July. She had seen Robert digging an irrigation ditch out in back of one of his father's houses and asked him up to the house. After iced tea and small talk, they were in her room, and she was naked, and she turned and bent over and told him to pull her hair back and choke her with his belt. He didn't have a belt. "Does it have to be my belt?" he had said. "What?" she said, as though he wasn't even in the room. The moment passed, and she became politely wicked, finding the sight of Robert with his shorts around his ankles laughable. "Please," she had said, "be a dear and climb the trellis down so the maid doesn't see you."

Robert sits at the table, watching as Sherman digs through his remaining clothes piled on the bed.

"What were you in town for?" Robert asks Sherman.

"Sophie's into these gems. Topaz and germanium. I don't know. She's got a whole book about them. A self-published book, mind you. And there's this conference in Chicago and I figured, well, we should at least see the football stadium and touchdown Jesus and all that if we're going to drive to Chicago. I'm originally from Buffalo—I was a carpenter there, but then some things happened, you know, and I decided to move down to Florida, where I got a job doing grounds maintenance at a nursing home. That's where I met Sophie. She was selling her gems to the old folks. We shacked up after a few weeks, and when I came home she just wanted sex and to get something good to eat, and it was pleasant living with a woman who seemed about as easy to please as a goat. I talked about my work and she talked about hers and I doubt either one of us cared at all about what the other one was doing, which I think is a pretty good way to relate to another person. So, but, that's the problem here. Once we got on the road, I realized she was a firm believer in the power of these gems. She wasn't just trying to make a few bucks. I mean, I knew she felt strongly about making these necklaces and figuring out the meaning of each one and all that, but I didn't think she was one to believe in karma and spirits and talking to the dead. She was really fucking whacked about these things. Like, believing that where you put a gem in your house gave that house some kind of power or strength, depending. So, she's got these gems all over the car, and she's constantly suggesting our safety depends on them. I said one day, you don't really believe in this crap, do you? And she looked like she was about to explode, shouted for me to pull over, right here, at this dump. I dropped her off and drove up the campus and went to the stadium and it was just like any other place because I knew she was sitting here sulking like a kid."

"What about the cut on her face?"

"You know the crazy ones, you get to fighting and then you get to fucking, and so we're going at it and she grabs hold of one of these gems and cuts me here in the arm, and she tells me to cut her, and so I do, but I guess she didn't mean the face, because she's got the presentation tomorrow, and that's when she ran out and over to your room."

"Why don't you get some sleep, Sherman. I'll be up early. You can catch a ride with me."

"Geez, you sure?"

"It's no problem, really."

The next day, Sherman Young has two coffees ready and hands Robert a twenty-dollar bill for gas and snacks.

"Fresh start," he says, smiling, a boyish dimple in his cheek.

But as Robert drives, Sherman Young begins to remind him of his mother, who had spent her last years smoking cigarettes and drinking cheap wine, not caring about a thing. She would casually mention wanting to commit suicide as if it was no different than going to the post office. "I might as well just take all these pills at once," she had said to Robert one day when he visited her senior living complex in Plymouth. "Who would care? What's that smell? Is that cologne?"

"Yes, Ma," Robert had said.

"I don't like it."

"Back to what you were saying a minute ago."

"Oh, I'm just being funny," she said.

The same look of the close-to-defeated, barely-hanging-on, is all over Sherman Young. The scrappy, overconfident cowboy Robert thought he saw outside the motel the day before is not the man who sits in the passenger seat now, one leg crossed over the other, his face twitching in the fierce sunlight spiking through the windshield.

"I mean, we're supposed to be hunters, right?" Sherman Young says, as though continuing a conversation he and Robert have been having since stopping outside of Cleveland. "But everything we're supposed to hunt is packaged and prepared, even our damn women. What's the point?"

They pull off at a truck-stop diner somewhere between Buffalo and Rochester. Sherman Young spends a while at the pay phone near the bathrooms. Robert orders coffee and a Denver omelet. Sherman joins him at the table just as the food arrives. His face is bone white.

"What's the matter?" Robert asks him.

"I don't know. Nothing. It just all came over me at once."

"What did?"

"How nothing I've ever done matters, and no one will care when I'm dead."

NINETEEN

IRENE SMOKES A CIGARETTE BY THE WINDOW, WAITING FOR Phil Donovan to finish whatever it is he has to do in the bathroom right after sex. Probably whacking off, she thinks. He can't come. He says it's his medication. Irene, at first, believed it had something to do with her body—her sagging breasts, wrinkled stomach, and the blue veins now visible along her legs. But after a month of seeing each other, she doesn't know if that's the case, nor does she really care. Each time they make love now she imagines Phil is a handsome actor from a specific film—Jack Nicholson in *Five Easy Pieces*, Nick Nolte in *The Prince of Tides*, Robert Redford in *Out of Africa*. Their faces and bodies never age from film to memory. She has her orgasm and listens to Phil struggle until he's out of breath, and then she dresses and waits for him to leave.

She gets up and makes coffee. The boys will be home from the swim class in an hour. She had signed them up at the Y, where she was able to get an inexpensive membership based on her low income. Like all the men (boys, Neanderthals, troglodytes), even Nathan and Andrew have begun to slip from her understanding. They are sweet to her, but in the kind of way a distant relative is at a wake; she feels they know she has suffered a loss, but they cannot internalize that suffering. After work, she usually goes to Kerrigans on the water and has a beer before driving home to cook dinner. She is lonely. Phil is heavyset, with a bristly mustache that leaves her neck and cheeks red.

She pours the coffee, looks at it, then dumps it out in the sink and takes a beer from the refrigerator. Phil lumbers down the steps and grabs his boots and sits, lacing them up with such careful precision that Irene wonders why the same dexterous, knowing hands are incapable of maneuvering around her body.

"Okeydokey," Phil says, and stands. Irene cringes. Is there a man in this world who doesn't revert to childish sayings after sex?

"Is the coast clear?" he says, creepily, as though their act is secret instead of pathetic.

"Yes. The boys won't be back for another hour. You can go now."

Phil kisses her on the cheek. She flinches, not expecting that kind of affection.

"Maybe next time we can do it facing each other," Phil says, and leaves.

Irene hasn't taken a day off since she started working for the town. The long days of working what feels like two jobs, or three, if you count Phil, has finally hit her. She needs a break. She'd been running like this to take her mind off of Robert, but Robert is in the wind, and a trip will do her good. Tickets to Miami are cheap in August, and she doesn't mind the heat. If anything, she'll sweat off a few pounds. She calls Francine and asks if she'll be able to watch the boys for a long weekend.

"Are you reconciling?" Francine asks.

"With what?"

"Your husband, dear. I can't stand seeing boys without their fathers. All this new feminism stuff is making our men weak, don't you think?"

"I'll leave a check for groceries in the mailbox. Please remember Andrew needs to have his inhaler with him if he goes out."

"See?" Francine says.

Irene spends the first half of the flight in peaceful rest, then wakes to the sun beaming beneath the eyelid of the small window beside her. She opens the window and puts on her sunglasses. The plane sweeps over the coast, out to the ocean, finally descending as if to pluck a fish from the water, catching the runway with a thud.

She fidgets with the seat belt and grabs her bag, suddenly impatient, then flings her purse over her shoulder and steps out into the aisle, bumping into the man in front of her.

"Excuse me," she says.

"They haven't opened the door yet," the man says.

She knows that voice. It is Eddie Prince's voice. But when she turns, he's so thin, he's nearly unrecognizable. His skin appears to be dripping from the places where it used to make him look strong—in the shoulders and neck and thighs—now sloping off his sides and buttocks, his chest narrow, head shrunken and laced with curled lines. She doesn't want to feel superior to him, but it comes natural to her at this moment, as though she's back in grade school, the prettiest girl, the funniest girl, the girl who they all had said would be a major artist one day: she had a perfect steady hand, a graceful stroke, she knew how to make colors work, she had "perspective."

"Irene?" Eddie Prince says loudly, her name sounding as though it's being advertised over the intercom as the place where passengers can claim their luggage. "I must've been sitting in front of you this whole time."

"I thought I recognized that hair," she says, uncomfortable by her own words, wanting to take them back; his hair is much thinner now, graying, and there's a boil on the back of his neck, which she had first seen when she had sat down. That boil on a stranger's neck had taken away her appetite, and she let the sheepish, chubby boy beside her have her extra bag of party mix, which he opened with enormous pleasure, glancing at his father in the next row to see if he noticed he had two bags now, then carefully emptying one into his palm and putting the other bag in his pocket to save for later.

"Please," Eddie says. "I'm a complete mess." He coughs into a punched fist, a deep, heavy cough. "Lymphoma. I have an appointment with a top specialist down here. Second opinion, though I don't see how he would know any more than the doctors in New York."

"Oh, no," Irene says. "I mean . . . no, they can't be right."

She looks into her purse for something she doesn't need and retrieves a piece of gum. She offers a piece to Eddie, who takes it but doesn't peel off the wrapper.

"Are you alone?" she asks, bitterly, as though she knows it's wrong to ask, but their history, the coincidence of being on the same plane.

"They don't know," Eddie says. He coughs hard into his fist again. Irene places her hand on his back. Finally, he catches his breath. "My family, I mean. I haven't told them yet."

He takes the piece of gum out of the wrapper and pops it into his mouth. As he chews, white spit gathers in the corners of his lips.

Irene can't look at him. She huffs and stands on her toes and sees an old woman being helped out of her seat by a young steward who holds the woman's hands like they are two pieces of finely wrapped glass ornaments.

"I hope I don't get old," she says aloud, and only because Eddie is there, wanting him to accept this idea, though she would have said the same to herself, and often when she sees how difficult it is to be old, to require assistance in public and need help in private, she wishes for a sudden death.

In the gate area, Irene and Eddie stand near the blue arrivals-and-departures screens. Eddie spits his gum into the trash. They walk together to baggage claim. Irene reaches for his hand, awkwardly grabs hold of two limp fingers, and lets his palm seize the top of her hand, the little finger and thumb clamping over it and moving horizontally. It can't be easy, she thinks. But they are on the fringe. How they suffer is nothing compared to how the rest of the world suffers. Over there a bar alight in neon holds plump-faced people drinking tall glasses of foamy beer. And there is a bounty of candied fruit and salted caramel pops and flavored water. And there are head-sized sandwiches stuffed with meat and cheese slathered in mayonnaise. You desire so much and leave with nothing. This will make you feel good, as though you possess self-control, when, in reality, to buy and buy and buy—"purchase" is the word you were taught—is the only way to keep everyone on their feet, alive, in a sense, producing what you wear on every part of your body, down to the diamond ring you have slipped onto your right-hand finger, scraping against Eddie's callused palm.

"I don't have any bags," he says.

She looks at him absently.

"I can wait if you want to catch a cab together."

"Oh, that's okay. I'm renting a car."

He seems dejected. He has only one place to go.

"I can come and see you," she says quickly.

"I'll only be here a day and a night."

"Still, if you give me the name of the hospital."

He gives her the name and she snaps her forehead by flicking her middle finger off her thumb—a fun thing her father used to do to her when she was a little girl—and says, "Got it."

"It was good to see you, Irene," Eddie says.

"You, too, Eddie."

After she collects her bag, Irene starts toward the car rental outlet. Eddie is standing by the window, watching the yellow cabs pull up to the curb, collect their passengers, and pull away.

"Eddie?" Irene says.

But Eddie doesn't appear to hear her. He stays staring out the tinted windows with his hands in his pockets. Irene watches the shadows of people pass by with their luggage. She steps closer to Eddie, and finally he turns toward her. She smells his stale breath—he's breathing heavily—and kisses him on the lips, lightly, without pressure, or intent.

At the car rental desk, she convinces a small man with a pockmarked face to give her a free upgrade, from a midsize sedan to a convertible. She is thicker in the middle and back, but what weight she has put on doesn't show in her face—smooth, bright, with thin lines of age curled around her lips. So to act like a sexual being is not outside her power yet, and men, this man, if shown the slightest suggestion that she is willing—a closed-lip smile, eyes lowered, hand on hip—might just think he has a chance to put his dick inside her.

The car is yellow with a black interior. A bee, motor buzzing as she feels the weight of the vehicle pulling her out of the lot. She flies through the city, over the MacArthur Causeway, sunlight dancing on top of the waves. At South Beach, she parks outside the Full Moon Café, where the diners look at her from their lunch plates—maybe she is someone important, maybe they have seen her somewhere, maybe she reminds them of someone—as she tosses her shoes into the backseat and walks out onto the warm sand. She pulls down the straps of her dress. A slight wind tickles her legs. No one knows her here. No one can tell her she's ugly or fat or too old to be wearing this kind of dress.

She stops at a fruit vendor on the beach. He has strawberries, red and plump. A warning, a memory, tells her she can only indulge in three or four. She was allergic. She knew what it would feel like once she bit into the fruit. Like a giant hand squeezing her throat. More than three or four and she'll break out in hives, her throat will close up, and she might be found on the shore of the beach, a withered artifact, herself.

The vendor has cut up a dozen and packed them into a plastic cup with the back of a spoon. When she was six or seven years old she hadn't known she was allergic. She relished the sweetness, and the black bumps like poppy seeds she tried to break in half with her teeth. It was only a minute later, after this instant joy, that she felt her tongue go numb and the air stuck in her chest. She panicked, grabbed her throat, ran into the living room, but her mother wasn't there. She knocked a lamp over and ran upstairs and tried the bedroom door, but it was locked. She kicked and punched the door until finally her mother opened it. Her father was lying on his back with his pants down.

"Oh, God, you're choking," her mother said.

Irene shook her head. She was sweating furiously.

"Cliff, call an ambulance."

Her mother walked Irene down the hall to the bathroom, rubbing her back, telling her to keep her eyes open, that her eyes could breathe. She ran the bath and helped Irene into it.

Cliff came to the door. "They're on their way," he said. Irene covered her private parts. "She doesn't look good," he said.

"Thanks, Einstein."

"It was just an observation."

"I'd like to observe you putting on something decent," Irene's mother said, and Irene nodded confidently, as though these sudden developments had become a diversion for what was happening to her. She felt like she could breathe again once her father was gone, as if he had been the one choking her.

She could hear the sirens nearing the house. Irene's mother dried her off and helped her get dressed and carried her outside. The paramedics quickly put her in the back of the ambulance, and Irene's mother held her hand while they administered a shot into her thigh. Then the night in the hospital, the rattling of the air conditioner, and her mother standing by the window with her arms crossed.

"Where's Daddy?"

"In the lobby," her mother said. "It's hard for him to see you like this."

"Like what?"

"Oh, sweetie."

Her mother came to the bed and brushed her hair aside and kissed her forehead.

"Hospitals make him nervous, that's all. Nothing's wrong with you. It's just that strawberries aren't your friends. You have to remember that. They're an evil fruit."

An evil fruit, she thinks. How gratifying.

She pays for the strawberries, and, for a while, she sits on the beach with her eyes closed, listening as the waves grab the sand and rake the shells and seaweed and stones back into their folds. She eats one of the strawberries, slowly, with great pleasure. That's it, she thinks. All that matters is this: the sand, the water, and a berry so sweet. There cannot be anything more perfect in the world. The waves, the sun, the sand. She closes her eyes. She remembers the old bungalow on the beach. The phony artists lying naked and stoned under the moonlight. Then there was the day before the day everything had changed, and she was here, on this beach, fifteen years ago, the same waves, the same sun, the same sand.

She eats two more strawberries before her skin begins to warm. Flushed red spots appear along her arms. She has eaten her limit. The light has begun slowly to melt across the horizon like a spread of honey. The sky has turned pink and a few stars are visible along with the moon. She loves to see the moon in daylight. There is something otherworldly about it, an occasional reminder of infinite strangeness.

Irene remembers reading from one of Sybil's New Age books that once you die you become a point of light and inside that light is everything you have ever lived and dreamed and thought, so that each point of light is like some fantastical world of your own devising.

She continues along the beach, then walks a jetty out to where the moss grows, nearly losing her footing. She steps back and stands looking at the clear aqua-blue of the water. She sits on the rocks and dips her feet in the water. Radiant, luminous fish gather about her toes, then swim off. For the next three days, she wakes early and walks to the same spot, but she never sees the fish again. In the airport, and on the flight back to Boston, she looks for Eddie Prince, but she never sees him again, either.

PART II

NATHAN AND ANDREW

2017

TWENTY

ANDREW LIES IN BED WITH HIS EYES CLOSED, TUGGING AT HIS limp penis, as Kirsten, naked beside him, reads from her tablet some new self-help book, whose belief system she'll follow for a week or two before giving up.

Andrew imagines he's a warrior in some Viking land, about to go into battle, and the young, golden-haired women of those hills are ready to please him before he ventures off into war. He feels something, a slight tingle, but then Kirsten sputters a laugh. He turns to her, and she covers her mouth with the back of her hand.

"What?"

"Nothing."

"No. Something. Say it."

"It's just, you look sort of ridiculous. It's hard to believe this is what boys and men do when they're alone."

"Ridiculous? Maybe if you—"

"Oh, please. You never had these problems when we were in college."

"Back then I was actually attracted to you."

"So now it's my fault you can't get it up?"

"It's your fault you don't care if I get it up or not."

"Stop it. I do care. Come on. Keep going. It's entertaining."

"I'm not trying to fucking entertain you, Kirsten."

She moves onto her side and plays with his curly patch of chest hair. It's just enough to be touched. He pushes her arms back and holds her wrists above her head.

"Now you're ready, Daddy," she says.

He feels the warm pull of her insides and closes his eyes again. A warrior with his giant sword, the woman tied up, whimpering at his massive piece of justice.

"Remember, don't pull out. Dr. Larry said my eggs are really fertile this time of year," Kirsten says, matter-of-factly.

"Fucking Christ," Andrew says, and his penis slips from her like a small fish in a hand.

"What? Keep going. It felt good."

"I can't fuck and think at the same time."

"Yes, you can. You're brilliant at multitasking."

"Stop calling him Dr. Larry. You're not a five-year-old and he's not a pediatrician."

"I like calling him that. Makes him seem less intimidating. Now come on. Back in."

"I can't. All I can picture now is Dr. Larry massaging your eggs like meditation balls."

"Oh, God."

Andrew flings his legs over the bed, gets up, and goes into the bathroom. He runs the faucets, biting his hand in rage.

Nothing frightens Andrew more than being a father, except maybe other people's noses. Sometimes he'll look at a nose and his stomach will knot up and his legs go numb. For five to ten minutes, all he sees are noses—wide, narrow, pudgy, pinched, bulbous. He'll hide in his office and breathe in and out into a paper bag. But the idea of being a father, of him becoming part of another, with all the same tics and demons and fears, sends him even farther into a debilitating panic, and he's lucky to get out of the cubbyhole under his desk by lunch if suddenly he's thinking about Kirsten's eggs, a pooping puking pissing baby, reading it stories, acting as if he cares that it discovered a neat rock, or that the drawing it did of a house with Mommy and Daddy bigger than the house and the sun smiling is some kind of fucking masterpiece. According to his friends and coworkers, these early years are supposedly the best ones. So, Jesus, what must it be like when they're ten, eleven, twelve? He remembers how annoying he was as a kid, how for an entire month, all he did was skip everywhere. Why? He can't remember. He just skipped from the kitchen to the living room, and down the street, and through the school hallways. Then one day Chris Schroeder called him a fairy, and he went home and told his father, and his father said, "Maybe think about not skipping so much."

Andrew looks at his limp cock in the mirror, stretches it out, pushes it in, slaps it, then lets it hang there like a piece of dripping skin. He studies it for discrepancies—a mark, a bump, a discoloration—because it makes sense for a man of thirty-seven years to look, even if he's frightened by the possibility of finding something new on his body. A few years ago he had discovered the scar across the back of his head when he finally gave up trying to cover his baldness and told the barber to go ahead and shave it to an inch. The barber held the mirror in back, and he saw the white line like a backslash carved into his head. He had asked his mother what had happened, where did this scar come from? And she had told him his father had tried to get him walking earlier than normal for a baby, had him up on both feet, and when he stepped forward it really did seem like he was going to walk—"You had such a confident look in your eyes, looking at me"—and he took one step, fell, and hit his head on the coffee table, hard, apparently. Why didn't you catch me? he had thought to ask, though he understood why, he understood her shock. Seeing a falling thing, no matter what it was, always made him stop, forget, and watch, and anyway they had stitched up the gash and she cried for hours and had said she felt guilty for years and, again, when he had called her about it, she had said, "Andrew, I'm so sorry," and cried—so pathetically emotional. "Okay, Mom. It's okay," he had said. "It's not like it hurts or anything."

Then, as if waking from a bout of sleepwalking, he remembers what it is he's trying to do in here. He has to get rid of this stuff inside him. It isn't good for your health to hold it in. Coming is a natural stress reducer. He read that somewhere. And, Jesus, if anyone is stressed, it's him.

Just in the last month, his mother had taken a fall on the icy steps leading up to the Wequaquet town hall. Since then, she's been suffering bouts of dizziness and forgetfulness. Photos were taken of the steps, where it should have been salted down, but she wasn't interested in suing.

"The town is practically bankrupt as it is."

"Maybe you should see a doctor," Andrew suggested.

"I have a doctor. Dr. Sawyer. I doubt he'd appreciate me wasting his time with a little fall."

"But if you fall again."

"It's those lousy old steps, Andrew. You want to do something for your mother? Make a donation. Maybe we can rebuild the town hall with some decent flooring, and an elevator that actually works, and a heating system that doesn't require us to practically freeze to death in meetings."

"I'll look into it."

"Oh, you'll look into it, will you? That's cute."

"I thought you might be difficult, so I made an appointment

with you to see someone at Mass General. He's a friend of mine. The very best. I'm covering all the costs."

"What did I say?"

"I know what you said. But I'm asking for me. I want to make sure you're okay. Is that such a bad thing?"

She looked at him with surprise, as though he had startled her with a memory of himself as a boy.

"No, it's not a bad thing," she said. "Will we have lunch afterward?"

"Anywhere you'd like."

But when the time came, they did not go out to lunch. They did not leave the hospital until the following day.

The tests showed three tumors in her brain. She could see them in the ultrasound imaging. In one frame tiny clouds had shifted and broken apart inside her, or had always been there; in another the tumors were lit up in bright orange coloring, like tiny suns emerging from darkness.

"Tell me," she said, looking at the doctor looking down at his notes, and when he raised his head he stared just right of her, guilty, despite himself.

"I'm sorry," he said. "We'll do everything we can to make you comfortable."

Andrew thanked him. Irene nodded. They were left in the office alone, as though the doctor had come to visit them at some neutral site, where one might be prone to control their emotions when given bad news.

"Not much of a bedside manner, that friend of yours," Irene said to Andrew on the ride home. "You should look someone in the eye when you tell them they're dying. Don't they train for that kind of thing?"

"I thought he was fair and honest. It's not easy for him, I'm sure."

"Not easy for *him*? What about me? Of course you'd be thinking of how hard it must be for your dear friend, but not your mother."

Andrew sighed.

"His hands were a different color than the rest of his body. Did you notice that?"

"Must be from washing them all the time."

"His nails were perfectly trimmed."

Andrew started to say something then pretended to cough instead.

"I'm not scared, honey," his mother said, lying, the way she had lied to Andrew about his pet bunny, Baloo, dying of natural causes, when he had seen, from the kitchen window, Nathan squeeze the life out of him.

Poor Baloo, he thinks now, standing in the mirror, holding a tube of hand lotion.

Don't think of Mom, or Nathan, or Baloo. Concentrate on not thinking. Wasn't that when sex was best? Wasn't that when you were most present?

It used to be that when he was on the road, Kirsten would talk dirty to him. But time and routine have taken from him his sexual desire for her. He tries flipping through images of past girlfriends, all of them now mothers (he believes), flabby, unhappy, annoying; then to porn, women bouncing on cocks with their tits flailing about like swinging speed bags. When he was young, porn was new and engrossing, and he had waited until his parents were in bed and Nathan had begun snoring to look at the then stills of women in magazines, half-naked, lying on some tropical beach somewhere. He would imagine he was there, and what they might say to each other, and what they might do; ask him to rub down their shoulders with coconut-scented lotion, playfully pull at the strings of their bikinis; at first, they would hide their breasts, and then let their hands drop. He didn't even need to dream about touching or tasting them, he was done by then. But he can't find his way back to those thick-legged, country blondes he had fantasized over when he was a boy. He needs to feel the hot whisper of a woman's voice in his ear, her fingers flittering across his back like a score of butterflies, the push of her hips against his, the warmth of her insides as he enters her. He has to return to those first days with Kirsten. That winter, when he saw her outside the dorm, the cold channeling off the lakes, rising from the gorges, burrowing through the stone edifices.

In college, Andrew would wake early and put on coffee. He'd pull a wool blanket over his shoulders and sit at his computer, clicking through the *Globe*, the *Times*, the *Post*, the *Wall Street Journal*, the *Ithaca Journal*, and the *Daily Sun*. He had never been interested in politics, but it had become clear during his first semester in college that he needed to have some point of view. Hunkered down in his shared apartment, listening to Wu-Tang Clan or A Tribe Called Quest, a rhythmic collaboration with his two-fingered key stroke, the words "High Alert" were in the top right-hand corner of every paper. The most read articles, depending on the paper, mentioned "Anthrax," "Terrorism," "Bin Laden," "WMDs," and "Tom Brady."

On occasion, Andrew met with a professor he had grown close to, Dr. Danberry, who taught a course on business ethics, in his large leather-smelling office with windows looking out onto the snowy campus quad. They drank bourbon and arm wrestled. They agreed that the greatest poet of the twentieth century was Cassius Clay. They discussed literature and world history and the current futures markets, reasons for their rises and falls. Cold winter in Brazil, wait for the price to drop on coffee, then buy it low. Andrew looked forward to these meetings. He found most of his classes simple and unengaging. But Dr. Danberry challenged Andrew's sense of self. He taught Andrew that the problem we can never solve is the perception of our own self-worth.

During his second year in school, a few undergraduates threw themselves off the Cascadilla Bridge. Occasionally, Andrew stood at the center of the bridge and thought of how it would feel for those few moments after the jump. He remembered the time his father had hung him over the Wequaquet River Bridge and how if his father had dropped him, he would not be here. And he wondered if his not being here would change anything. He'd wet himself. In the back of his father's Wagoneer, he kept his hands under his butt so as not to leave a stain on the seat.

Shepherd, his roommate, had said one night, "Dude, we're lucky to be alive at this point in time. Our parents had an enemy—communism: Russians and Asians and hippies. But we have everyone, even ourselves. We are all enemies. No heroes, just villains. It's sort of orgasmic when you think about it."

Shepherd related everything to sex. He loved love but was never in love. When he brought a girl back from the bar, he turned up the volume on his computer: Tom Petty, Van Morrison, Cat Stevens—the usual suspects of an inexperienced kid. Still, Andrew knew the squeaking sound of bed springs meant a girl's breathless gasps would follow, and then Shepherd's grunt as he came. Andrew watched the girls as they stumbled drunkenly past his bed to leave.

What was his secret? Andrew wanted to know.

"There's no secret," Shepherd said. "They're drunk and bored and rich. They don't have any good stories to tell. What else can they do?"

This sounded perfectly depressing to Andrew.

Because of their schedules, Andrew usually saw Kirsten Staples in the dining hall on weekends. She was the first vegetarian he had ever met. Her tray looked like a small garden alongside a square of yellow cake. She ate alone, slowly and thoughtfully, without a book in front of her or headphones on. Sometimes she closed her eyes after a bite as though savoring her last taste of honey. Andrew wasn't afraid to talk to girls, but there was something about her he couldn't hold on to. He had grown into a handsome young man; gone were the thick eyeglasses, wimpy arms, and hairless legs. It was as though he'd hit puberty later than most boys, and after daily gym sessions for the past couple of years, except for Sunday, his chest was wide and his arms muscular, and he used his college loan money to buy new clothes—button-down shirts, khaki pants, and a sport jacket for when he met with Dr. Danberry. He had a sharp chin and kept a bit of stubble about his face, shaving every other day, and never wore a hat for fear of going bald.

One day he passed Kirsten sitting on a bench near the clock tower, then stopped suddenly and looked at her turning the lens on her camera. She held it to her eye, then moved the camera aside and looked up at him.

"Can I help you?" she asked.

"Yes," Andrew said, surprising himself. What did he need help with? Think. "I need to celebrate and I thought you might be interested in celebrating with me."

"What are you celebrating?"

"I've finished something I think will change the world."

"So I'd be celebrating with a world-changer?"

"Maybe."

"And I'd be a fool to turn down the offer?"

"No, you wouldn't be a fool."

"Do you know what I was just looking at before you stepped in the way?"

"What?"

"See that boy over there?"

Andrew looked. The boy was clearly a freshman on orientation. He had thick glasses and neatly combed hair; a campus map fully unfolded, covering his torso.

"See how confused he is? No idea where to go, too afraid to ask. Before you came by, he had stepped off the curb and stepped back. It was the second time he had done that. He keeps staring at the map and pushing his glasses up and looking around at the buildings. I've been waiting to get the perfect shot of him."

"Why?"

"Because *that* is fear."

Andrew glanced at the boy again.

"Don't help him," Kirsten said. "He needs to learn to be afraid."

That night Andrew and Kirsten ate pizza and shot pool at a local bar. They were half-drunk, bumping into each other, joking at first, and then Andrew grabbed hold of her and they stayed that way, walking side by side as though they needed each other to stay upright. They stopped at the entrance to the Stone Arch Bridge. Andrew knew then that as time went on, he would have to share with Kirsten his more intimate, secret thoughts. But not now. Not at this moment. Now he had to kiss her to keep from thinking at all.

Andrew's cell phone starts to buzz. He checks the face of his phone, an unrecognizable number—857 area code. Better take it, he thinks, maybe I won a sweepstakes. Any and all sweepstakes offers that cross his path via the Internet, hotel counter, restaurant, wherever, he goes in for. He doesn't care about the prizes, mostly, the luxury cruise or four-night ski vacation. He simply wants to win.

His hands are slippery from the lotion, and as he picks up the phone, it glides out of his grip into the toilet. With the toilet brush, he struggles to get the phone over the seat, guiding it to the rim, then losing it through the rhombus-shaped hole in the bristles. Finally, with a flick of his wrist, he catapults the phone out of the bowl and the face smashes against the wall. He leaves the phone where it is and washes his hands until they're red and throbbing. He tucks his lips in and, with the long nail on his forefinger, picks at a poppy seed stuck between his front teeth. He only manages to push it farther back and cuts the gum line with his fingernail.

All his life, Andrew seems to have suffered stupid injuries. He's never broken a bone or been concussed or had a real sickness of any kind (except for slight asthma when he was young), yet he's prone to episodes of unexpected pain on regions of his body he never worries about. He may sprain an ankle stepping off a curb, or pull a muscle in his neck looking twice before pulling out onto the highway. A few years back, he developed a pimple in his nose he let Kirsten pop with a sewing needle. Then it got infected and the left side of his face began to harden and he had to be taken to the emergency room. The doctor there said if Andrew had waited any longer, he'd have died; the infection was tracking right toward his temple.

"Think about never picking your nose again," the doctor had said just before delivering a cortisone shot to Andrew's rear.

Andrew washes his face and brushes his teeth, checks his nose hairs, clips a few, and sneezes. The blackhead is now a red spot on the tip of his nose. He studies his balding head, hoping to see a sprig of hair between the two leaves above and below his ear and around his head. Andrew's father had once said that hairless people are weak. That stout and certain tone of voice seemed perfected by a sense of wisdom lodged in Andrew's brain like a bullet shell. His father's declarations were impossible to forget. Andrew sprays his scalp three times a week with a European formula called Pousser, which is supposed to provide surprising results, according to the advertisements he's read online. He has considered toupees, but after two weeks of wearing one in Del Mar, California, he developed a score of scabs from scratching the top of his head while he slept at night.

What did it matter what his father had said anyway? His father has been in prison for the last eighteen months for tax evasion, Andrew the only one willing to make the seven-hour drive once a month to Allenwood. They have exchanged thirty-six hugs, played eighteen hands of Gin, walked nine times in the open courtyard during the warm weather, where his father smoked and talked.

"Son, my mind is so clear these days," his father had said just last week, when Andrew had gone to ask if there was anything he needed to bring. Andrew has already found him a small, one-bedroom cottage, having paid a year's rent in advance.

"Please, Dad."

"Really. I don't see walls anymore."

"You need to start thinking about what you want to do next."

"Next?" his father had said, and smiled. "That's funny."

But always there was a next. Andrew didn't trust his father's sudden serenity.

"Things have a way of working themselves out, Bud," said his father, the prophet Kelly.

And maybe they did, Andrew thought, but he couldn't trust a man who'd run from every problem he had ever caused, and made no apologies.

Andrew, on the other hand, has been going about things the right way, and doesn't he deserve some recognition?

He's a senior VP at Birken and Associates, a financial consulting firm located in Boston. He and Kirsten have a four-bedroom, three-bath home in Brookline, decorated with Buddhist artifacts and paintings by up-and-coming artists touted in the *Globe*. They take weekend getaways to Manhattan, the Berkshires, Kennebunkport. They eat small plates in big chairs at restaurants where the prices are never listed. King and Queen in the Country of Oz. The only problem seems to be that there is no problem.

Andrew opens the medicine cabinet and checks Kirsten's bottle of meds, shakes the pills out in his hand and counts three less from yesterday. Last winter, she had broken her ankle ice-skating, and ever since has kept a prescription of painkillers from various doctors in the city. Andrew has guessed that a good deal of her indifference toward him lately is a result of her inability to give them up. Or maybe it isn't indifference, maybe the pills grant her a kind of absentmindedness, yielding the noise inside her head.

Kirsten is up, the television is on downstairs. Andrew dresses in jogging pants and a T-shirt. In the living room, Kirsten has her foot raised on a pillow. She doesn't look at Andrew when he comes down the stairs.

"Gym?" she says, condescendingly.

"*The Real Housewives of Beverly Hills* marathon?" Andrew says.

She throws a magazine at him on his way toward the front door. He picks it up and looks at the cover. Some pop star squeezing a plastic bear of honey into a bowl on her lap. He puts the magazine in his gym bag, lowers his sunglasses down over his eyes, and assumes his carefully constructed presence away from home.

Andrew revels in the old musk smell of the locker rooms, baby powder, shaving cream, combs dipped in Barbicide. He changes and does twenty push-ups on his knuckles, then jogs out onto the main floor of the gym to begin his session with Malcolm, a former navy SEAL, who does part-time surveillance for a private security firm. Malcolm tells the most improbable stories: sniper stories, government conspiracy stories, organ-trafficking stories. Andrew is attracted to how foreign Malcolm's life is to his own.

"You remember that chick who used to come in here?"

"What chick?"

"The one with the fake tits and big ass. You know, her name was some month. June or May. I forget."

"April."

"Yeah. That was it. April."

"So what happened?"

"She got hit by a bus. She was just walking across the street. Then. Bam!" Malcolm punches his fist. "Bits of her everywhere. You can't even feel all that bad for her, considering she must have gone like that." Malcolm punches his fist again.

Andrew curls dumbbells until his biceps burn, drops the weights with a thud on the foam-matted floor. Today he is training in order to keep from breaking apart. He boxes the heavy bag, completes thirty-one pull-ups, and spends twenty minutes on the bike.

"Anyway," Malcolm continues once Andrew is off the bike.

"I'll bet the bus driver is suffering worse than anyone, except maybe the people on the street who got bits of April on them."

Malcolm has Andrew thinking about the worst, which leads him to wonder whether or not he appreciates being on earth as much as he should.

"Good set today," Malcolm concludes, and slaps Andrew on the back. "Be careful out there, amigo."

On his way home from the gym, Andrew sees a group of high school girls jogging alongside the road. He slows down, pretending to be cautious. A few wave at him and smile, then laugh. He can feel his cock stiffen.

But back home, Kirsten is asleep on the couch, her arms above her head, hands holding her elbows as though propping up a triangular object. He forces them down to her sides. He kisses her on the cheek, a faint smell of cinnamon lingers about her face. At the beginning of their marriage, Andrew had visions of cookouts with the neighbors' kids and his kids and cold bottles of beer in a cooler on the back porch, Kirsten and the other mothers discussing potential private schools while the men played horseshoes and joked about Midwesterners. But when clients and coworkers showed him baby pictures, he felt a twinge in his chest, like someone twisting the muscle between his ribs. He couldn't imagine having a family with Kirsten. Or with anyone for that matter.

He grabs a beer from the fridge, then sifts through the drawer of nonessentials—matchbooks, various pens from various hotels, playing cards—for the bottle opener. He notices a card for a therapist in Bourne. Karen Shelby. He can't recall Kirsten saying anything about a therapist. There's a cell number on the back of the card, for emergencies. He picks up the house phone and, just as he's about to dial, the phone rings in his hand.

"Kelly? Is that you?"

It's Will McGrath, one of the VPs from Birken and Associates.

"Yes."

"I've been trying to call you all afternoon."

"It's Sunday, Will. What couldn't wait?"

"I guess you didn't hear the news?"

Silence as Andrew waits.

"Birken's dead."

"What do you mean dead?" Andrew says, stunned.

"What else could I mean? He's dead. Splat. Literally. He was skydiving over the Maldives, and his parachute malfunctioned. Was he Catholic? I think I remember seeing him—"

"I have to go, Will."

"Sure. Right. Give my best to—"

Andrew hangs up the phone. He walks by Kirsten on his way upstairs. She, like most people, is more beautiful asleep.

TWENTY-ONE

AMAZINGLY, THE MORTICIANS HAVE RECONSTRUCTED BIRKEN'S sixty-eight-year-old jaw, going so far as to paste hairs above his upper lip. Whatever else inside him that was knocked loose or spilled out from the free fall is unnoticeable; his chest is full, shoulders pushed back, hands placed one on top of the other in peaceful repose.

Kneeling at the coffin, Andrew looks at Birken, then at the line of impatient men and women in their let's-get-this-over-with poses.

"Thank you, sir," he says in a whisper.

He shakes hands with Birken's wife, and his son, he guesses, a tall man with a thin mustache, who, in disregard—or protest—of his surrounding is dressed in jeans, wearing a derby hat. As he walks out of the hall, he regrets not having said more to his dead mentor, and then it hits him that Birken is dead. He is nervous about death, about becoming a dead man in a coffin people pray over. The nervousness makes him have to pee. He finds a fountain in the rosary garden and goes there.

Early that afternoon, Andrew drives up to Birken's estate in Newburyport. In his newly leased BMW, he follows similarly expensive, freshly waxed cars through the high arching timbers adorned with ivy and clusters of red berries, to where the procession ends near the multicar garage built to resemble an old Cape Cod cottage. In seconds, a valet opens his door and gives him a ticket and says, "Sorry for your loss."

Directed by another servant down a pebbled walk between the main house and the garage, Andrew catches a glimpse of a Birken through the window and stops suddenly. The Birken in the window doesn't move.

"That is a wax statue," the servant says. "I believe it was created by Mr. Birken's son. He has a great affinity for his father. Please."

Andrew follows the servant to the back lawn, which slopes down toward the ocean, where the white swell of waves seems frozen along the dark water's surface. Round tables are assembled about the lawn, and he is directed toward one, where he sits and introduces himself to a group of old-timers who have flown in from around the country. They talk around Birken's death, about the bad news coming down, layoffs, restructuring, branch closings, and the risk/reward of doing something like skydiving.

"A quick death is preferable," one partner says with an easy nod.

After a while, Andrew excuses himself and walks toward the buffet table, which is sectioned into hot and cold food by a giant ice sculpture of Birken's head. He pours himself some water, then takes the ice pick in hand.

"Drive it into his eye," Birken's wife says over his shoulder.

She's wearing a garish black dress with diamond sequins. Her throat looks like a mangled hand.

"Miss?"

"They say when you're with someone for as long as Lawrence and I were together, that when one dies, the other dies soon after. But I intend to stay alive for a very long time."

Mrs. Birken laughs and takes the ice pick from his hand and stabs the sharp edge into the ice-crusted eye. Flecks of ice splinter into the air.

"This was my son Gordy's idea. He's the artist. There's no doubt I'll receive a bill before his father's head even melts."

"I'm sorry" is all Andrew can contribute, and as he mills around the patio he grows depressed by the idea that when he dies, the best he can do with a ton of money is have his friends and family and coworkers throw a party for their own amusement.

Suddenly, he can't breathe. It feels as though a thousand tiny insects are crawling up his spine and over his shoulder, gathering in his chest and gnawing away at the meat between his ribs. He drops to the ground and holds his hand over his breast. Then he blacks out.

He wakes in a hospital bed, his gown bunched up, blanket twisted around his legs. He's had a restless, dogged sleep. The tube lighting overhead partially blinds him. He turns his head toward the window. It is night.

He calls for a nurse.

She explains he's had a panic attack and asks if Andrew has been experiencing a high level of stress at work, if everything is going well at home, if he may have experienced any suppressed emotional trauma as a child.

"Who hasn't?" Andrew says.

Rest is the recommended course of action.

For the next three days, after the incident at Birken's funeral, something lingers in Andrew's chest, near the heart, a nerve ending pinched, and this something spreads throughout his body, arresting him so that at times he can do nothing but lie in the antique tub Kirsten loved so much she had specially ordered it, with his arms across his chest in an attempt to hold himself together, feet dangling over the rim, a warm washcloth on his forehead. When he has the energy, he performs small jobs around the house. He repairs the rusted hinges on the cabinet doors; tills a small plot in the backyard and plants seeds for basil and tomatoes and lettuces; builds a shed out of scrap wood to house his gardening supplies as well as the pot and the tiny green bong he has recently bought off a hippie in Harvard Square. He takes long walks through town to the park and sits on a swing, absent-mindedly kicking his feet out, stoned.

When he returns to work the following Monday, Andrew feels there is nothing left inside him. He can't concentrate when the other VPs hold a conference call to discuss the company's fourth-quarter fiscal outlook. At lunch, he walks to the deli on the corner with only a faint beat in his heart. He eats from the sad buffet until he's tired again and goes back to his office and sits in his high-back leather swivel chair, turning slowly, then stopping to look out at the city, at the fog of heat that swamps the buildings. He thinks about how easy it would be to disappear.

In bed that night, Andrew hears a faint sound from somewhere else in the room. He gets up and listens closely. It's coming from the iPod player on the bureau. "Soothing Ocean" is playing on Kirsten's iPod. The white noise seems to work for her, as do the pills, because she's sleeping heavily, wrapped in the comforter like a cocoon. But "Soothing Ocean" has the adverse effect on Andrew, because "Soothing Ocean" sounds nothing like the ocean. The ocean is a beast growing stronger, moving toward the shore, smashing the shore with its fists.

TWENTY-TWO

GREAT CLOUDS OF BREATH RISE FROM THE SAN FRANCISCO Peaks. An American flag hangs limp from a thirty-foot flagpole in front of a Jack in the Box. For Lease signs hang crooked on storefront windows, abandoned malls and office parks empty and decimated like some kind of ancient ruins. On his way to the 7-Eleven down the street from his motel room, where he's been living for the past year or so, since returning from his fourth and final post, this time in Kandahar, Afghanistan, Nathan Kelly imagines how hundreds of years from now people will pay good money to see these national treasures, take flippant, humorous photos, and purchase commemorative junk.

Two police cruisers are parked behind a rusted truck in back of a fast-food restaurant, blue and red lights spinning. The driver of the truck is bent over the hood, handcuffed, his head pressed against the metal, eyes crazed, dark and venous, like cracks in clay. Nathan lights a cigarette and fishes through his duffel bag for a prescription bottle, shakes the half-full bottle like a rattle, and tosses it back in the bag. He looks at his watch, quarter past, flicks the cigarette out into the road. At the 7-Eleven, he buys a six-pack and a candy bar and sits on the curb drinking. The cool wet stream enters his belly. The candy bar is old and stale. There's a number on the package to call if you're not satisfied. He presses the candy bar between his palms and sucks the chocolate away from the peanuts before tossing it in the trash bin. He licks his fingers, staring at the mountain in the distance. An orange tinge of light blankets the peaks as the sun begins to rise.

He passes an abandoned house with broken windows and a front door boarded up with plywood spray painted in different colors—signs and symbols of local gangs. A cracked toilet lies in the yard. Cautiously, he steps off the curb and surveys the roadside, his eyes moving back and forth, swaying steadily. He can still feel the padded lining of his helmet and the green cloth chin strap snug across his jaw. His clothes are already damp underneath the body armor. He's out on patrol. It's April 2008 in Sadr City, Baghdad. Or is it just after Thanksgiving in 2006, when those retired cheerleaders came over swinging their saggy tits over the turkey and stuffing? Either way, it was early on in his tenure, early enough that he still believed there were rules in modern warfare. But on the ground now, everything he has read and learned about warfare is wrong. The hajjis strip dead soldiers of their uniforms and weapons, wear and use them in battle. In the smoke and flame and dust you can't tell what's what or who's who. Missions have no beginning and no end.

PFC Quinton serves as the Tank Commander in the lead Humvee, Recon Group 1 (RG1). They call him the Principal, because he knows every army regulation in the book. It would almost be nerdy if it wasn't so impressive. He refers to himself as an American Fighting Man, because that is what the manual tells him he is. Staff Sergeant Rodrigo, squad leader, rides in the backseat near the radio. He smokes two packs of cigarettes a day but still holds the company record for the fastest mile. Specialist Everitt, a twenty-nine-year-old from East Texas, mans the .50-cal up in the turret. He has hooked up for a two-year enlistment solely for the action. And Private Silk is the driver and mechanic, the least desired position, but that's what he's asked for; he tells the platoon leader that if he isn't driving on the lead truck, he'll lose his fucking mind.

The PL is in RG2, the second RG in the patrol, trailed by the Buffalo, a boat-shaped truck with an armored arm and claw used for handling IEDs, and RG3, which is helmed by PFC Stanton, with West in the passenger, Nathan in back on the radio, and a medic whose name nobody knows. He has a faded cross on his helmet. It doesn't mean anything out here in the desert.

The mission is the same as always: clear the assigned routes to provide freedom of movement for US and Iraqi security forces, and local nationals. There's one new road on the patrol tonight, route Shamrock, a road used by US patrols traveling between BIAP (Baghdad International Airport) and FOB (Forward Operating Base) Crazy Horse.

When they're moving in single file, Nathan can't see the convoy unless he looks around the driver's head, so he just stares out the window to his nine. Any cars that come too close, unless they're in heavy traffic, on a side road, are warned through intercom. You never know if any of the cars are loaded with explosives. If a car doesn't heed the warning and continues to drive close to the patrol, a warning shot is fired. If that doesn't do it, the next shots are fired with intent to disable the vehicle. The next shots after that are to kill.

Piles of empty cartons of milk, canned foods, used diapers, chicken parts, fruit rinds, and the like create a median between the two lanes on the new route. Some shops are open for business. Here a fish market to their right, carts with huge orange and gold carp on them. Here a small herd of sheep near an open area between two buildings and a slaughter station where a couple of unlucky animals hang by their legs, blood draining into a pool on the ground.

Crowds of people cling to their vehicles as the unit rolls past. Nathan closes his eyes for a moment, tries to imagine he's a rock star and these are his fans. But it doesn't work. They aren't really people to him anymore. They're potential threats, no different than a sack left by a curb or a curiously erected pile of rocks.

Maybe it feels right this way, being numb to the human element. The chatter on the radio, gunshots echoing through the streets, explosions in the distance all give him a chance to forget the past. He's supposed to be playing ball; it's all he's ever been good at. But he'd fucked that up, and, so, what were his choices? He'd been recruited by Syracuse, Rutgers, and UMass. In Amherst, the night before he was to meet with the head coach, he went out with a group of juniors and seniors to a house party somewhere off campus. One of the players put two fifths of Southern Comfort in his hands, then duct-taped his fists and said he'd either have to drink or risk severing a finger trying to break the glass. So he drank. He kissed two girls, who then kissed each other. He rolled in the mud outside. He danced, and broke the bottle over his head, tasted the blood, like tongue against metal, and someone tied a red dish rag around his forehead so that he looked like Rambo. In the morning he woke up to use the bathroom and saw someone had drawn a penis on his cheek, the tip pointed at his mouth. He undid the rag around his head and scrubbed his cheek vigorously. Some of the ink remained, but it could easily be mistaken for dirt. As he walked back to campus, the fog of drunkenness wore off, but a new pain shot through the bottom of his left foot, making it impossible to keep his weight distributed evenly between both feet. He limped toward campus and sat on a bench outside the practice facility. When he took off his sneaker, he saw the purple rings around the swollen bulb of his ankle, and he knew it was broken. He remembered the story his father would tell him when he was a boy, how he'd had a spike driven through his leg during a rugby scrum. His father had a scar. Nathan, a hangover.

He hobbled to a nearby convenience store and called for a cab. The driver took him to the local emergency room. The doctor gave him painkillers, a brace for his foot, and a crutch. He called another cab, and the driver took him to the bus station. He had eight dollars left of the forty his mother had given him for the trip. He bought a six-dollar ticket, one way, to Chicago. The other two dollars he spent on fried eggs and hash browns. When he was finished with his breakfast, he asked the cook for a bag of ice. He sat on the bus with the bag of ice tied around his ankle, the painkillers pulling him under. Every so often he opened his eyes to the purple light that shone through the darkened windows.

Maybe he could've gone in the following year, but his first step was never as fast as it was in high school, and he'd already blown off his potential recruiters, making him a low-end Division Three prospect at best.

Instead, he did some light demolition work for a local crew, working his body back into shape. He bought a truck for a thousand dollars cash, and when the cold came, he drove south to El Paso and found work digging trenches for an irrigation company. He was big and strong and healthy. He ran five miles a day, and every day he passed the same billboard for the army. They were offering a hundred bucks and a free watch just for coming in to talk. Depending on how nice the watch was, Nathan thought, he could pay his weekly rent just to listen to some guy bullshit him about sacrifice and freedom and sacrificing his freedom. He couldn't tell his mother, though. She didn't believe in fighting, or war, or guns.

Baghdad isn't a city. It's a killing field with buildings. People walk around blast craters and dead bodies as though they're construction sites or fruit carts. Armored vehicles mounted with .50-caliber machine guns crush everything beneath their tracks.

Nathan doesn't really know what he's looking for. Do any of them? To properly disguise and hide a roadside bomb, one must conceal them, so if the insurgents do it right, then they shouldn't be able to find any. When they do find them, it's a mistake.

On route clearance they never have face-to-face interaction with people. They are a mounted patrol, scanning the roads through their beat-up RGs—cracks in the bulletproof glass from gunfire, divots in the armored V-hull the size of baseballs—the battle scars of route clearance. Nathan has heard stories about explosively formed projectiles (EFPs). How they go in one side of the RG and out the other. They are the weapon of choice in Shiite neighborhoods. Sunni sections of Baghdad only mess around with deep-buried IEDs. EFPs are usually encased in a curb or a curb-like structure and placed along the roads, angled up toward the height of the Humvee, RG, or Stryker. They usually come in multiple arrangements, so you'll have anywhere from three to five molten copper projectiles being fired, covering the entire length of the vehicle. When the patrol leaves the Sunni neighborhoods, they stop looking for signs of deep-buried IEDs and start looking at the curbsides, scanning for cracked cement, command wires, unearthed dirt.

And it still frightens him, even now, walking along the curb down West Fine Avenue in Flagstaff, Arizona, that if a molten copper slug the size of a softball can penetrate the side of an armored RG, imagine what it does to human flesh.

Nathan hears Red Platoon going through radio checks. RG2 is having coms trouble. There hasn't been a day when all coms have been up and working.

"Buffalo, this is Red Six, radio check, over."

"Red Six, this is Buffalo, over."

West rips off his headset and steps out of the truck.

"It looks like this is going to be another exciting day, guys," he says.

"I wish I had today off," Stanton says, and coughs.

"I got tomorrow off. I plan on spanking my monkey all day."

"Where'd you get a monkey?"

They drive a stretch of road on the border of the Sunni and Shiite muhallas. Open fields to the right, scattered shacks and a cluster of buildings to the left. The road is lined with freshly painted curbs. They roll through an old dusty blast crater. The street is empty. Soon they close in on a checkpoint—a few cement barriers and two unlucky IA (Iraqi Army) soldiers sitting out in the middle of a battlefield. They drive through the checkpoint and down Route Amsterdam, nearly the end of the patrol. For the fourth straight day they come up on what looks to be another hoax IED.

"Red Six, this is White One, they're watching our TTPs, over," West says.

"Roger that, One."

Tactics, techniques, and procedures: TTPs. That's what these hoax IEDs have been about, but you never know for sure. This one is a duct-taped box on the side of the road, under an overpass. Whoever put it there is watching. They watch how the entire patrol stops. They look at which vehicles scan which sectors, how the Buffalo moves up through the formation to approach the IED. They can't push through until it's safe. There's a window of time for them to take on fire, or be hit by a real IED hidden along the road where they have halted.

The giant steels on the Buffalo hack open the box and a bunch of bricks fall out.

"Red Six, this is One, it's just a bunch of bricks, over."

"Roger that, One, Charlie Mike, over."

Most of the platoon lives for typical night patrols, where the risk is high and you never know what's coming. But Nathan thinks it's better to know you're going to see action than not to know. The not knowing is the hardest part. Patches of idle time are not good for soldiers. Nathan tries to keep his focus. The rumbling of the RG motor acts like a metronome, and suddenly he remembers playing hello by squeezing the rolls of his belly together in the mirror when he was a boy. He laughs at that boy now. He had been chubby, in an almost womanly way—skin soft and hairless. The older kids in grade school moved like wolves from behind the trees in the woods behind the playground, holding branches to use as whips. They struck his thighs and butt and legs. After the beatings, he had picked at his scabs in class and tasted the blood. He put the scabs in his locker along with candy bars, PE clothes, and posters drawn on with Magic Markers. He sniffed the tips of the markers. He ate everything his mother put in front of him. Remember the little chocolates she hid in your coat pocket? He cried, but his mother held him. She had said he was handsome. "You'll see." He had begun each day with a careless optimism. At the bus stop one day, when he was eleven, he shared a chocolate with the slow girl. She was bigger than he was but had a small head. She said she wanted to be a pilot. She would never be a pilot. She pretended to fly down the street after she put her hand down Nathan's pants and pulled on his thing. He ran and sweated and lifted and sweated. He climbed the bleachers every morning. He could still hear the metal echo of his footsteps over the birdsongs at dawn. He ate and grew and ran faster. By the age of sixteen, Nathan had grown a foot taller than most of the other kids in school. He made the football team and played the line. "Don't let them move you back," Coach had said. He wore his jersey to school and fingered the best-looking girls. He drank in the same woods where he'd been whipped years ago. He whipped younger, chubby boys, who had soft, womanly skin. Sometimes they screamed and he struck them harder.

Waves of chatter from the radio, gravel crunching beneath the treads, the inner acoustics echoing in the hollowness of his stomach. He's so in tune with these codas, he barely recognizes the sudden blast of horns and drums in a collapse of symphonic symmetry that brings the entire ensemble of sound to a stop. He only hears the percussive beating against his eardrums, and for a moment the darkness ahead explodes into beautiful light.

The next he knows the PL is yelling, "RG One!"

"Are they okay?" Nathan shouts.

"No, they're not okay."

Nathan pushes the heavy armored door open and jumps out, along with the medic. It's quiet. So eerily quiet. And dark. Nathan hears the armored latch moving from inside RG1. Someone's trying to get out. When he wrenches the lock open, black smoke flumes out from inside the RG. The first person he sees is Rodrigo slumped over in the backseat across from the radio. The medic pulls Rodrigo out and slings him over his shoulder.

Rodrigo moans.

"That's a good thing," the medic says. "He's feeling pain. He's alive."

Nathan helps the medic lower Rodrigo to the ground. They run back to the Humvee. Nathan wraps his arms around the next body, Silk's. His leg is hanging on by a few strings of ACU material just above the knee. And when he picks him up, he sees Everitt facedown beneath him. He drags Silk to the cold pavement, unconscious, unmoving. Then Nathan jumps back in to get Everitt, but Everitt's legs are wedged between the rear seat and the smoldering radio—he can't move.

"Get me the fuck out of here," Everitt says. He still has a big wad of chew hanging in his bottom lip.

"I'll get you out," Nathan says. "Don't worry. I got you. I promise."

In the flume of smoke, Nathan sees how it happened, how Everitt fell from the turret and the shrapnel must have taken out his legs. Nathan turns to the door to get some air and clear his eyes. That's when he sees Stanton and West.

"Fucking help me," he yells.

Stanton climbs up through the smoke and comes back with a fire extinguisher. He hands it to Nathan, who sprays down the radio. The smoke intensifies. He jumps out of the truck. When he hits the ground he hears his ankle pop, that fucking ankle, and he falls beside Rodrigo. Rodrigo's been peppered with shrapnel; his face is bloodied and his left eye is swollen shut. His right leg continues to spit dark purple blood.

"Rodrigo, hey, you're going to be all right. Okay?" Nathan says.

Rodrigo's eyes rove around almost majestically, as Stanton and the medic pull him up into the RG.

Nathan grabs a roll of duct tape from his pack and wraps it around his heavy combat boot and treads where the ball of his ankle has begun to push against the cattle hide. On the other side of the Humvee, Nathan sees Silk, one arm bent behind his back, the other folded under his chin as if trying to pick his hand up off the ground.

"I can't breathe," he gasps.

"Medic!" Stanton yells.

"No, right here," Nathan says. "I can help him right here."

It's an open space, on a hard surface, and he can work under the spotlights from the other trucks.

"You best wait for the medic," Stanton says.

There's no time to argue. Stanton is his superior and Nathan has to follow orders. They put Silk on the orange plastic spine board and load him into RG3. Rodrigo is still slumped over on the rear right seat. There's just enough room for Nathan to crouch inside where it's dark. The only light they have to work under is from the lighter they found in Rodrigo's pocket.

Silk starts to slide off the spine board. Nathan pushes his shoulder against his side to hold him in place while the medic fumbles through his aid bag and pulls out an IV set.

"Come on, Doc," Nathan says, as the pie-faced kid spikes the IV bag and primes the line.

He hangs the bag from the ceiling of the RG and opens up an 18-gauge catheter, then puts a restricting band on Silk's arm and feels for a vein.

"I'm going to have to fish around," the medic says.

"The fuck you mean?" Stanton says. "This unit's got no use for a medic who can't save nobody."

"Okay," the medic says, cowering in the faint light. "Here." He opens his bag and takes out another kit with a longer needle and wider tubes.

"I got to penetrate the sternum in order to infuse fluids through the bone."

"Come on, Doc," Nathan says.

The medic sets up the Fast1 and plunges it into Silk's sternum.

"Listen for a pop," the medic says, and pushes down as hard as he can.

There's no pop, no drip. The medic squeezes the bag to force fluids in. The drip chamber fills up but the fluids don't flow. Silk reaches over toward Nathan. He's trying to speak, but he can't. Then he's dead.

They have to leave him there and turn their attention to Rodrigo. Why is there only one medic anyway? Nathan thinks. He checks Rodrigo's dressings, then cuts off some of his boot to get a look at his foot. It's bloodied but superficial.

"So?" Nathan asks.

"He's going to be fine. The shrapnel's all in his face and legs."

"That doesn't sound fine."

The medic shrugs.

"One for two," Stanton says. "That's not a very good percentage."

It feels like hours before the medevac arrives. The medevac hovers between the telephone poles and low-hanging wires, and lands a hundred yards north of their patrol. West slings Rodrigo over his shoulder. Nathan and Stanton carry Silk out on the spine board, then go back for Quinton and Everitt, who are also dead.

In RG3, Nathan sits in the rear seat and leans his head against the cold bulletproof glass. They spend the rest of the night sitting on that road watching RG1 burn. At one point the medic says something about remembering to breathe. Nathan can't stop it. He breaks his hand on the medic's face. The medic takes it like a boxer. He snaps his nose back in place and breaks open an ice pack and hands it to Nathan. While he sleeps that night, the sound of pathetic whistling, like a child trying to play the flute, fills the campsite.

Memories are detonators.

Nathan needs to stamp out the fire in his head.

Iraq, Afghanistan, the heat, the cold, it all runs together now. He never meant to be a lifer. He never quite felt he was in the right place. He was killing time waiting for the bigger purpose. Then he was killing people. Now he's killing time again. But he gets a check from the government, free medical, no dental, now that he's out.

The wind picks up. Cones of dust look to be dancing on their points. The lingering taste of beer and cigarettes coats Nathan's mouth. A quarter mile down the road is the bungalow where Mason has been living ever since he got his toes blown off in Afghanistan. He wears a special boot that causes him to limp and makes a loud, clomping noise like a horse hoof. He says he's known in Kabul as the medicine man.

Before Nathan reaches the door, Mason hobbles out in his underwear, glasses crooked on his nose, holding a smoldering roach in a pair of tweezers.

"Okay, okay," Mason says, as though expecting this visit. "Let's get you figured out."

Mason is in that rare state where he seems to have lost all concept of time. He has a serene glow about him. Maybe it's the pot and pills, but in this moment Mason appears to Nathan to be unburdened, living without a past.

Stretching out on a worn green couch and turning a fan toward his face, Mason gestures with his hand for Nathan to sit.

"So?" he says. "How do you feel? Specifically, I mean."

"I feel like my skull is breaking apart," Nathan says. "I see all things all at once."

"I have just the dose for you," Mason says excitedly, plucking a bottle from a group of bottles on the coffee table, then opening a metal tackle box.

Nathan hitches his shoulder. He doesn't like sudden movements.

"Oh," Mason says. "You've been diseased."

He tosses the bottle to Nathan.

"What's this?"

"That," Mason says. "That will take you to the calm."

Nathan twists the cap, plucks a round yellow pill from the bottle, and places it on his tongue, waiting for a bit of saliva to gather in his mouth in order to swallow it down.

"And these, too," Mason says, tossing another bottle, and another. "Might as well."

He proceeds to give Nathan blue ones and muted green ones and, "What's this color," he asks. "Cantaloupe?"

"Listen, Nathan," Mason's voice like a warning, "picture the mind as a hotel. In this hotel, there are endless rooms and floors, and elevators ascending and descending to different times in one's life, to dreams and faces, wants and projections, scenes, smells, small chocolate candies melted in your coat pockets, fears. And sometimes further back, beyond your life. Into distant lives of others that are part of you because you have shared the same blood, the same world."

Nathan knows the hotel well: the place where he visits all the people remembered and imagined, a retreat of sorts, a comfort, yet, like hotels often are, mysterious, full of despair. The long, carpeted hallway one walks at two in the morning when the front desk clerk is half-asleep and the lone bellhop is smoking outside near the valet stand. Soft, recognizable music plays in the lobby. This is the slow, seemingly endless moment before everything changes.

Nathan feels a strange sense of gratitude for Mason's attentiveness. The same as when his father would ask him about this or that grown-up matter when he was a kid: What do you think of the new homes I'm building up on Shootflying Hill Road? Who would you put your money on in the Oilers versus Packers matchup? Don't you agree the government should issue a flat tax and be done with it?

Mason places his hand on Nathan's knee.

Nathan flinches.

"It's okay," Mason says. "No one is going to hurt you."

Bright light envelops the room. The sun is supposed to be a healing force, but the light stabs him like a lance to the chest.

"You poor thing," Mason says.

The next day, Nathan wakes still dressed in his army-issue service uniform, what's referred to by his fellow defenders of the flag as a bag of smashed asshole. Even though he's been out of the army for a few years now, his uniform affords him free drinks, appetizers, and the occasional piece of trim. There's a girl beside him, snoring noisily, her lips dry and cracked from too many cigarettes. Nathan vaguely remembers her, the way she hooked her leg around his at the Rambler, a bar just down the street, and her breath on his ear, and her pinky finger wriggling around his ass.

His phone is ringing somewhere. There, just under her left breast. He presses two fingers up into her tit and levers the phone to look at the screen. Then he pulls the phone out and answers.

"Andrew?" he says. "What time is it?"

"Six in the morning, where you are."

"That's right."

"I wouldn't have called if it wasn't something important."

"I'm sort of busy," Nathan says, and looks at the girl, flat out on her belly with her legs spread, a tattoo of a spider on her rear.

"Mom's sick."

"She's been sick."

"She's worse. They found tumors in her brain."

"Plural?"

"It doesn't look good."

"No, I wouldn't think tumors in your brain would look good at all."

"Are you drunk?"

"Not nearly."

"There's nothing they can do for her in the hospital anymore. Now she's home."

"And so are you?"

"Yes, for a little while."

Andrew's voice sounds shaky in the way it used to get when he was uncertain.

"Do we have an ETD?"

"A what?"

"How long until—?"

"Oh, man."

"What?"

"Weeks, months. She's asking for you. What more do you want?"

"I don't have much dough."

"I can spot you for now."

"I'll need to settle my affairs here, first."

"Can you try and make it? I'll have your ticket paid for."

"I can try."

After he hangs up, Nathan sits still for a few moments, or seemingly still (his right leg has twitched involuntarily since his first tour), trying to understand why he feels so close to nothing. He should cry, or throw something, or do both at the same time. But he feels fine. He has a craving for pancakes.

The girl stirs and turns over on her side, revealing a pearl white, stat-graph scar along her belly—the shaky hand of an old country doctor who had just run out of whiskey.

"What's going on?" she asks, rubbing her nose with the back of her hand.

"My mom's dying."

"That sucks. Can you pass me a smoke?"

Nathan hands her the open pack. She sits up and pulls the sheet around her like a cloak, takes out a cigarette, which Nathan lights for her. She blows out a stream of smoke, while appearing to be thinking of something worthwhile, eyes squinting slightly, maybe just a stray lash in her pupil.

"I think I lost a contact last night," she says. "Did I lose a contact last night?"

Nathan stands and pulls up his jeans and buckles his belt. It almost doesn't seem right to leave this one here alone.

"Check out's at eleven," he says, as he pulls on a black T-shirt. "If you don't mind."

"Whatevs," the girl says.

That's a new one, Nathan thinks. Then he remembers the pancakes, and he grabs his wallet and smokes and keys.

"Take care," he says, and lets the door slam shut behind him.

TWENTY-THREE

ANDREW IS WAITING OUTSIDE HIS CAR IN THE VISITOR PARKING lot at the Allenwood Federal Correctional Institution in central Pennsylvania. He has driven most of the way in the rain, and the cloud cover, darkening the daylight, has made him feel doubly confined. He crosses his arms, then stuffs his hands in his pockets. He guesses there's no specific way to stand to greet your father after he's been released from prison.

His father pushes open the door holding a packing box in his arms. They meet on the crosswalk, and his father gives Andrew a quick kiss on the cheek, his lips wet from chewing on a fresh stick of gum, then hands the box to Andrew. As they walk back to the car, Andrew looks at the self-help books and loose-leaf papers inside the box, along with a wallet, a comb, the Cornell sweatshirt he had sent his father last October, a couple of T-shirts, a pair of running shorts, and a sad, misshapen ship's-wheel lamp, which Andrew takes out of the box and examines as though it has been put in there by mistake.

"I made that in wood shop class," his father says.

"Nice," Andrew lies.

"It's a piece of shit."

His father sleeps for the first leg of the trip, his mouth parted, eyes lifted, as if dreaming something precious. At a rest stop on the other side of the state line, Andrew gives him some money for a coffee and a pack of cigarettes, and the two stand outside the bathrooms, watching the travelers pull in and out, fat and unforgiving with their overfull minivans, shaggy dogs, and picnic lunches.

"So," Andrew starts, once they're back on the road, "did I tell you my boss died last week?"

"When would you have told me that? I didn't see you last week."

"I thought you might be interested to know."

"How are you taking it?"

"Fine, I guess. I'm not sure. Apparently there's going to be a lot of movement inside the company now."

"You're thinking promotion, then?"

"Possibly."

"I guess that's a good thing. Though, when you move up because of something like this, part of you will always wonder whether you earned that promotion."

"Just because a man died doesn't mean I haven't worked hard."

"And just because you've worked hard doesn't mean you deserve a promotion."

"Why'd I even bring it up?"

"Don't get sensitive, Andrew. I'm happy you're in the position you're in. That's all you can do really, put yourself in a position to move vertically. You can't help what happens to people in other positions. What I'm saying is it might be a burden. That's all."

"I'm well aware of what a burden is."

"Don't be rude."

"I didn't mean it that way."

"Of course you did. I am a burden. I can admit that. Go on, pull over. It's been awhile since I last drove a car."

He drives fast through the blankets of dark and lightless highways, a mist of rain pebbling the windshield, the wipers smoothing the rain away.

"This is quite a ride," his father says.

And that's all he says for the next three hours.

Andrew's father scared him when he was a boy—his size, black eyes, the way he emphasized the *An* in his name when he shouted for him to come to the dinner table. But he showed him love, too, held him delicately when he cried, nicked his chin when he acted up. But this isn't why he feels the old man deserves a break—his reasons have more to do with a general anxiety over letting go, that if he doesn't help, his father will be gone forever.

The cottage Andrew has rented for his father is nestled in the pines near a small pond in Wequaquet. There's a short charcoal grill on the porch; a pan, two bowls, cheap bent silverware, and a miniature refrigerator in the kitchen; an old, musty green couch and a thirty-two-inch television set on a nightstand in the living room; and a stiff twin bed with a set of linens Andrew took from his house. A lingering odor of burnt coffee beans from his morning coffee still hovers in the kitchen and living room, which are nearly the same size and only separated by a scratched wooden table with two folding chairs.

"This will do fine," his father says, after touring the house.

They unpack the boxes of old clothes Andrew has been storing in his basement, and decorate the place with a few framed prints not unlike a seasonal landscape scene hanging on a wall above a bed in a highway motel room.

While his father sets his toiletries in the bathroom, Andrew flips through the pages of a self-published self-help writer's guide, poorly bound, a clip-art copy of a hand holding a pen scanned onto the cover. The book is titled *The Keys to the Self-Help Kingdom*. The author, Henrik Corbyn, has selected a photo of himself looking very worldly in a canvas-colored shirt with a neatly trimmed goatee, and around his neck many necklaces of various stones, elbows propped up on a desk with his hands together and two index fingers held in a thinking man's position just under the chin.

From inside the cover, Andrew pulls out two folded pages of white, lined paper, and unfolds and presses them flat on the table:

Power Presence!
By Robert Kelly

Chapter 1

> *"There's always the day before the day everything changes."*

Let me start by saying that I'm not perfect. It took me losing my wife and kids, going bankrupt, and spending three years in prison to realize that. But there is more action when the world is falling apart. More fresh starts and do-overs and clean slates; there is the feeling of renewal, of having the body split open, the soul purged and purified, and everything done wrong laid out for examination.

Let me start by saying that I'm not perfect. It has taken me three bankruptcies, two divorces, and one short term jail sentence to admit that.

Then, in his father's doctor-like scribble, a note in the margin:

> ***The key here is***
> ***to motivate the***
> ***reader right off the***
> ***bat—introduce the hook—***
> ***positive seeking people***
> ***want instant answers***
> ***not prophecy—the body split***
> ***open? Sounds gruesome.***
> ***Strike that.***

It has taken me fifty-seven years, a failed marriage, bankruptcy, and three years in prison to finally realize I'm not perfect.

But there is more action when the world is falling apart. More fresh starts and do-overs and clean slates; there is the feeling of renewal, of having the body split open, the soul purged and purified, and everything done wrong laid out for examination.

But it is that moment when your world is falling apart, that you can finally be honest with yourself. I had nothing to be proud of. I was humbled. I examined my past and admitted my failing. Then I was free.

HOOK:

Once you get rid of the past you can finally live in the present.

One morning, eight months into my two-year stint in Allenwood, a bright light caught me as I was sitting on the toilet thinking about the time my father had taken my dinner plate and dumped the meat loaf and string beans onto the floor of the mudroom where we kept our shoes and jackets, ordering me to eat off the floor if I wanted to act like an animal at the table. I was eight years old. The light coming through the caged glass enveloped my memory and erased it. I could feel my heart pumping. I clenched and unclenched my fists, staring up at the sickly yellow auxiliary lighting that passed for darkness in prison. Suddenly I felt released. This feeling, I later understood, was the unexplainable power of the present.

Andrew hears his father's heavy steps on the hardwood floor in the hallway, and he quickly tries to stuff the pages back into *The Keys to the Self-Help Kingdom*.

"Curious?" his father asks.

"A little."

"There's money to be made selling clarity. Books, DVDs, digital downloads, apps, and who knows what in the future—possible holograms, bright beautiful people guiding the sad and searching through their day."

Hope turns to disappointment turns to exhaustion. Why did he always get suckered in by his father's enterprises? Inevitably, each one was just another scheme. Andrew will nod and ask uninspired questions, time ticking away on his watch face—how much time has he wasted with his father's plans? And when they didn't work out, how his father acted as though they had never existed. The last one he had was last month, written out in his prison cell on yellow legal paper, his least inventive: the dissolvable meal, a pill containing all the nutrients, vitamins, and calories you needed to complete a two-thousand-calorie diet, minus the chewing. "Not to mention the health benefits," he had said. "And think about how many people we will save from choking or chipping a tooth or food poisoning," and when, weeks later, Andrew got up the courage to tell his father that he had to pass on the idea, his father said, "People love to eat, I don't know what I was thinking. Now I'm looking into kiosks, all different types of kiosks, you can put them in airports and shopping centers and parks, rent them to whoever checks out, they can sell Seventh-day Adventist literature for all I care, as long as they pay the rent each week, always a check in the mail, like collecting royalties, kiosks across the country, KELLY AND SONS etched into a small steel plate on the side, with a phone number and e-mail address, this is the future, sell and move, sell and move, people need change, only the old keep returning to the same place, and the same place grows old with them."

His father will never follow through. Something else will come along, something bigger and more profitable, something untapped, like undiscovered oil buried deep below a square of unexplored ocean. Andrew has cataloged his ideas in his memory. ATM machines, inflatable air dancers, super vitamin packs, nicotine lozenges, antiaging face creams, helicopter rides, and chocolate face-moldings for lavish corporate gatherings. And what if he raised enough capital, gathered the right group of investors, even asked Andrew to take a loan out in his name? If, say, he became a multimillionaire, a trailblazer, a man remembered. The same, Andrew thinks, because, for his father, there is no goal, only a constant, unattainable imagining of possibilities just outside his reach.

His father pulls up a chair beside Andrew, picks up the papers, pats them down so the stack is even. Andrew can smell the sweet mint and coffee of his father's breath.

"But it's not just another scheme," the old man says. "I really feel the present. I had an awakening in there. Now I just need to figure out how to sell it. This Corbyn guy has it down. He says how you need the audience to sympathize with your upbringing and good intentions, your successes and failures, your unique, hopeful vision once faced with so much adversity."

He picks up the book from the table and flips through to a dog-eared page.

"Listen to this: 'The past is fiction. You can never know what it was like to live back then as yourself. You were not the you you are now. Just as we cannot truly know how the Romans and ancient Greeks lived or the Neanderthals. There are fossils and cave paintings and marble busts, but these are locked behind museum doors, reimagined by the viewers who stand before them with their own thoughts and emotions and ideas of past civilizations. The beauty of art is that a painting is never finished because it is never looked at the same way twice. So, too, is the beauty of the mind, always changing the person you were into the person you are. So it is our present perspective of the past that controls our fate. Can we move forward? Or will we root ourselves in historical fiction forever?' "

He shuts the book and looks at Andrew with his unblinking, black eyes.

"Is that not the most powerful thing you've ever heard?" he says.

"It's pretty powerful," Andrew says.

"Pretty powerful? That's all you have to say?"

"I think so."

"You think so?"

"I bought some steaks," Andrew says, turning from his father. "They're in the fridge."

The following week, when Andrew stops by to check on his father, he hears laughter from inside the cottage, and through the screen door he sees his father sitting at the kitchen table drinking bottled water with a red-haired woman not much older than Andrew, slender, in a cotton spring dress, her legs crossed, brown boots halfway up her calves. How, he wonders, is his father able to move in, move on, so easily, no matter the place, no matter the circumstance? The woman is holding a dog in her lap, a Jack Russell terrier with a brown face divided by a narrow patch of white fur down its nose.

Something about her, Andrew thinks, with that dog and those boots and that red hair.

"Andrew, don't stand out there like a loon," his father says. "Come in, meet my new friend . . . what was your name again?"

"Millie," the red-haired woman says.

"That's it. I don't know if I agree with that name for you. I think Rebecca, or, possibly, Vanessa. Something with an *a* at the end."

Millie gives an affected laugh, as if by doing so, she is joining him in this bout of flirting.

"Your father's a hoot," she says to Andrew. "Here I am, looking all over for my Rudolph, and he's curled up on the front steps outside like some kind of lion cub."

"Do you live around here?" Andrew asks.

"Sort of."

"Pull up a seat, bud," Robert says.

"Yeah, bud," Millie says.

"I just came by to check in on you," Andrew says. "I didn't mean to intrude."

"Why do you need to be checked in on, Robert?" Millie asks.

Robert pulls up his pants leg, revealing the home monitor bracelet strapped around his ankle.

"I'm not a pedophile if that's what you're thinking."

"That's good to know."

"I'm just a crook."

"We all got our secrets," Millie says. "Some worse than others." She turns to Andrew and winks. "Any-hoo." She rises from the chair with her dog held in her arms like a fragile gift. "I'll let the two of you alone."

"Oh, but . . ." Robert says, then stops himself. "Sure. You got better things to do than hang around with the likes of us."

"No, no. That's not it. I think it's important to spend as much time with your family as possible."

"That's true," Robert says.

"It was nice meeting you," Millie says to Andrew. "And it was nice meeting you, too," Millie says again, this time in a slightly gruff voice, holding her Jack Russell terrier up by her face to make it appear as though the dog is speaking.

After she leaves, Robert can't stop from smiling every few seconds.

"God, I miss a good woman," he says solemnly, with a hint of desperation.

Andrew wonders if his father has had a good woman since leaving his mother, and, if not, is it her he misses?

TWENTY-FOUR

ANDREW, LYING IN HIS OLD BED IN HIS OLD ROOM IN HIS OLD house, now has time to ask himself when last he had truly been happy. Sometimes his memories of the Cape make him feel something akin to happiness. Such as when he used to ride his bike past the marsh, across the train tracks, then farther down the road to Long Beach. The time he discovered an old motorboat tied up to a rock at the edge of the landing. He untied the rope and pushed the boat out toward the landing and got in and pulled the cord. The engine wouldn't start. He checked the tank and saw that it was full. He had brought tools this time and took apart the engine, carefully laying out each part in order to find the missing piece. It was simple really. There was no spark, no way to get the fuel to the motor. He spent awhile chipping at a flat stone and fit it in the engine and put back together the parts and set the motor on the boat. He greased the wheel with his spit, then pulled the cord. The small engine turned over and a blast of black smoke flumed out. He shifted the lever back and forth and up, and went slowly out into the bay and past the docks and around the blue striped buoy he saw in the distance, until bringing her back to the landing. He cleaned his hands in the seawater and gathered his tools and looked at the boat, feeling accomplished.

But the memory disappears, and here he is now, living with his mother, ashamed, guilty, scared, alone, and unhappy. He has been lying in bed for the better part of the morning, listening to his mother's unceasing cough. The heavy rains of late, and the pollen in the air, don't help her condition. He has also started to ready himself for his brother's arrival. What does Nathan look like these days? More important, how will he act?

It has been ten years since he's last seen his brother, the day after the wedding, when they drank beers underneath the Wequaquet River Bridge and planned a trip to go fishing in Maine sometime in August. But neither of them liked to fish, and Nathan was gone before the end of July.

In his socks and underpants, Andrew walks from the guest room to the kitchen and opens the refrigerator door. There is nothing inside the fridge but a jar of pickles and two cans of beer. His mother lives like a bachelor. He'll have to run to the store later.

He cracks open a beer, drinks half of it in one, long gulp, then walks through the swinging door and into the dining room, where he looks out at the street through the bay window. A gang of kids on bikes are circling around the entrance to the driveway, hands pressed forward on their handlebars, their loud chattering indecipherable from that distance. The kids begin to pick up speed, as though feeding off one another, then zoom down the street toward the hill on Southbay Drive, which hundreds of years ago fishermen would climb back up with their catches.

Finishing his beer, he begins to relax and take stock of the house, of the large painting of the cat in the dining room, which always frightened him as a child, making him feel watched by this cat, this hungry cat about to lap up the spilt milk before her, then to the mantel above the fireplace, where he places his beer can beside the wooden horses his great-grandmother had brought over from Sweden. One has broken and been put back together with glue. He studies the zigzagging crack along its leg and flank. Some splinters of wood have gone missing forever. He belches.

"Andrew," his mother calls.

He rushes into the living room.

"What is it, Mom? What do you need?"

"I just wanted you to help me work this thing."

She pinches the remote control, holds it away from her face as though it is something foul. He turns it over and sees that the batteries have fallen out where she taped them in after losing the cover. Nothing in the fridge, but plenty of batteries stored throughout the house. He crouches down and rubs his hand underneath the couch. His mother nudges him with the toe of her soft slipper. Batteries taped back in, he hands her the remote and places a cushion underneath her feet.

"Thank you, honey."

"What else do you need? Are you hungry?"

Suddenly his mother is on the verge of tears. Her hands tremble. The remote falls from her hand.

"Sometimes you're horrible," she says.

"Mom," Andrew pleads, because these sudden shifts in mood are near impossible for Andrew to process, with his own similar shifts in mood.

"Just horrible."

"I didn't mean anything—"

His mother waves him away.

"Where's your brother?"

Andrew's earpiece buzzes. He looks at the phone—Dad.

"Here," Andrew says, handing his mother the remote. "Watch your show."

He walks back through the dining room and into the kitchen before answering his father's call.

"Can you pick up the papers for me?" his father asks before Andrew even agrees to come by.

"What about that coffee shop on the corner? Don't they have the papers?"

"Just the liberal ones."

"I might be awhile."

"Where am I going?"

Andrew presses the earpiece to end the call. He breathes in five seconds, holds five seconds, breathes out five seconds. He's been watching a series called *Self-Preservation in the Age of Anxiety* on YouTube. Nearly an hour of the ten-hour series is spent on breathing techniques. They work as stopgaps when he needs to move from one anxiety-inducing scene to another. He had never realized how incorrectly his breathing had been before.

"That was Dad," Andrew tells his mother.

"Oh, is he out of prison?"

"He's been out."

"Good for him. Maybe all of us—me, you, your father, and Nathan—can have lunch together sometime."

Her bitterness is new, culled by her anxiety, her sickness, the replacement of what could be with what could have been. Andrew accepts her sarcasm, no matter how disparaging it is—given her attitude on that particular day. He accepts it, accepts her. He has become all the men she once knew and loved. He listens, reacts the best he knows how. He's become adept at taking the brunt.

But the sneering tone of her voice causes Andrew's chest to

tighten, and for a moment he is short of breath, which, when short of breath, breathing technique six in *Self-Preservation in the Age of Anxiety* instructs one to find a safe place to stand with one's arms above one's head, like a tree, in an act of receiving, while trying to remain conscious of only your body, slowing the heart rate, returning to a steady breathing pattern.

"I'll be back soon," he says, and quickly rushes out of the room.

"You've always been such a good boy," she calls after him. "Maybe that's your problem."

Andrew drives to the corner of Main and Southbay and pulls up at the penny candy store where nothing costs a penny anymore. He picks up the *Herald* and *Post* and *Times*; the first two he remembers his father reading back to front because he says they tell the truth and still keep the lines on the games in the sports section. The *Times* he uses to get the coals started on the grill.

Andrew tosses the papers into the backseat and drives along Southbay, glancing out at the ocean, at the soft swells, the seagulls perched on the empty lifeguard stand. This has always been the best time of year. The tourists haven't yet arrived, the beaches are still empty, and you don't have to pay to park your car close to the shore. Maybe later today, after he visits his father, maybe he will drive back down and dive into the water and swim out to the old floating raft and lie back on the mossy wood, the way he had when he was a kid.

Truth is, since he's been home, he can't imagine leaving. In a sense, his mother's dying has offered him sanctuary. He remembers early summer cookouts when the kids in the neighborhood appeared alongside the adults, like ghosts from a mist. And in the backyard on those orange sky evenings, Andrew would study their legs, their calves and knees and thighs. Some of them were red. Some brown. Some were hairy. Some were hairless. Mrs. Landslow's veins wound around her legs like ivy. How confident they all were when they laughed and shook hands and lit cigars. They mimicked a bullet to the head, a dancing pastor, a man on fire, a dog taking a whiz on a tree, a cripple. They were never the same person twice. When the adults had finished eating and were slightly buzzed and nostalgic, they joined the kids in whatever game they were playing. Mr. Dunning snapped his pinky finger back behind his ring finger during a game of Horse. He snapped it back to the children's delight. "Ewwww!" they screamed. Andrew's mother felt faint and needed to sit down. She had a big cigarette between her fingers and when she smoked it she coughed until her face went scarlet and patted her chest and said, "What the frig is in this thing?" And it was ninety degrees and humid. The mosquitoes got fat and died in the grass and on the patio furniture. On nights like these, when he wasn't being watched by their father, Nathan gorged himself on grilled meat and bread and pasta salad. Andrew watched him sneak back for a third and fourth hot dog. He always took three scoops of ice cream when the other children took one. Whenever he passed by a table, he grabbed a handful of potato chips. Inaction made him nervous. The more he ate, the sleepier he got. Once the plates were cleared and the adults had their drinks and the other kids were playing Wiffle ball, he went into the kitchen and snuck a Kit Kat from the drawer where his mother kept their high-test-score rewards. Andrew caught him and said—what did he say?—something about his shorts bunched between his red thighs as they always were when they ran around in summer, or the pimples on his cheeks and chin, or his chunky upper body. "Fat Tits," he had called him. "What are you doing with that Kit Kat, Fat Tits?" That's what he had said. And he still regrets saying it.

He pulls up his contacts on the screen in the console. Then says, "Call Kirsten."

The other end rings once, then goes to voice mail:

Hi! This is Kirsten, but you probably already knew that, or, if you didn't, maybe this is destiny. Either way, leave a message!

Andrew doesn't leave a message.

He speeds past the beach and rolls down the windows.

The panic starts again as he passes the Tidewater Hotel on the hill opposite the beach, taking the curve in the road, where the ocean is eclipsed by the giant triple-decker houses standing on the rocks, and Southbay turns to Eastbay, and all the subdivisions his father and grandfather had built up since moving to Wequaquet fifty years ago with names like Horseback Run, Garrison Court, and Meadowbrook Lane, with For Sale signs and open house announcements planted in the ground.

As he turns onto the gravelly road leading up to his father's depressing cottage, he stops short of the tire ruts in the shallow, muddy yard so as not to scratch the rims on his BMW. A part of the person he still is cares about these things.

For a moment he wishes he hadn't agreed to see the old man, but in the window, his father's shadowy frame raises up the thin curtains, and he knows he can't leave now.

Andrew is certain his father wants more than just to touch base. Since his release, over a month ago now, his father has ditched his self-help book on obtaining clarity and taken up Andrew's mind space with various propositions, such as selling authentic Cape Cod beach grass, acai berry powder, and, just last week, time shares at the El Presidente Retreat in Costa Rica. Andrew wonders if his father isn't losing his mind, though, each time, he transfers some money into the old man's account. When his father's efforts fail, he blames Andrew for not going all-in. They had a chance to hit the big time. If only.

"I guess you're already big time," his father has said more than once, bullying Andrew into upping his ante toward a future investment.

Andrew collects the papers and steps out and into a patch of sticky mud. He throws the papers in the driver's seat and rips out the *Times* sports section and wipes the mess off his shoe sole. He dips the sole in a puddle and rakes the bottom of his shoe against the stones in the driveway.

On the small, unstable front porch, his father takes the papers and puts them down on a plastic table, hugs Andrew, and kisses him just next to his lips.

"You look good, Dad," Andrew says.

"I'm running again, just down the street and back, and lifting weights. I use these stretch bands. It's all about resistance. Are you hungry? Want lunch?"

"I could eat."

His father puts together a couple of sandwiches—turkey wraps with mustard—and pours two cups of coffee.

His father has always been a fast eater, possibly from his time in the army, or, more likely, to make a quicker getaway from Red at the dinner table. Still impressed, Andrew studies the Pollock-like drops of mustard left on his father's plate.

"You're not hungry?" his father says. "This is all I eat now—lean meats, eggs, legumes."

The word "legumes" rolls around in Andrew's mouth like a marble.

"I feel better than I have in years. I'm meditating now. Do you meditate?"

"Not yet."

"You should meditate."

As Andrew finishes the first half of his wrap, his father starts out as he always does, asks about Nathan, says he hasn't heard from him in a while.

"It must be difficult. Having to transition back to this lush life."

"He's had enough time to do it, don't you think?"

"They take a piece of you when you leave."

"I didn't know Iraq and Germany were so similar."

"Don't be a smartass," his father says, pinning Andrew to his chair with his dark eyes. "What about your mom? Anything new on that front?"

"The same."

"I've been meaning to call."

"She'd appreciate that."

"Right. Well."

Bases covered, his father starts to explain his plans for the future, how he's been contacted by Corbon Dennison, a venture capitalist out of New York, who his father had met in prison, and this Dennison has summoned his father to procure his knowledge of the real estate market, whether it's a good time to buy, which his father believes that if you have the money then it's always a good time to buy, has said it to Andrew during any and every father-and-son talk they have ever had—"Buy property. They can't take it away from you." Who were they? Andrew had often wondered as a boy. Always there was a "they" lurking outside the boundaries of their lives, paying close attention to their every move. When finally he had discovered who "they" were—tax collectors, bank managers, property attorneys, building committees, politicians, women—all of whom played one role or another in severely damaging his father's financial stability, not to mention his integrity, Andrew started to understand why his father had run off all those years ago. Andrew had been working with "them" since he graduated college. In fact, up until just recently, he'd been one of "them."

Dennison had nearly the full amount needed to buy the old Tidewater Hotel, boarded up and vacant for the past decade, a junkyard of used auto parts and miscellaneous metals delivered, dumped, and stacked behind a loose, wind-stripped fence.

"You know my position," his father says, pulling up his pants leg to flash the blinking anklet. "I can't be anywhere near this thing."

"Right," Andrew says, and drinks from his mug. The coffee tastes strong and stale, like end-of-the-night diner coffee. Andrew nearly spits it back into the cup but instead swallows the sludge to show his manhood, always challenged when he's with his father, no matter his age.

They sit, slightly hunched, Andrew in his khakis and polo, his father in sweats and a mock turtleneck, the cool summer afternoon, and the light barely visible through the pines.

"I have to use the bathroom," Andrew says after a while.

"Take this in with you." His father hands Andrew his plate. "And make another pot of coffee. The grounds are in the top cupboard."

Andrew puts the plates in the sink and runs the faucet. He sighs in relief, an intermission, finally. He finds the large can of coffee and spoons the grounds into a filter, pours the water, and listens as the machine gurgles and whines.

How lonely it is to wait for something.

He walks into the bathroom and shuts the door. He recognizes the burnt-match smell, a politeness his father issued after taking a shit, most likely a habit formed from having to share a bathroom with his sister when he was a boy. Andrew washes his hands, then taps the puffy skin under his eyes, looking in the mirror, the wrinkles that have formed at the edges and webbed out but stop before they reach the edge of the cavities. And here are the long, unfurled hairs sticking out of his eyebrows, the unshaven cheeks and chin, the small crop of curls that spring from the opening of his collared shirt.

Taped to the medicine cabinet is a piece of lined paper with the heading:

THINGS TO WORK ON

1. Be Patient
2. Express Remorse
3. Eat Healthy Foods
4. Exercise Routinely
5. Secure Thy Self

Andrew despairs in picturing his father sitting down to write out such a specific mission statement, choosing where to place it, where he will be reminded of the things he needs to work on. In order to achieve what?

He remembers showering with his father when he was very young, how the water sprang off his father's hard, thick forearms and the white met the tan edges of his skin from where his sleeves were cut and the sun couldn't reach and the bushy hair in the middle of his chest and around his navel and penis, how it collected in the drain and he asked Andrew to pull it out so the drain didn't clog. His rough hands on Andrew's wet body, his skin red from the heat of the water, turning Andrew around and soaping up a washcloth, scratching his skin, making it even redder. Andrew had wondered if he was that dirty that he should be scrubbed with such force. His father picked him up and held him close to the water spitting from the showerhead. Andrew had always taken baths with his brother, not showers, had played in the bath, had had his mother's soft hands massage his head with shampoo. But this was how men bathed. His father placed him down carefully outside of the tub and told him to grab a pair of towels. They walked out of the bathroom, Andrew's towel trailing behind him like a sweep train. He was moving away from his mother and toward his father. He didn't know what it was, then, but he took pride in having achieved something. But if what he had achieved has all led to this—an old cottage, bad coffee, sad lists taped to the medicine cabinet door?

He opens the medicine cabinet and sees on the single rack tubes of foot cream, toothpaste, and lotion. In the cabinet underneath the sink is a small leather bag that contains years of toenail clippings. Strange. But not unlike the collection of gray hairs Andrew keeps in a plastic ziplock bag tucked away in his shaving kit.

One more glance at the list, the phrase "Secure Thy Self" catches him and, in his head, he repeats the phrase as he pours the coffee and returns to the front porch.

Outside, his father lights another cigarette, crosses his leg over his knee, and lets his foot dangle. Andrew remembers how he would grab at his father's foot and his father would pull his foot back and tap Andrew on the top of his head with his toes. Come to think of it, his toenails were always perfectly trimmed.

"Just imagine," his father says, "a world-class hotel here in Wequaquet. We'll have luxury and affordable luxury—a view of the ocean, a view of the garden, separate but equal. Everyone will be treated the same. Guests must wear shoes and a shirt in the lobby, and a suit coat in the dining room. We'll have an

Olympic-size swimming pool, restaurant on the patio overlooking the ocean, fitness center, putting green. And here, look."

What the Cape is, and always has been, is a refuge for the rich, spending a month or so in houses bought and kept up through the off-season by a local hire. Then there are the minivan families, who save all year to spend a week in a motel off Route 28 with two springy mattresses and a bath running only cold water, park their asses on the beach, eat fried clam rolls, and play putt-putt with their kids.

His father unrolls the blueprints, which up until now had been hidden in a tube just behind a potted ficus tree. The initial outdoor design shows, in pencil drawing, a victory-style casino look with a central lobby, two wings, and a wide sloping lawn in front.

"It's one of those deals you don't pass on, a home run."

A slam dunk or a hole in one or a sure bet, Andrew thinks.

He looks over the other sheets, unsure of what the measurements and all mean, but, by the size of the property, he can tell that this is a lengthy, arduous deal, which could fall apart at various stages over the next year or so it will take to build, including Stage One—Today.

His father knows how to get things done, on the quick, skipping the lines with a bill squared in his palm. And Andrew knows a project of this magnitude requires certain palms to be greased. And at present, mulling it over in the way he used to mull over his own investments—by examining the negatives first—he isn't so sure the small town he grew up in needs any sort of upscale hotel. The real whales who summer here rent houses on the bluffs, hire Portuguese maids, and send for girls in Boston.

"So, what do you think?" his father asks indifferently, as if not asking at all.

Unsure of what to say, Andrew sips his coffee like a child sipping hot chocolate, both hands around the mug. He looks up at his father with a willing expression. He wants to please him. There is still nothing he wants more.

"I think it can't miss," he says.

TWENTY-FIVE

A WEEK AFTER HIS BROTHER'S CALL, NATHAN BUYS A BUS ticket for Phoenix so he can make the flight Andrew has booked. He sits on a bench out back where the buses are parked and smokes. Then he pops one of the blue pills Mason had given him on his last visit to the bungalow. Home seems so far from this dreary cement-stamped station.

On the bus, Nathan stashes his duffel and sits in the aisle seat toward the back. He unties his boots, yanks them off, and sniffs the insides.

An old man in black Velcro sneakers looks back at him, then turns ahead. He looks back again.

"What?" Nathan says.

The old man smirks.

"We used to have real wars with real enemies you could actually hate because in a way you respected their guile. Now we fight terror. We fight a word. There's no wonder we can never win or lose. Our enemy is a ghost of the imagination."

"Fuck off, pal," Nathan says.

"Exactly," the old man says, and faces front.

At the gate check in the airport, Nathan stands in line sweating furiously in the wake of impending authority. The only thing he has of any importance, or worth, is his old military ID, the prescription bottle filled with a combination of other prescription drugs—Klonopin, Xanax, Ambien, Zoloft, and five or so purple, diamond-shaped muscle relaxers from Brazil, all provided by Mason—and two changes of clothes. He puts the items into one of the gray plastic crates on the conveyor and watches them enter into the big metal box to be inspected. A lady with a mechanical wand directs him toward a body scanner. "Belt," she says. He slips off his belt and puts it on the conveyor with someone else's phone and shoes and money clip, a hundred-dollar bill pinched under the clasp.

Inside the scanner, he lifts his arms to mirror the shaded, unisex human form in front of him and looks down at his bare feet, his untrimmed, yellowing toenails. He steps out and is searched again on the other side. The man behind him is also being searched. The TSA agent passes over the bullet pieces that had broken up in Nathan's shoulder during his second tour in Tikrit. Nathan pulls down his shirt and shows the man the scar.

"Just think," he says, "six inches to the right and we would never have had such an intimate moment together."

"Let me thank you for your service," the agent says, not looking him in the eye.

Nathan picks up his materials from the conveyer and snatches the money clip.

In the terminal lavatory, he slips the hundred-dollar bill into his coat pocket and ditches the money clip in the trash. He sits in the stall at the far end, locks the door, and lights a cigarette. He takes three quick puffs before extinguishing the butt in the toilet, then pops two Klonopins and follows that with two Xanax. Barring any screaming infants, he thinks, the pills should knock him out before the plane takes off.

Only when the plane wheels slam against the runway in

Boston does Nathan wake. A terrible pain crests across his shoulders and springs up into his neck. He senses the man in the next seat staring at him and turns slightly to see him with his left eye.

"You drooled on my shoulder," the man says.

"Sorry about that."

"Middle seat, a stranger's drool on my only blazer, and I'm ninety-five percent sure my wife is sleeping with one of my cousins."

"Not quite the American dream?"

"My cousins are all so fucking good-looking. Their brains are mush, but they got these giant arms and big bulging shoulders and they all speak with this phony Greek accent, pretending they didn't grow up in Bridgewater."

"Maybe they have small penises."

"In my dreams," the man says, sullen. "Too bad we all went to school together. They're hung like horses."

The man sits on his knees holding his carry-on. He's small, blubbery, and sad.

"Look at these people. It's like they want to stay on the plane longer. Carrying their entire wardrobe—all you need is a blazer and you can go anywhere. Unless someone drools all over it, then I guess it's a good idea to have more than one blazer."

Nathan, no longer paying attention to the pathetic stranger, thinks about his mother, how to approach her, how to make it seem like he's doing well so that she won't worry.

The line moves ahead like a slow funeral procession, and he shuffles out into the gate area, through the traffic of ruddy-faced travelers, and out beneath the gray sky, surrounded by the smell of smoke and burnt coffee beans, the dropped consonants and phlegm-clotted laughter.

Nathan boards the Plymouth/Brockton bus for South

Station. Rolling over the lunar potholes, he's reminded of the terrifying intricacies of this small, gloomy city he knew as a kid, chasing after his father who strode through the crowds as though they were invisible, and later when he was a teenager and would ditch school and catch a ride to Haymarket Square, and find a bar to serve him and his buddies, who had all grown enough stubble to look close enough to twenty-one. The way the roads dip under Boston Harbor as if falling from the earth, how the buildings appear crooked, built on the waves surrounding them, the flagrant grayness of the city itself, from the pale sky to the pale faces.

He arrives at South Station and out into the oil-rich air with the smell of exhaust fumes and overfull garbage cans, and stands listening to a raggedy-looking addict play Bob Dylan's "It Takes a Lot to Laugh, It Takes a Train to Cry." There are no coins in the musician's guitar case, no dollar bills. It's tough for a street musician these days; no one deals in cash anymore.

On the train, he studies the passengers, most communing with their phones and tablets. They work in a kind of rhythm, along with the rushing of the train—whirling, symphonic—it all seems a natural movement into the day, and for once in a city, the people flow around and over him, as though he is a loose rock in a rushing stream, soon to be carried away to some new destination.

The cold is a charge, an input. Nathan has always felt comforted being close to the ocean, as if a giant hand is ready to receive him, though not today. And this, along with the smaller joys he had when he was a boy—the walks he took along felled autumn leaves, swiping his finger across the crystallized windows of storefronts in winter, the smell of cut grass and damp earth on the baseball diamonds, dangling his feet over the harbor bulkhead in summer—now appear distant and unattainable. Where have they gone? Brief flashes, scenes infused with color congealing into a mass of bleak gray; times when he could feel what it was like to be the person who felt things.

Nathan walks with the crowds—their haunted faces have the unhealthy pallor that clings to the skin during frantic times—unceremoniously roaming the coffee-stained brick neighborhoods of Beacon Hill. Zombies. Human flotsam. What is that line from *Under the Volcano*?

"The Lighthouse, the lighthouse that invites the storm, and lights it!"

He heads downtown and into the State House, where his brother's wedding had been held, when? Nine, ten years ago? The last time he had been in Boston, just home from Iraq, his mother begging him to wear his uniform, his brother begging him not to.

He rides the elevator to the top floor and enters the large reception room, where, from the ceiling-high windows on the top floor overlooking Back Bay, he can see the ocean dimple from the light rain. He remembers how it was to dance with his mother, and his sister-in-law and her mother. How beautiful they all looked. Andrew's father in-law had made millions selling bathroom fixtures to fast-food restaurants, and though his left eye twitched feverishly, his voice had the relaxed tone of a father reading his child a bedtime story. He was Jewish and heavy, and it took five of Andrew's bullnecked friends to lift the man up on the chair as they danced the horah. But it was that moment with his mother, when he put his cheek against hers, as they stood by the windows in the waning end of the celebration, while guests were collecting their coats and asking one another which bar they should meet up at, when he felt a warmth in his body so infantile, so new, he gripped her tightly, attempting, he guesses, to pull her into him, so that he could feel this heat and comfort he had somehow known was about to disappear.

Nathan pictures the scene so clearly, he feels it must hold some kind of significance.

Then the wedding party was gone, and only his father was still there, sitting at a cluttered table with his legs crossed, smoking a cigarette and touching the ash into a half-drunk glass of champagne.

"Jews and fags," he had said. "It used to be you could make a joke every now and again. Not anymore. They lock you up, call it a hate crime."

He dropped the half-smoked cigarette into the glass, looked past Nathan to the diminishing crowd.

"Do you think it will last?"

"I do," Nathan said.

"He's underwater now," his father said, not to Nathan so much as to himself. "He'll never be able to come up for air."

Nathan's father had taken off one of his snakeskin boots, shaken a pebble out in his palm, then flicked it carelessly onto the table.

Approaching now, a sharp-featured young woman with a harsh New England face—thin lips, cat eyes, sunken cheeks—"Sir, we have a wedding rehearsal beginning this afternoon," she says. "You will need to vacate."

"Vacate?"

"Leave."

"I know what it means."

The woman scratches her cheek with the tip of her white painted fingernail.

"My brother was married here," Nathan says. "Andrew Kelly. I was the best man."

"We have many weddings here. This is a very popular space."

"I gave quite a memorable toast, as toasts go."

And it was memorable, in a way, if only for the fact that he had cast Andrew as a nerd and Kirsten his savior. Locked away in his dorm room, reading advanced microeconomic theory, his eyes like red stones, not so different from when he was a boy and stayed up all night putting together a puzzle of Monet's *Water Lilies, Evening Effect*, or playing chess against himself (an invented opponent of Russian descent named Boris Popov). Nathan thought Andrew would never come out of it, never meet anyone if all he did was study, until he met Kirsten; and here he paused and looked toward Kirsten, who sat at the head table with an air of impatience and annoyance, the folds of her dress like a cream custard, so perfectly frozen about her. A lone uncle or old college roommate of Andrew's whistled inappropriately. Nathan, seeing her face, turning to the light, said of love, "How crazy it makes a man; how perfect it makes a woman," and emptied his glass of scotch to arrhythmic applause. "To love and peace and the absurdity of happiness," he closed.

"The absurdity of happiness," he repeats aloud, thoughtfully.

"Please, if you wouldn't mind, sir," the woman says.

Nathan has never felt comfortable being called "sir," whether in a regimental sense or as a regular citizen. He looks out the windows, to the graying clouds hanging over Back Bay, and the clock tower. A pair of seagulls perch there like carved statues.

"Okay, then," he says.

Once outside, he queues up with a school field trip, boys and girls in ugly soft orange T-shirts, chanting some horrifyingly senseless song—*1773 is when we dumped the tea, our taxes were hiked and the British were psyched, so we threw their love in the sea*—clearly the work of a first-year, overzealous high school teacher whose hope has yet to be zapped.

Nathan walks alongside the group. They visit the Old Granary Burying Ground and meet with the headstones of Paul

Revere and Samuel Adams and Thomas Paine. The teacher explains that these men were heroes in their time. Nathan stands behind the children, nodding thoughtfully, thinking, if I were teaching this class I would say something like, "Children, they were heroes for certain men, thieves and slaughterers for others. Who knows, we may have been better off had the British won." The teacher moves on to another grave, and the children weave through the headstones, playing a game of Can the Dead Feel This, jumping as high as they can and landing with a thud on the browning grass where so many tourists have walked before. As is true in most American cities still recovering from the recession, the local government is unable to provide sufficient maintenance for its most treasured monuments, trusting an innate respect for the dead that children are incapable of possessing because they are, as of yet, unafraid, that possibly they have awakened the ghosts of these supposedly triumphant men.

"John Adams was a pussy," Mr. Putter had said one afternoon during Nathan's sophomore social studies class, and he had always remembered it. A couple of days later Mr. Putter was put on leave, and Nathan never saw him again. He guesses now that Mr. Putter's trouble wasn't unusual; it had something to do with booze and regret and boredom, of being a white, American male stuck with the derivative seed flowering rows and rows of dull lives.

Nathan leaves the group of children and walks through the Common to the Public Garden, between the overhanging elms, the fecund-smelling flowers, and bubbling fountains, saluting George Washington: "You tall, stone-legged son-of-a-bitch." Only one unhappy-looking couple is out in a paddleboat, their arms wrapped around their bodies, bicycling toward the center of the pond.

He sits on a bench and picks up the metro section of the *Her-*

ald, which has been left on the place beside him. A spider crawls up the page and skitters along the broadside onto his hand. He presses his hand to the bench and the spider crawls off. "B1, Above the Fold: A pregnant woman shot in the stomach: double homicide. The shooter had intended to kill someone else. He expressed his sorrow in court, pled not guilty. B1, Below: A girl kidnapped by her own father, who hung her by the feet in the basement of his house in Fall River. She is okay now, the paper says. Back home. Safe and Sound. B1, Right Column: Corruption, toll hikes. B2: The Mayor's relationship with an old, blind white woman, who may or may not be a mystic he visits regularly. B3: Whitey Bulger, who'd been caught by the FBI on a tip given from a former Miss Iceland, is said to be living a decent life behind bars." Nathan's father had admired the gangster, said he was smart enough to rig the lottery and cash his own ticket.

"B11: Weather today: cloudy and mild with a chance of rain."

Nathan rolls up the paper, sees that the spider has returned, and goes to smack it dead out of natural instinct, but stops himself just as the paper is about to land, lets it unfurl there on the bench, and watches the spider crawl back across the columns. He stands but doesn't move, like one of those statues of colonial heroes, face motionless in a godlike expression. Some boys are pushing each other, pushing one boy more than the others. They are playing Captive, a game Nathan had played when he was young and had scabs behind his ears. He, like this boy, was always picked first to play the captive. The boy is pudgy with thick, bowl-cut hair and a red-cheeked face. The captive boy has five Mississippis to find a way out or else he will starve—which might not be a bad thing—and be forced to playact his own death for the amusement of everyone watching. The only way to get out is to push through the boys hard enough that their arms break free. When he had been inside the circle, Nathan ran with all his might through the boys' arms, tripped and fell, muddied his shirt and pants. The boys had laughed at him. They had called him fat ass. He rolled over onto his back. He had cried from confusion. There was no way to win the game except to know it was a game. The boys shove the captive from one cruel troll to the next, smacking his head, pulling his arms, tearing his shirt at the collar, kicking his ankles. Grown men walk past and look back. Perhaps they remember what it was like to be inside and outside the game, surrounding or being surrounded by each other.

The boy is on the ground now, covering his head as though from nearby gunfire. He will never be free, Nathan thinks. Even when the bullets stop and the dust settles, he will live forever inside this tiny circle trying to find a way out.

Nathan continues on, past the T-shirt and souvenir vendors at their stalls, smoking, selling, rapping with one another. He takes the stairs to the subway tunnel and catches the next train. He needs to move, to be moved, to feel the rails beneath him, the car rattling back and forth. His elbows brush against the arms of strangers. He feels the tiny bumps on their skin. He hops on the Red line for Braintree. The T bumps along the rails like an old trolley car, except in the old days you could see the man at the controls: he greeted you when you got on and said, "Have a nice day, folks," when you got off. At least that's how Nathan imagines public transportation used to be. Now he can barely hear the name of the station as the train approaches the snuff-stained cement landing of each dreary outpost along the north-eastern shore.

If he hadn't fully felt the effect of the drugs over the course of the flight, and his brief walk through Boston, Nathan feels them now as his legs turn gelatinous and he finds it necessary to sit in an empty seat near the automatic door. Through cloudy vision he sees a subway car full of drooping heads. Then the heads fall off and roll from side to side with the shimmy of the car. The heads knock against each other like bingo balls in a cage. Their pupils dead and unwavering. The headless workers grip the rails above, armpits clenching a coat or tablet or sheaf of papers, knees wobbly, legs ready to fold. They are as alive as insects, all nerves and instinct. One by one, they reach their stop, pick up their heads, and fit them back on their necks. Their eyes begin to move like the faces on battery-powered dolls.

It occurs to Nathan that if it is true what Mason had said about the mind being a hotel, then his hotel is set for a riot. The people on the subway car handling their bags, punching the keypads on their phones, staring blankly at the advertisements overhead, are waiting to check in, and he, Nathan Kelly, a thirty-eight-year-old with faulty wiring, acts as a porter of sorts. Then there are those who sneak past while he isn't paying attention. How, then, is he able to spend so much time at the door of the hotel, while also inside the hotel, and here on this train? Surely he, too, has taken up a bed in other hotels. His family, past lovers, friends, and, quite possibly, the woman sitting beside him curling her hair around her finger while reading a textbook on music therapy all have offered him a room for one night, if not longer, in their own hotels.

"The human race, bored with itself, has not changed all that much," Mason had said once, while lighting a roach, inhaling, speaking distinctly through coughing spurts. "Distant worlds are invented to entertain as mystic storytellers did in tribes thousands of years ago. We are a fearful race. So we retreat to inner worlds with infinite freedoms, where one can go backward or forward in a matter of seconds, never having to be present, never having to be—"

"Hey!" Nathan, startled, looks across at a yellow-haired boy.

"You're bleeding, Mister."

"Bleeding?"

"From your nose," the boy says.

Nathan swipes his finger under his nose and examines the runny red liquid.

The boy hands him a tissue.

"I get 'em sometimes, too," he says. "Ma says to plug it in there to stop the bleeding."

"My mother used to say the same thing."

Nathan breaks off a piece of the tissue and stuffs it in his nose to stanch the bleeding.

"I look ridiculous, don't I?"

"Yup."

The boy gets off at the Quincy Adams Station.

"See ya later," he yells back, and how sweet, the way he runs, trying to keep pace with the train, Nathan struggling inside his head to become a memory or to be lost forever, because, surely, they will never see each other again unless in remembrance.

Between the shadows in the light of the station, Nathan looks at his nose, the tissue hanging, like a petal unfurling from his nostril. The muscles in his rib cage tighten under his left breast, the pain like a sharp blade twisting into his skin. He sits again and pops a few more pills, no longer discerning between colors—they all seem to have the same effect.

When the train reaches the Braintree stop, Nathan pulls the tissue from his nose. On the station platform, two men stand together holding their hands up against the wind to the flame from their matches as each lights a cigarette and exhales the gray smoke upward. Nathan bums a smoke, and the three stand together like transients with nowhere to go, connected by smoke and idle time.

"You ever see the purple martins in Virginia?" says one of the men.

"Haven't," the other man says. His arm is in a cast up to his elbow and the right side of his face looks to have been badly burned some time ago.

"You?" the man asks Nathan.

"I've never been to Virginia," Nathan says.

"What about 'em?" says the man with the burn scar.

"No reason to tell you if you haven't seen them."

"If we'd seen them, what would you tell us?"

"It's a feeling. I can't explain."

"Look at that," says the burn scar.

"A beauty," says the other man.

"Better than those goddamn purple martins, I bet."

Nathan follows their gazes toward the fully decked black BMW that has inched its way into the lot.

The horn sounds.

The three men stare, lovesick for something they will never have. The door opens and Andrew's face appears, full and puffy under his too-small Red Sox cap. He flicks his wrist for Nathan to come over.

The other two men start, and Nathan grabs the one with the burn scar by the shoulder.

"Hey, bud," says burn scar, turning and putting up his fists.

"At ease," Nathan says. "That's my ride."

TWENTY-SIX

ANDREW HASN'T SEEN HIS BROTHER SINCE THE WEDDING MORE than ten years ago now. He was big then, in the shoulders and chest, and when he hugged Nathan after the toast, Andrew could feel the hard muscles in his brother's arms packed in his suit jacket. He's surprised now by how thin Nathan looks. For as long as Andrew can remember, Nathan had always been big, his torso a solid block, his neck a column of stone, chest wide and thick. His greatest asset, and the thing Andrew had admired most, was his strength. But here's his older brother now, tall and ratty-looking, field-stripping a cigarette before stepping off the curb. The same Nathan who one afternoon, when they were boys, cutting through the Dunkin' Donuts parking lot on their way home from school—Andrew walking his bike, and Nathan carrying a plastic bag of sweaty clothes from phys ed—were stopped by a group of high schoolers, who ripped Andrew's bike away from his hands and tossed it on the pavement, where it bounced and landed in a crooked position, almost instantly taking on the look of something thrown in a trash heap, pounding their chests like apes. Nathan, calm, too calm, turned to Andrew and said, "Go home."

"But my bike."

"I'll get your bike."

The older boys spat at Andrew as he walked in the other direction. Nathan bull-rushed the biggest of the three, and he was knocked down by a blow to his side. The boys kicked him in the arms and head, pushed his face in the mud. By the time he blew the dirt from his nose and wiped the mud out of his eyes, the boys had reached the other side of the street. Andrew had watched it all through a split slat in the fence that separated the doughnut shop from the empty field in back. Nathan's face was covered in mud, eyes dark and mean. He pushed the bike across the parking lot. Andrew ran home. He didn't know why. Nathan was trying to protect him, but Andrew was scared.

He gives Nathan a brief hug, feels his brother's hip bone sharp against his side.

"You look good, Andy," Nathan says. "Can I still call you that? Andy?"

"I'd prefer you didn't."

"Okay. Right."

Nathan, sitting in the passenger seat of Andrew's BMW, cheekbones jutting out, chin sharp and distinct, shoulders slumped forward, reaches in his pocket and pulls out a crushed pack of cigarettes.

"You can't smoke in here," Andrew says. "I'm leasing this. Not that you could if I wasn't."

"Understood."

His brother puts the cigarette pack on the dash. Andrew stares at it as though it's a weapon. The seat belt signal begins to flash, drawing his attention away.

"Do you mind putting on your belt?"

"A lot of rules here."

"Does it remind you of the army?"

"Not even close."

Nathan puts on his belt.

"Ready to roll," he says.

Andrew pulls out onto the highway and drives south toward the Sagamore Bridge.

"How was the trip?"

"Uneventful."

"Spend some time in the city?"

"A little. The chaos appears to be in relative order."

"Not as bad as the Middle East, though, I'm sure."

"You'd be surprised at how easy things move when there aren't any rules."

As they hit the bridge, Andrew notices how his brother's leg twitches, and how he gnaws at the hard skin around his fingernails, bringing his hands to his face in short, blunt motions. He's on something, but Andrew can't tell what.

"You look good," he says.

"I look like shit," says Nathan. "Hey, remember counting the boats on the canal?"

"Yeah. You always cheated."

Nathan doesn't seem to hear him, or else ignores the comment, looking out the window as the dark draws down and begins to meld with the water below.

There were times when Andrew had felt a certain emptiness that came from missing his brother, his presence really, his whereabouts, not only here but elsewhere. He wanted to place him, picture him, and know for certain he was still alive.

When Nathan had set off across the country to find himself, or whatever you wanted to call it, he would e-mail Andrew and tell him how amazing it was to stand at the top of Big Sur and watch the ocean crash against the rocks, or the thin big-breasted women in bikinis on the beaches in San Diego, how in the Sonoran Desert the stars were so close and bright it felt like you were living in outer space. Deep down, Andrew knew that his brother's drifter lifestyle would not last long, and though at times, especially in the brutal cold during his freshman year in college, he envied his brother, he also pitied him. Nathan could never really sit still.

"How is Mom coping?" Nathan asks.

"She has her moments of clarity. Sometimes you can tell she's not all there, the way she looks at you, she's not really looking at you but at something else, like a memory, like you're already gone."

"To know you're dying," Nathan says, "I almost kind of envy those guys that caught a bullet or an IED, quick and painless, let the living suffer."

Andrew sighs.

"If you wouldn't mind limiting the darkness to your own thoughts," he says.

His brother raps his knuckles on the window.

"Pull over for a second, will you? I need a smoke."

"Nobody smokes anymore, you know that, right?"

"I do," Nathan says. "Or is that what you meant?"

Andrew waits in the car as his brother stands outside, the night nearly settled, the orange glare of his cigarette end glowing then dulling like a warning signal.

The day before graduating from Cornell, Andrew had been up all night with Kirsten, holding her hair back as she retched in the toilet, most likely from the fried rice and tofu she swore had pork in it at the Chinese buffet they'd gone to downtown. During the brief recess between her bouts of vomiting, he received a collect call from Nathan.

"Hey, bro."

"Where are you?"

"El Paso."

"Texas?"

"Things didn't work out in Cali. Boring story. I thought I was in love. I wasn't. I'm joining the service."

"What are you talking about?"

"They give you a free watch and benefits."

"Are you joking?"

"About the watch?"

"Be real for a second, will you?"

"Don't worry about me, Andy. I just wanted to congratulate you. I wanted to tell you how proud I am of everything you've accomplished. I wanted to tell you that I love you."

Nathan wanted to tell Andrew, or he was telling him? Either way, Andrew had never heard his brother say those words to him before.

"Thanks," he said.

"No problem. Now go get drunk or something."

Nathan had hung up, but Andrew stood there with the phone in his hand, listening to the silence on the other end; his brother gone. He could see only Nathan's strong, wide back and bulging shoulders, and the brown, leathery faces of the people walking past and around him, as though he was somehow carving a trail through this place where he did not belong. He heard his name crack through the bedroom door, and Kirsten's dry, sad cough. He felt the weight of responsibility, not as a chore, but as a remuneration, because here, in his helping, he was valued.

Andrew turns up the radio using a pad on his steering wheel. He speeds through the tiny villages, past the colonial meetinghouses and churches and general stores, and down the industrial lane, passing slow-moving trucks on the left, then free for a stretch, kicking the speed up to seventy, eighty, nearly ninety miles an hour. The hum of the engine has a calming effect. He lets up on the gas and eases into a full stop at a traffic light, waiting with his head resting on his straightened forefinger, thumb shortened and pointed upward. The dense, muddy smell of the salt marshes sweeps through the open windows as they pass over the wooden bridge toward the beach. He slows before the raked land in front of the dilapidated Tidewater Hotel. When they were boys they would raise each other up to look into the bathroom windows at women showering behind plastic curtains. Empty cartons of food and soda bottles and beer cans are strewn across the property. The building looks as though it's about to fall inward at the slightest touch or breath of wind.

"Let's get a drink," Andrew says. "Mom's probably in bed by now."

The sky finally clears; the pale glow of the moon is rounded by rings of light. All the world's fantastic possibilities lie before them.

Kerrigan's on the harbor, the bar in a shed with its weathered slats of wood, stripped paint, ropes tied around the cleats on the dock holding whalers in place. The grounded tugboat has been turned into a seating room where children explore the console while their parents wait for their overpriced fried clams, and though there are signs commanding patrons not to feed the seagulls, they had always and would always toss the undercooked fries from the bottom of the pile into the water and watch the birds dive after them.

Andrew orders a shot of Jameson and a Bud Light. Nathan asks for water with a slice of lemon.

"You're making me drink alone?" Andrew says.

"I'm on certain medications."

"Probably for the best then."

Not that the medications are the problem. Drinking whiskey in the same glug-glug way they used to drink apple juice at the dinner table when they were kids had made both Kelly boys nasty as sin. He can't help but remember when he was sixteen, and Nathan was just about to graduate from high school. Andrew had been half-asleep, listening to his brother bang around downstairs on his way back from a Friday night party in the Pines, where everyone in Wequaquet used to go after the football game, and he broke through Andrew's bedroom door, lifted the lid of his hamper, and urinated on his dirty clothes. The time Nathan had to drive out to Truro and pay a fifty-dollar fine to have Andrew let out of protective custody wearing one shoe. Together they had once spent an entire afternoon drinking from a bottle of Southern Comfort, then pulled up a half-dozen lobster traps, and brought them back to the house and poured the lobsters out into a pair of beach coolers in the garage, and passed out on the back lawn laughing as they traded turns screwing up dirty tongue twisters. Later that night, their mother refused to let them back in the house, called the police. One of the cops punched Nathan in the gut and the other whacked Andrew in the knees with a switch. They took the lobsters and left the brothers out front—Nathan with his face in his own vomit, Andrew curled up in the mud, as if to embarrass their mother even more, as if to say, with swift violence, "Can't even take care of your own kids."

Andrew clicks Nathan's plastic cup of water and downs the shot, then cringes and chugs back the beer. A golf tournament is on television. A player in pink and gray plaid pants lines up a putt like a rifleman with one eye closed. He addresses the ball, then steps away again, kneels, stands, sets his feet, and strokes the ball toward the cup where it hits the edge and spins in then out. The player snaps the putter over his thigh and carries the two pieces in either hand like torches toward the hole, lowers to a knee, and, with the piece that held the putter head, taps the ball into the cup. It strikes him as kind of sad, this skinny little guy whose entire world revolves around a ball and a cup.

"What's the saddest thing you've ever seen?" he asks Nathan.

"The saddest thing?"

"Yeah, like something that just made you feel empty inside, like there was no hope for anyone?"

"Probably this guy got his dick blown off."

"That's too obvious."

"I thought it was sad."

"Wasn't everything over there sad?"

"Pretty much."

"Out with it then."

"Okay. You want to know the saddest thing I've ever seen? And I'm not bullshitting, either. The saddest thing I've ever seen was out in California, before the army. This childish-looking man alone on a bench along the boardwalk, dressed in a yellow collared shirt that barely fit over his belly and made it look like he had women's breasts, eating a chocolate-dipped ice-cream cone."

"Why is that sad?"

"Because the guy had given up and it made me think, still makes me think, about at what point do you finally give up?"

Andrew feels a surge of electricity hit his side. He is no different than that man, just in better shape.

He watches as a pair of golfers hit their approach shots onto the green. Then he finishes his drink and puts a twenty on the bar.

"Time to go," he says and slides his keys across the bar. "You drive."

TWENTY-SEVEN

"Tomorrow you will be a new person," his mother used to tell Nathan. Sometimes the thought was so frightening, he couldn't get back to sleep. She'd follow what she had said with a kiss on his nose, or, when he began to cry, holding him tight against her chest. She meant what was past would stay past. But that is false. His remembering her lie makes it so.

The following day, the first he has been home in ten years, Nathan wakes early and passes his mother's door, ignoring her coughing fit, carrying his boots out onto the front step, where he ties the laces, stretches, and then takes his brother's car out for a ride. He has an idea to keep busy around the house with repairs. He returns an hour later with three giant bags from MegaWorld.

"I bought steaks and deodorant and house paint and coffee and an electric screwdriver," Nathan says.

"I'm guessing you forgot to pick up a crossbow while you were at it," Andrew says.

"What are you, un-American?"

"Give me a break."

"Here, I got you something."

Nathan reaches inside one of the bags and pulls out a stuffed monkey. The monkey is holding a half-unpeeled banana by its groin and makes spastic jerking motions when Nathan pushes the button on its rear.

"What am I going to do with this?"

"That's the point."

Nathan replaces all the bulbs in the house. He brings the old ones out back and stomps on them with his boots.

That afternoon, while Andrew is out, their mother's coughing gets so bad, Nathan brings her a cup of ice chips. What can he say to comfort her? Since Iraq, he has simplified death. You are here, then you are not. When he was a boy, had he felt nurtured? Loved? He can't say, can't remember. His mother spends most of her time in bed. But she isn't interested in having the television on or reading a book; she simply wants to lie there. He fluffs up her pillows and tucks in the sheets. She kicks the sheets out.

"Don't put me in a coffin just yet, honey," she says.

He sits on the edge of her bed, their hips touching, and tries to smile, but looking at her wide, yellow eyes and crooked wig and white, cracked lips, it is too sad.

If he had escaped death during his years in the army, it was a miracle. Since he returned home, he has simply been lucky. The day he'd gone riding ATVs out in the desert and rolled over a half-dozen times and walked away with only a few scratches on his arms and knees; the pilot light in his neighbor's house that blew him back on the ground and singed his eyebrows; the stick-up kids at Cherry's Donuts who put a gun to his head while he sat in a booth on a sleepless night, staring out the window at the glare of the sign on the sidewalk as though the sun had fallen flat, and when the one kid pulled the trigger a stream of water shot into his partially opened eye, and they laughed and ran out of the shop with forty bucks and change.

At dawn, the next day, he drives to the beach, to the far end where he used to go when he was younger. The tree where the older boys had thrown his clothes had been torn down and only the stump remains, hollowed out and rotted. Maybe the shoreline had moved an inch or two up the beach. He lets his hand pass along the sea grass, plucks a strand from the dune, and holds it between his teeth as he chases after the seagulls gathered around an extinguished fire pit. Then he lies on the sand; the thrashing of the waves and wind soothes him to sleep.

He wakes to a low, rhythmic chanting. He can't make out the words. But there, at the shore, a dozen or so women, all of them very old, their hair tucked under swimming caps and their wobbly thighs and backsides stuffed into one-piece bathing suits. One of them shouts, "All right, ladies!" and they flop into the water. Though, once in the water, they are graceful, swimming in unison like a flight of birds out to where the orange curve of the sun colors the water a soldering white.

The women brave the breakers and they shout and sing out and dive down to the sea bottom, their toes wiggling up above, then rise and laugh and yell. Great swaths of pink and gold hang above them in the sky.

One of the women stands up, wet and jittering, removes her cap, and shakes the droplets of water from her hair and body like a shaggy dog. She sees Nathan, already shivering in the cold morning air.

"Are you planning on swimming?" she asks.

"I hadn't considered it, but it looks like you're all having a lot of fun."

"We certainly are. We're called the Ice Breakers. My name's

Marion. The rule is you have to be over sixty years old to join. I can tell you're a long ways from that."

"I can still swim with you even if I can't join the group, right?"

"Of course," she says. "But, it's cold as hell in there."

Nathan dives in with only his boxers on. He holds his breath and goes underwater, pushing up with his palms to go deeper. The water is dark in front of him. Here, in this soundless, infinite chamber, he is free.

TWENTY-EIGHT

On the first of October, Kirsten calls with genuine concern over Andrew's well-being.

"My well-being is just fine," Andrew says.

"And your mother?"

"Hanging in there, I guess."

"Well . . ."

Andrew feels that hated word, and the pause that follows, like a thumb pressing hard between his eyes. The things he misses, the things he doesn't, maybe it will be these casual conversations when they eventually, finally, taper off.

"I just thought," Kirsten says, "since it's getting colder, you would want to pick up some of your things."

But that is real pain, real loss, that she doesn't want to see him, wants more for the pieces left behind of him to finally be removed.

"You know, your suede jacket and boots, and scarf."

The one she had given him on his birthday two years ago, which he has never worn.

"Andrew?"

"Yes. Okay. I can be there this afternoon."

Andrew's house feels to him like an embassy in a foreign land, vaguely familiar, but not ever again as home. Kirsten dutifully greets him at the door. Her lawyer, standing next to her, greets him as well, along with a squat, ball-shaped woman with a large folder of papers under her arm.

"What is this? An intervention?" Andrew says.

"Your wife—or ex-wife—is it ex, yet?"

"No," Kirsten says and smiles. "Soon, though."

"Either way, she has begun—had begun, is my understanding—while the two of you were cohabitating—to look into adoption—

"Which is a long, and somewhat traumatic, though pleasurable, experience, a mix, really, if everyone involved keeps each other informed, and you, Andrew, correct? Andrew Kelly? Yes, you, being the breadwinner, such an antiquated term, but, the one to support said child, really, along with said mother of child, Kirsten, beautiful Kirsten, what a heart, we had to inform you that we have found a child, a baby, actually, without a healthy living situation, actually, terribly unhealthy, she was found in garbage, not a can or dumpster, mind you, but a big pile of garbage, fish heads, soggy dumplings, overcooked noodles, oh, my, I can't even imagine, they hosed her down at the orphanage, ran many tests, she is of perfect health, and sweet as honey, here."

The lady hands Andrew a photograph of the Chinese baby. The Chinese baby has a gruesome harelip, and gentle, peaceful, black eyes. He looks past the photograph, then it hits him—life has moved on. Sure, they had talked about adoption well before the breakup, finding surrogates, or even joining Testing All Parents Inc., an idea Andrew sort of loved, because you got to be a parent for a couple of hours at a neutral location and then you said good-bye until next week. Even if the kids were in a bad mood or didn't feel like eating their hamburgers, he could get them to laugh by making farting noises like his grandfather used to when he was a kid, and once he was back home, he felt like he'd done something meaningful. Kirsten had noted all of this in her diary, and had the diary authenticated by a notary, and the diary was there, on the kitchen table where he used to eat his Honey Nut Cheerios every morning.

"And to what capacity are you, Mr. Kelly, responsible for paying child support for this—for—is there a name?" the lawyer asks.

"Fiona," Kirsten says with pride.

"How wonderful," the ball-shaped woman says.

"Quite Irish, indeed," the lawyer says. "Capacity or no capacity, we have a full record of your past and future earnings, stock holdings, capital investments, and the like . . ."

Kirsten was asking for three thousand a month, the lawyer explains, plus ten thousand toward the initial processing fees, which includes standard rates for government-handled paperwork, round-trip airfare, two weeks of accommodations in Malibu for the mother and daughter to get accustomed to each other, food, medicine, a Mandarin language instructor, a Mandarin dialect coach, and the monthly transport of a Chinese mother's milk for up to one year. She will also require a nanny, for, as a single mother, she must not feel overwhelmed in order to satisfy the criteria by which children are placed.

The seriousness with which Kirsten, her lawyer, and the ball-shaped woman from the adoption agency speak about each clause and addendum, raising objections to strike from the contract any needed health insurance past the child's eighteenth birthday, as though doing Andrew a favor, agreeing with each other on specifics like organic baby food and an addition to the house called the Learning Wing, lit by natural light through painted glass windows and full of brain games and talking stuffed animals, makes it clear he cannot deny the ultimate request.

For a moment, Andrew wishes he had brought his lawyer, but perhaps the fight is not worth it, perhaps that is still part of his old self and to give in to Kirsten's demands, no matter how ridiculous, is the price he must pay for letting go.

When the whirlwind of talk has died down, Andrew finds himself with a pen in his hand. After he finishes signing the paperwork, Kirsten hugs him and puts her cheek to his shoulder.

"Would you like some cookies?" she asks. "They're not very good."

He takes a bite of one of the three cookies she has handed him in a folded napkin, tastes the baking powder and vanilla that hadn't been mixed enough, holds the bite in his cheek as he walks to his car, then spits it out into the street. The remaining cookies he eats as a penance during the car ride home. He sighs as he hits traffic coming through Plymouth. He had planned to meet his father at the construction site for the Tidewater but now feels deflated and tired, looking forward to a deep sleep. He powers down the windows and within seconds feels a sharp nick to his ear. He cups his ear and pulls over into the breakdown lane. He looks in the rearview mirror. His earlobe has swelled to the size of a potato, the hornet still happily buzzing about the dash. Andrew picks up the folder of documents his wife's lawyer had given him and smashes the hornet dead.

He drives to the Urgent Care in Harwich. The waiting room is full of coughing children with snot dripping from their noses, and old, aching women. The receptionist has him write his name and the time and his affliction.

"Isn't it obvious?" Andrew says.

"I can't rightly assume anything," the receptionist says.

He sits down next to a boy with a mark on his arm taking on

the form of a growing tree, from tiny whiplashes that had to have come from a massive jellyfish. The boy's eyes are red from crying.

"I'd rather have that than this," Andrew says, pointing to his deformed ear.

The boy smiles and sniffles, and wipes his nose with the back of his hand.

What Andrew sees in the boy's eyes, though, is something he knows well, the freshly formed realization that nowhere is safe.

Nearly an hour later, Andrew has his ear drained and the lobe patched over. He can't find his insurance card, and has to call Kirsten and tell her what has happened.

"How do you always end up in such ridiculous predicaments?" she says.

The receptionist hands him a bill for a hundred and forty dollars.

When he finally returns home, it is past midnight and the house is dark. He retreats to his room. He wants his mother's help. He wants her to rub the ear in magic ointment and blow on it to cool the burning. What he really wants is to again be the boy who knows this kind of magic, whose scrapes and scratches heal easily. He tries to concentrate on one of the books his father had recommended he pick up, which he had laughed off then but found himself, not more than a week later, laying down sixteen bucks for: Dr. Stew Buckwald's *Upload My Human Side*. But he cannot concentrate. His ear is pounding so badly. He needs a drink.

He grabs a beer and an ice pack, then goes to the living room and turns on the ancient Zenith, the same one he used to sit in front of every Saturday morning, playing video games. His mother only gets basic cable and at this hour the only thing on are infomercials. He asks himself what kinds of people buy cheap knives and self-help audiobooks and vibrating belly bands. People like you, he thinks. People who get stung in the ear by hornets. He's the one watching, the one compelled to pick up the phone, to get a pizza cutter for free if he calls now. Now! He dials the number on the screen, somewhat surprised at how gullible, how easily convinced he is by the ad for the Ninja Knife Set. He holds the phone to his good ear, listens as it rings a half-dozen times before a woman with an Eastern European accent finally picks up.

"Good morning," she says. "Your interest in Ninja Knife?"

"Yes," Andrew whispers.

"I need credit card," the woman says.

"What's your name?" Andrew asks suddenly, not knowing why he wants this information.

"My name?"

"Yes."

"Anna," the woman says. "This important to you?"

"Not really. I was just curious."

"Your name I do need for purchase."

"Andrew Kelly."

Anna laughs.

"What are you laughing about?"

"Joke from someone here."

"What's the joke?"

"Nothing, Mr. Kiley."

"Please," Andrew pleads, as though this joke is something of great importance, that without it, he cannot stand the day ahead.

"Ovi, he work with me, he say before you call, 'What is difference between American woman and Romanian woman?' I say I don't know. Then you call and we talk about Ninja Knife and then he take call from someone else wanting Ninja Knife, but now he finish and say to me, 'American woman thin to look beautiful, Romanian woman thin because there is no food.' I think it maybe sound better in my language."

"It's true, though," Andrew says.

"You think so?"

"Sure."

"I tell him that. Then it is not really joke. We have plenty of food, actually, but no money to pay for it. Maybe there is different joke we can make about that. So . . . you want Ninja Knife, yes?"

"Does it come with the pizza cutter?"

"Is that what they told you?"

"No one told me anything. I saw it on television."

"Then they tell you on television. I type information about pizza cutter and you get pizza cutter. Now I need credit card number, Mr. Kiley, sir."

"Kelly. Hold on."

Andrew grabs his wallet and takes out the credit card. Stuck to the credit card is his insurance card. Between them is a gluey piece of gum. He pulls the cards apart and reads the numbers off his credit card to Anna, then waits as she puts them into the computer.

"How long until I get the knives?" he asks.

"Four to seven days of business," Anna says. "Is this okay? You won't be cutting too much before then, I hope."

"Yes, fine."

"I think maybe you are lonely and not wanting Ninja Knife as much as wanting to talk to someone."

"I think you're right."

"I know. I can tell. I work here three years and most people don't want knife, they want talk, and so I talk to them, but because I talk to them I miss sale of knife for other people who call and maybe really want knife and my boss get mad, but he think my eyes are nice eyes. He say, 'I cannot let go of your eyes,' as if he can hold them. So I'm lucky to have job."

"I miss being with someone."

"I think I understand what you look for. But I cannot talk sexual on phone. Our conversation is taped and my boss he will know I talk sexual and maybe my eyes won't save me."

"I wasn't looking for sex talk."

"I think you are not so different from many people. You don't want to be alone."

"So what do I do?"

"You buy Ninja Knife, receive free pizza cutter, begin cooking, take mind off loneliness."

"I see," Andrew says, disappointed that they have come back around to the knives.

He gives her his address and repeats his full name, which she repeats back to him, and on hearing his name, he believes it possibly to be someone else. He had wanted to be on the radio when he was young. He taped his own show and played the tape for his mother, who pretended to laugh at the funny parts, which Andrew cued her to by opening his eyes wide and pointing and saying, "Listen."

"Okay," Anna says. "I have your information and you purchase Ninja Knife Set and receive free pizza cutter. This will arrive in four to seven days of business. Do you have any question for me?"

"Are the knives as sharp as they say on TV?"

Andrew hears her whisper something away from the phone. Then he hears a man laughing in the background, most likely the Ovi guy.

"Now we have new joke," Anna tells Andrew. "Of course they're sharp! They're the sharpest knives in the world."

He waits.

"Are you okay, Mr. Kiley."

"Yes," Andrew says. "I'm okay."

"Please wait patient for your knives," Anna says. "Thank you and good night."

"Good night, Anna."

Andrew hangs up the phone and shuts off the television. He sips his beer, then puts the still cold bottle to his earlobe. In the dim lamplight, he grips his other hand tightly around the handle of an invisible knife.

TWENTY-NINE

EVEN IN THIS NOVEMBER CHILL, WET SUITS ARE NOT ALLOWED in the Wequaquet Polar League for Women over Sixty. And even though Nathan is not technically a member, and will never be a woman over sixty, he has been swimming with the group every Sunday for the past month and a half. His being the only man, and a patriot, makes him a welcome rarity, and often the women invite him to join the group at the Dunkin' Donuts up the road when they have finished their swim, an invitation he has accepted each time—sitting in one of the chairs circled around a square table, chatting about how Wequaquet used to be—except today, because today, when he dives into the ocean and swims out to the first break and treads water along with the group, listening as they exhale and chirp and shout, cracking open the silence of the sea at morning, he lets go, lets himself drop beneath the water's surface, then farther, because the cold is not enough to energize him, nor is the thought of drowning; it is the brief passage from consciousness to unconsciousness, that narrow tunnel he is trying to get to, where he knows he is most himself, most alive. He comes up for air. He hears the women call to him. Their swims are brief, and they don't waste time getting back to their cars. He waves them off, then goes underwater again. Not until the fifth time does he feel his head start to lighten and his heart beat steady. He readies for one more dive below, knowing it is possible he might not come back, but the same, he thinks, is possible if he does not try to satisfy this need.

The space there is absolute emptiness, or fullness, a feeling of being present, of time infinite, of sand between his toes, the crack of gunfire in the desert at night, a paper cut, a head butt, the ringing of a bell above a storeroom door, coming, going, flying, sinking, dying, driving, and touching Erin Mark's soft inverted nipple in the sixth grade on the moss-dressed rocks beneath the Wequaquet River Bridge.

When he finally rises—the memory of his father pressing his hands together above his head and calling out, "Shark," to him and his brother—Nathan is revived, though disenchanted, like an addict, both relieved and panicked, he has made it through to another day.

Swimming to the shallow water, he stands and walks along the shore, his fingers crossed behind his head, elbows spread wide. Turning slightly, he sees a figure up ahead, a beach chair tipped over, her arm raised, then gone in the water, fighting against the waves.

Not more than twenty yards away he stumbles forward, exhausted but pierced with urgency and, like a boy who stumbles often and never tires, runs faster, with awkward movements, the sand shifting beneath his feet. He dives into the ocean and grabs the woman's hand and pulls himself into her, lowering and leveraging himself against the thickened sand beneath him, and swims her to shore.

He drags her on his shoulder, falls, and rolls her onto her side, so that she collects sand in her hair and on her skin. He is exhausted. But, with his adrenaline pumping, he turns over and pushes away the strands of hair stuck to her face, puts his lips to her mouth and pumps her chest, then turns her onto her side so she can spit up.

He is breathless and tired, and rolls over onto his back, feeling the blood beat throughout his body.

Then he hears her, like some faint sound from a dream about to be gone forever.

"Nathan?" his mother says. "Nathan."

THIRTY

Chapter 2

"The past is a bomb; idleness its ignition."

There are three kinds of fortune: good fortune, bad fortune, misfortune. I have experienced them all, and survived. I am a survivor of the unappreciated diseases that make for good gossip. I have had money. I have had no money. I have been cheated out of money. I have lived in a mansion, a studio apartment, a stinking motel room. But no longer will I go against my purpose in life, to live in what I like to call, the sphere of the every-moment.

Sure, it was horseshit, but, maybe, given his father's recent congenial attitude, the calm manner in which he spoke, the brief embrace each time Andrew stopped by—and he was stopping by more often than he ever thought he would—maybe there was something to this new age, present-living crap. Maybe the sphere of the every-moment, or whatever, is just what he needs right now.

His breath quickened and his lungs contracted and tightened. He slowed and walked the shore with his fingers clasped behind his head. There were no other runners on the beach. It was late and the bugs were out, nipping at his shoulders. The water crested over his shoes. He took them off and unrolled his socks and stuffed them in his shoes and held them in the crooks of his fingers. In the distance he could see the Tidewater Hotel, the frame already set, the rooms defined. He saw them occupied with lovers old and young, families, and loners on reprieve. The sign still stood like some kind of legend to his childhood. Maybe it should stay. Keep one thing from the past. Because there is history here, tradition; he is preserving an institution of proper etiquette, impeccable service, and savoir faire. He is challenging his own reckless self, the boy who cut up the sod on the putting green outside the hotel's casino entrance; who, when he was fifteen, watched as his father, dressed in a fine stitched sweater and pleated, plaid pants, accepted an award from the local charter for businessman of the year. He listened to the applause echo in the high-ceilinged dining room with the green felt spread and nailed to the floorboards. He took in, from the children's table off to the side of the room, the waiters standing back behind the table with a cloth over their arm, eyes scanning the room for whichever table needed their attention.

A year later, Robert had brought Sharon Price here on their first date. Red had told him to tell the waiter to put the meal on his account and gave Robert a ten-dollar bill to leave as a tip. When they were seated, the waiter placed napkins across their laps. Another waiter came and filled their glasses with sparkling water, and yet another placed a basket with warm Parker House rolls and whipped butter in the middle of the table. Robert was confused which waiter to tip. He and Sharon shared a house salad with raspberry vinaigrette dressing, and both ordered the same meal of clams and linguine in a red sauce. The first waiter described the desserts, and Robert let Sharon choose, hoping she wouldn't pick the crème brûlée, which tasted to him like nothing more than expensive pudding. She chose the crème brûlée. For the rest of his life, the women he went for always chose the crème brûlée. At the end of the meal, the manager asked to speak with Robert privately. He walked ahead of Robert toward the men's room, and while a man was groaning loudly from inside the stall, the manager explained that Red's account hadn't been paid in six months.

"Quite a high number," the manager had said.

Robert, not yet bold enough to challenge authority, asked if he could pay his bill by working at the restaurant.

"When can you start?" the manager asked.

"Whenever you want."

"Tonight, then."

"Tonight?"

"Or we can ask the lady if she'd like to take care of the bill."

Later that night, after he dropped Sharon Price off at home, he drove back to the Tidewater and washed the pots and pans and dishware, mopped the kitchen floors, wiped down the tables, pushed the vacuum cleaner over the green felt flooring, and took a dozen black bags of garbage out to the dumpster in back.

The money had come through. But there were stipulations. First, Andrew had to handle the account along with Dennison. His father would take a small finder's fee and be paid a minimum salary, just enough to prove to the government that he was working. The plan, simple; the execution not so much. The stigma attached to the Kelly name has made it nearly impossible to bring a reputable contractor on board. Not so different from someone bouncing a bad check in a convenience store and having the check and photo taped to the register, the framers and electricians and plumbers have since lodged the Kelly name deep in their minds, equated the sounds of the letters together with distrust, dishonor, and general hatred. Even Andrew, who was known in town to be both dependable and accountable, was forced to pay up front for the lumber needed to build the additional wing.

Dennison has been unhappy with the stagnation, deeply invested in something he doesn't know much about. But Andrew's father has staved him off awhile longer. And Andrew isn't planning on going anywhere soon.

Even though it's more costly, Andrew has hired private contractors from out of state—Pennsylvania and Connecticut and New York. Travel expenses and housing off-Cape cost more than the construction itself. Dennison has brought in another partner, an off-putting man with a face like a waffle iron, who hails from Sunny Isles Beach, Florida, and is as silent as a silent partner can be.

In these last days, before the winter cold sets in, the old Tidewater Inn is torn down, the land bulldozed over and raked back. Then the foundation is set, and though neighbors complain about the constant banging during the day and the hum of the lights and generators at night, the same as they had complained about the wind turbines out in the bay, the hotel is back on pace to open next summer. The town council cannot complain about how grand it will look, the business it will bring to town, state congressmen, local retired athletes, judges, CEOs, CFOs, COOs. The old Cape feel emitting from the stained clapboards to the copper-lined rooftops and the circular entrance, where Andrew's father has added a towering flagpole to the plans, another hefty piece, for which Andrew cut a check, handed it to him before he even finished explaining why it was so important to represent the country in such a manner.

The site is grand, glorious, and tangible. Andrew and his father stand on the stiffening earth, the cold early December air blowing off the ocean, dismissing the steady beep from the monitoring device around Robert's ankle.

"Not to be overly dramatic, son," his father says, in an overly dramatic fashion, "but this hotel will resurrect our name. The Kellys will live in the halls and rooms and elevators, for a hundred years or more, or until the ocean finally swallows us whole."

Later that afternoon, as Andrew and his father approach the cottage, Andrew sees Rudolph sitting obediently, as though awaiting his father's return. His father crouches down to greet the dog, while Andrew goes inside to use the bathroom, passing by pages of the manuscript flung about the floor, drawers opened, cushions upturned. Perhaps his father was letting off some steam. Perhaps the present isn't as peaceful as his prophecy asserts.

Pissing, thinking about "Securing Thy Self," Andrew hears, from outside the window, a flurry of steps along the pebbled drive, and his father shout, and then quiet.

He walks tentatively down the hall, lowering, looking out the window, where Millie, the red-haired girl with the dog, Rudolph, is holding in her hand the ship's-wheel lamp his father had made in prison. He looks to his right and sees his father struggling to get to his feet, slipping on the rocks and falling onto his side. Rudolph licks the wound in his head.

"Rudolph!" Millie shouts. "Stop that, Rudolph."

Andrew, heart pounding, blood rushing up to his face, full of fear and raw instinct, closes in on the front door, in order to hear what Millie is saying.

"Jesus. This is really pathetic, you know. All right. You can get up. I didn't even hit you that hard, for crying out loud."

"You think a man living like this has something to steal?" his father says, on his knees now.

"Crooks are usually unassuming," Millie says. "But I didn't come for money, necessarily. I just figured what the hell, might as well get all I can, which, apparently, comes to approximately three tanks of gas, enough to get me back to Spartanburg."

Robert stands and backs toward the deck chairs on his patio, sits down, positioned now to see Andrew in the window if he were to raise the blinds.

"You probably never heard of it."

"What's that?"

"Spartanburg. South Carolina."

"Oh. Sure. The Spartans."

"You probably never even looked at where the checks were coming from. Just cashed them and stuffed your pockets, let the faceless idiots suffer."

"I see. Listen—"

"I have to say, that little self-help book of yours is just about worth all the aggravation it took to find you. I'm both slightly impressed and seriously disgusted. I mean, really, I've never laughed and cried so hard in my life."

"A person can change. I've had a lot of time to think about what I've done."

"You always hear people say that when they get out of prison. But then, you read about the recidivism rate. Something like seventy percent, I think, end up back in prison."

"But what about the other thirty percent? That's where I am. Somewhere in the thirtieth percentile."

"I might take your sincerity to heart if you were honest with me. Perhaps I should consider not hitting you in the head again." Millie makes like she's going to place the lamp down, but when Robert instinctively thrusts his hand out to grab it, she quickly raises her hand, steadies the lamp like a ballplayer holding a bat, and whacks him in the head again.

Robert falls off the chair, groaning.

"Damn it," Millie says. "Now I got to tie you up. I really didn't want to exert myself like this."

Millie pulls Robert's hands together and tightens them with vinyl straps, then fixes another set of straps around those ones and ties them to the deck chair. She does the same to his ankles, pulls the strap tight above the bulky home monitoring device.

"At least you know you're being monitored," she says.

"I have some things in the works here," Robert says, his head ringing, voice sounding like an echo in his skull. "Things you can be part of if you have any sense."

"Any sense? Wow. My father had sense. He had sense enough to give you his life savings for a mud pit in Tennessee. Now he lives in my kid's room. He was a dedicated and loyal man. Luckily my mother died before she could ever see how sad it got for him. He used to be a fighter pilot. He has a bunch of medals. My kid pinned them to his backpack. When I get home from lunch I hear my father crying in the bathroom. He sits on the toilet and cries. He worked at a power plant for forty years. He can't even get me a discount on my electric bill."

"I don't know what to say. I'm sorry. I mean, that was a long time ago, and I wasn't the only one involved. Honestly, my intentions were good."

"Fuck your intentions," Millie says, and levels the lamp, which is now missing the ship's wheel.

"Okay, wait," Robert says. He bows slightly. "My son. He's well-off. He can help you and your father, and your kid. What's your rent in Spartanville? He'll pay your rent for a year."

Millie turns. And, for a moment, Andrew believes they are looking right at each other, as though to affirm the next logical step. Then, he sees she is crying. She can't be more than thirty years old, face round and pink. Her eyes are crossed. She has braces. Her breasts are flabby and her belly hangs over her waistband and pulls up her shirt at the sides. There's a tattoo on her arm of Winnie-the-Pooh, which she must have gotten when she was much younger, because now it looks like a spread of honey with a daub of blood in the middle.

He feels sad for her.

"You know this is bigger than money," Millie says, wiping her tears with the back of her hand, then turning away from Andrew toward his father.

"I know," his father says.

"This has to do with the soul, with good and evil, heaven and hell. Are you starting to get the picture?"

"I'm sorry. I truly am."

Perhaps here, in this moment, Andrew thinks, his father has finally accepted blame. Though Andrew is unable to tell from the bare expression on Millie's face whether or not his apology is enough. Either way, something has to be done. Andrew fires out the door and sacks Millie, pulling her to the ground. Turning, he sees his father has flipped the chair over so that he is on his side. Andrew hooks Millie's leg, and together they perform some lunatic dance before crashing to the deck boards.

When the police and paramedics arrive, they find Millie inside the cottage, hands and feet bound in rope tied tight with a bowline knot. Andrew is icing his hand in a bowl. His father is sitting on the couch, pressing a bag of frozen peas to his head. He can't thank Andrew enough, and so he doesn't thank him at all.

Later, in the emergency room, Andrew, his hand wrapped and pulsing like another heart, wonders how someone could hate his father so much, she's willing to go to prison. She barely knew him.

The nurse wheels his father out.

"Two Kellys in one week," she says, and snorts and covers her nose.

His father's eyes are lowered, dulled by morphine. His forehead is wrapped in gauze, one hand pressed to the square patch covering the stitches, his other hand holding the tall, beak-nosed nurse's forearm. Andrew helps him from the chair and out into the front passenger seat of his car.

Andrew will want to tell his brother. After all, Nathan is a true hero.

He drives back to the cottage slowly, careful to maneuver around bumps in the road. When his father begins to snore, Andrew drives faster, glancing over to see if his father might wake. At a stop light, he reaches over and presses his thumb into the gauze. His father shoots forward. Blood begins to spread to the ends of the padding. He looks at Andrew, who passes through the intersection, slightly gratified.

PART III

THE OUTER CAPE

THIRTY-ONE

GLIMMERING SPECKS OF DUST LIFT FROM THE COUCHES AND tabletops and cupboards as they walk past into the kitchen. The boys sit with their coffee at the kitchen table as their father sets the cribbage board down and deals the cards along the smooth wood surface of the table. All that can be heard inside the house is the hum of appliances and the faint voice of a sportscaster on TV. The three of them bend over as if in some silent prayer, examining their cards and the small cribbage board on the table.

"You spend so much time dodging death," their father finally says, setting down a spread of cards and moving his peg up the board. "Then the smallest thing, you know, the thing you can't see, it creeps right up inside you and steals you away."

Their mother starts coughing in the other room. They have left the door open through the night, taking posts in the living room, newly appointed watchmen.

They take their eyes from the board and listen until her coughing ceases, as though punishing themselves with the song of the sick.

Everything is in memory now. The red-painted candy store, the fishing pier, the dry spot beneath the Wequaquet Bridge where Robert had brought the boys to talk about manly things, the beach that had become smaller as the water drew farther inland, the way Irene shaded her eyes from the sun and looked out at the ocean her husband and children watched and wondered what went on inside her head.

"Let's call it a night," Nathan says, and folds up his hand, placing the cards on the table.

"I think that's a good idea," Andrew says.

Robert gathers the cards and slides them into the wooden pocket of the cribbage board.

Robert spends the night sleeping on the couch. His legs stretch over the armrest. He cracks his toes with immature pleasure until a boom of thunder shakes the house and the rain cascades hard and fast from the sky. Lightning splits the sky like a gleaming ax blade, thunder booms, the continuous rain. That's it, Robert thinks, loneliness. That's what keeps you in the past for so long, thinking of all the people you had known and come across and those that were locked away, the key waiting in a scent or touch.

He sits up and rubs his eyes, then inches slowly toward Irene's room. He watches her sleep, arms crossed above her head as though falling. Then, her eyes slowly open, adjusting to the pale light in the hallway coming through the open door.

"Don't hover," she says.

Robert sits on the edge of the bed and takes hold of her hand.

They love each other in the way that two people who have shared a past will always love each other. But he knows he has failed her, failed the children.

"Did you stay the night?" she asks.

"I slept on the couch. I thought my days of sleeping on couches were over, but I guess not."

"My legs are all swollen. It feels like I've walked to Ptown and back. Do you remember when I was pregnant, when I used to have to soak my feet for hours?"

"And you bent forward and sang to your stomach."

"I did. He could hear me. Not the words, but me. Waves of me."

Robert smiles.

"You weren't a very good singer."

"I'm still not."

Irene rubs her eyes and attempts to pull up the blanket around her legs.

"Let me help," Robert says, and rolls the blanket back above her ankles.

Her feet aren't swollen, but they are a bluish color.

"What are you doing?" she asks.

He presses the bottom of her foot with his thumbs, running his nail up the wrinkled crevice, moving toward her toes, covering them with his hands, massaging the sides of her foot. Then he moves to the other foot, developing a rhythm as though picking up an instrument he once knew how to play, remembering how to play, simple and flawed, but his own hand, his own style, recognizable to Irene.

No one else can see how beautiful he is at failing.

"We had some good times, didn't we?" she says.

"We did."

"And we loved each other, and the boys, and we were happy."

"We were."

"That's good," she says and closes her eyes.

Once she is back asleep, Robert bends down and smells her hair, the sweet scent of an almond split open. He whispers he loves her. Then he quietly leaves the room.

Irene feels the sheet lower and spread out over her, falling like a shadow, landing softly, covered by a blanket and her head pushed up, then let to drop onto the soft pillows.

Nathaniel and Andrew stand beside the bed. She grips their hands. They are a secret of images and patterns, lost, then found, then lost again; her creations, as she had made them, that very instant they came from her was the last stroke. Then they were changed and rearranged, damaged, challenged, called by different names, hung in other rooms, reemerged as new works, no longer hers, but of those people they had encountered once they left home.

"Nathan, you were so big," she says. "You were so beautiful."

"As a baby?" he asks.

She tries to speak.

"She needs to be resting," Andrew says.

Nathan kisses her on the lips. She strokes the hair on the sides of his head.

Then they are gone.

Irene struggles to free herself from the tucked sheet, finally kicking the end free and letting the cool air flow over her legs. She relaxes, listens to her heart pump hard, as if she has just finished a race, and is standing on the track with her hands clasped behind her head. She feels the flow of adrenaline, the sweat that pours from her body, the shakiness in her knees.

Uneasy on her feet, by the window, looking out at the boys as they stand on the lawn: Nathaniel smoking, Andrew checking his phone, both of them in unguarded postures. Then, in an instant, they are gone. Milk-white smoke still drifts upward from the finished cigarette Nathan has carelessly flicked away.

Beyond exhaustion, she lies in bed with her eyes closed and crosses her hands over her stomach. She exhales, feeling the final, fumbling rhythms of her body play out. And it is not a flash of white or a shot of dark. It is a passing through halls of color, which, she hopes, will never end.

At last, she is somewhere toward the beginning; not to be outdone by the big-breasted, wide-smiling, overtly sexual competitors in Norwalk County's Annual Junior Beauty Pageant, Irene Duffy, age sixteen, stuffs two plums in her bra and sings "Moon River" while standing uncomfortably erect. She is halfway through the song when she feels one of the plums release from the cup in her bra and travel down and out the chute of her gown. She stops singing and looks at the plum, which has rolled past her left foot and stopped in a small indentation in the stage. She can hear laughter, but when she dares to pass her eyes across the crowd, she sees her parents, mortified and stunned, and the judges looking at the plum as if it's the last breast in all the universe, and Eddie Prince with his eyes on her eyes, circling an extended finger as if winding up a spool, mouthing the words "keep going." She cannot remember the second verse of the song. So instead, she pops the other plum out of her dress and takes a bite. The audience erupts—no fakeness about this girl—and she regains enough confidence to pick up the other plum and toss it to Mr. Ockmann, the former mayor, long retired and recently widowed. Mr. Ockmann stands up and rubs the plum against his cheek, as playful an exhibition as he has ever given in all his years in the public spotlight. When the three finalists are announced, Irene is not one of them, nor does she think she deserves to be. But it is her plums that are remembered and immortalized in the history of Norwalk High.

THIRTY-TWO

Slowly, the summer slides into autumn. Locals return to the beaches with their dogs; the last of the fruits are sold or jarred; signs on the stores along Main Street read, SEE YOU AGAIN NEXT YEAR. Only the schools and the mall operate on a normal schedule. The rest of the people in town reduce their working hours, drink more often, return to gossiping about each other rather than complaining about tourists. On page 1 of the most curious locals' manifest is the fact that Nathan and Andrew Kelly are now living back home. Irene is sick, but her sickness is physical. Those boys, they have always seemed off. It was their father's doing. He left them right when they needed their father the most. Are you surprised? Don't you remember Kelly's own father, Red? You could hear him whaling on that poor boy all the way from Mulberry to Southbay. But Robert Kelly came back, too. Again? Again. When? Oh, six or seven months ago. Didn't you hear? I did, but I never thought he'd show his face in this town again. He had one of those home monitoring things around his ankle. Poor Irene. And those boys. Robert, too. Yes, him, too. He deserves some mercy. The Kellys. They're no different than any other family, I guess. They suffer under the weight of that name.

THIRTY-THREE

SINCE HIS MOTHER'S FUNERAL LAST WEEK, NATHAN HAS QUIT smoking and every morning runs along the beach, down past the Tidewater Hotel his father and brother had planned to open by Labor Day—Andrew going so far as to slide an official invitation under his bedroom door—but now has been postponed until the end of the month, due to their mother's death. Nathan has already decided he will not attend. That world is not his. He jogs the length of the beach, then up Southbay, until he reaches the Wequaquet Harbor. He sits in a coffee shop across from the harbor, watching the ferryboats shove off toward Nantucket. The tourists take day trips and return with luggage full of crap—T-shirts and coasters and painted seashells. Nothing is old or new. That's the problem with trying to escape, he thinks. There's no place for anyone anymore. Boston is no place; Baghdad is no place; San Diego, La Paz, Paris, Florence, Madrid, Las Vegas, Beijing, none of them truly exist.

Today, he finishes his coffee and puts a few dollars on the table for keeping the seat as long as he has, and walks down the harbor gate, toward the bulkhead, where the commercial fishing boats are docked, the hulls grimy, nets hanging limp, still dripping. Derek Coe, captain of the *Whisky Gun*, wears a baseball cap and has an auburn-colored beard. Nathan has been out with him before, a month back, for a quick shrimp haul. But he's heard Derek has gotten a contract to keep him out longer, bring them to different ports along the East Coast, and he asks if he can get a job on the boat. Derek says it's possible. Someone just backed out. He says he can't pay much.

"I don't need much," Nathan says.

The first day on the boat, Nathan empties his pills over the side. He begins each day at three in the morning with a series of stretches and a hundred push-ups and sit-ups. The physical exertion steals away the shakes from quitting the benzos cold turkey. He believes in something now. He believes he can begin again.

The work is hard and repetitive. Set the net, wait, close the net, wait. Hydraulics pull the net up and release the catch on the deck, sorting, and storing. He eats simply and spends his few hours alone reading by the stained lamp next to his bunk.

At port, he never leaves the ship. Some of the younger men think he's strange, and Derek says he might think about spending a night out in order to develop some camaraderie.

"It goes with the job," he says.

Down in the Keys, he hands Nathan a twenty-dollar bill and tells him to have a night.

The men like to go to a bar called Lacuna, where the well drinks are two for one. The locals there still respect fishermen and know their worth. The women are thick with round shoulders.

The men on the boat call Nathan Hero, or Big Hero, or Big H. Nathan can't tell if they're mocking him or not. They are strong, stupid men. They don't know what it means to go to war. They don't need to know. Nathan admires this about them. Most of the men are high school dropouts or pill heads or failed athletes. Some have grown up with only the boat and the sea. The ones who clean the deck and cabin are ex-cons, and they turn over at every port.

He pays for the first and second rounds and sits with a club soda at the bar while they drink at two wooden tables pushed together and play cards. Some of the men gather around the pool table and put quarters on the side and stare down the players until one scratches the eight ball on purpose.

"Hero," the one called Randy shouts. "You play?"

Nathan remembers what Derek has said about camaraderie.

"Cutthroat," Randy says.

The other player is a new guy. Nathan can't remember his name. He has oily hair and a mean, thin face.

Nathan takes up a pool cue and dusts the tip with the blue square and waits to see how the numbered balls spread out along the felt. He hasn't shot pool since the army, but it comes back to him the way most things do the first time you try your hand at a game you used to know well.

Nathan sinks all but one of the balls. The other men from the boat are by the table now. Randy's sitting on a stool drinking a long neck. He gives a hard clap. The new guy looks at Nathan, then at the table, then at Nathan again. He lines up his shot in the web of thumb and forefinger, but when he goes to strike the cue ball he barely hits it and the ball spins and nestles up against the side of the table. The other men burst out laughing and the new guy throws the stick on the ground and walks back to the table and sits with his arms crossed over his chest, sullen.

A few local girls tag along with the six men from the boat as they head back to port. One girl slaps Randy in the face when he takes his penis out to show it to them. Then the girls are gone and the men walk along the harbor, and some go down to the rocks on the shore, throwing their empty bottles into the sea.

Nathan sits on the hard sand and listens as the water touches the earth and pulls away. After a while, he can't hear the other men.

He understands how you need someone to protect you in this world or else you have nothing, and he thinks that must be the reason so many people believe in God or whatever, and why so many others are scared or crazy.

He feels now that he is everywhere the sea is, and this is his home, his purpose. But he is not without doubt, not tonight, having been out with the guys from the boat, drinking, shooting the shit, hearing stories about treacherous catches, nasty accidents where other men died, storms and sicknesses and seedy drifters. There is chaos everywhere. The goal, he thinks, is to survive the chaos.

As he pushes up off the beach, he hears a bottle break behind him. He turns and, in the swift final second of recognition, sees the jagged edges swing toward him. The blood pumps out of his neck and the new guy with his dead eyes is holding the end of the bottle. He looks at Nathan with a kind of disappointment, then turns and hurls the broken bottle into the ocean, before walking off, kicking up wet sand, the sound so familiar, so quiet, so peaceful.

THIRTY-FOUR

THE GRAND OPENING OF THE TIDEWATER HOTEL IS NOT WITHOUT its setbacks. First, it's been raining since early this morning, and the marble floor needs to be constantly attended to. Then there are issues with the catering service. They've forgotten the lobsters. What good is having a restaurant in a hotel on the Cape if there is no lobster on the menu? Luckily, the water has been unnaturally warm during September, and lobsters are cheap and readily available. In the few hours that are left, Andrew and the caterers empty out every fish house and supermarket within twenty miles, put the lobsters in a half-dozen tanks, and have the chefs boil them on an outdoor range away from the party. A group of kids have broken in through one of the windows in the east wing and ripped up the carpet and torn the television sets off the walls and drawn large, coming penises on some of the reproduced Monets. The entire wing is now closed off. Andrew's father has the idea to put up a sign that reads: RESERVED FOR PRIVATE PARTY.

"What private party?" Dennison asks when he arrives.

A dense fog has made it impossible for the Belgian's boat to dock at the harbor in time, but Dennison has showed up just late enough, with two young blond-haired women with skin the color of sand. Andrew and Dennison have met only once before, when Dennison came down from Boston to yell at whoever was laboring on the property. He reminds Andrew of the men at Birken's firm. Like them, and like Andrew not so long ago, Dennison thinks his money buys time, not work. He smokes thin, lady cigarettes and wears short, pink shorts and a navy blue polo. A diamond-encrusted bracelet around his right wrist matches his diamond-encrusted watch on his left. Most likely, Dennison had been ridiculed as a boy, and he is forever making those other boys pay.

"We had a setback," Andrew's father says. "Nothing to worry about, really. Everything will be running smoothly by next week."

"So there isn't a private party?"

Andrew notes that Dennison is half-cocked, and because he's very rich, he works now with the dangerous and damaging combination of power mixed with unchecked ignorance.

"No. There's no party," Andrew steps in. "But the west wing is sold out, and your suite is ready. We have an exciting tasting menu prepared once you get settled."

"Oh, my," Dennison says, looking back and forth at the two girls on his sides. "I'm so tingly I might just make a mess in my pants."

The two women fake a giggle, placating their rich host, whose tact Andrew can tell has completely unnerved his father.

A yachtsman wearing too much cologne lights himself on fire trying to get a match started for his cigar on the restaurant veranda; a child has to be given the Heimlich after swallowing a fat piece of overcooked steak; a seagull, having dived down through the sliding door left partly open to one of the rooms, sends an overweight couple running naked through the hall.

"This is what happens at hotels," Dennison says, bumping into the table where Andrew and his father sit quietly, nervously. "Life."

After dinner, the guests make their way to the lawn where fireworks are set off from the beach, lighting the sky in bursts of red, white, and blue. Andrew watches from the veranda, no longer worried about the night, because he is in it now, and the reporters in attendance will write what they want, and the guest reviews will start flooding the Internet before morning, and something else he cannot account for. He has to let it happen, let it come down, because Dennison is right, this is life.

Andrew walks down the long set of steps to the beach, then looks back at the hotel lit up in the floodlights and the people milling about on the lawn, and the flag curling in and extending out like a wave.

It's as though the Tidewater has been here forever. This is the place you are always returning to, even if you don't know it. He wonders where Nathan is right now, if he returned to Arizona or has ventured to some exotic locale, where no one can find him, and where he'll never be heard from again. Andrew hopes so. Nathan belongs out there, he thinks, with the odd and the infamous, a warrior, a loner, guided by a universe Andrew knows nothing about.

In a green dress and black top, sitting on the slope of a dune, a dark-haired woman, head turned slightly, gazes out at the calm waters, one hand under her chin, the other holding the stem of a champagne glass, the sandals she wore to the opening at her side and her toes buried in the sand.

"What are you thinking about?" Andrew asks her.

She turns the glass like a paper drum back and forth between her fingers.

"I don't know if I was thinking about anything, really. More like, I could see myself. Or, I mean, my past self. How pretty I was—or thought I was—how interesting everything around me seemed. All the questions I asked. The games I played. Pretending to be this or that."

"We had our own little worlds back then, didn't we?"

"Now everything is just average, *blah*. Eventually a slice of cheesecake tastes like dust, money feels like a weight, joy like a warning. Geez, listen to me."

Andrew has been listening. He feels in her words the same feeling he had the day of Birken's funeral, and even years before, when he and Nathan were kids and would run wild around the neighborhood, through hedges, climbing fences and hills and trees, always trying to top the other, to be king of some invented kingdom, and how it felt so deserved, and how nothing felt deserved anymore unless it carried with it a certain kind of risk, because risk had diminished over time, risk was calculated and avoided or else created and embellished to make it seem like the impossible was possible. No way would the hotel have been financed if there was too much risk involved. But the property had been appraised and construction costs prefigured and any kind of setback worked into the budget, and here they are now, celebrating.

Years later, when Andrew and Sara, the girl on the dune with the thick eyebrows, have married and moved into a small home on Block Island, they return to the Outer Cape, with their two daughters, to the beach beyond the Tidewater Hotel, and watch as the girls' eyes grow big and wide at the shimmering sand and giant waves and the other children jumping off the docks.

As in the old photographs he has kept, and his parents had

kept, the ocean is still the same, no matter how quickly and without warning the land surrounding them has changed and shifted. They play sharks and pirates and deep-sea divers. The games his father and brother had taught him. And everything Andrew had collected when he was a boy, he now gives away.

ACKNOWLEDGMENTS

First and foremost I would like to thank my family for their openness, love, and generosity of spirit.

Also, for their unconditional support over the years, I would like to thank Aaron Fagan, George Saunders, Max Diulus, Daniel Torday, Arthur Flowers, Chris Kennedy, Mary Gaitskill, Amanda Doyle, and Kevin MacConnell.

Special thanks to Sergeant First Class Phillip Jacoby.

This book would not have been possible without the guidance and support of my editors, Sarah Bowlin and Michael Signorelli, my agent, Claire Anderson-Wheeler, and the wonderful people at Henry Holt and Company.

Lastly, a note to my son, Colin Archer Dacey:

You are young now. But when you are older, and you come across this book, I want you to always know, despite what you may see, hear, or feel, there is love in the shadows.

ABOUT THE AUTHOR

PATRICK DACEY holds an MFA from Syracuse University. He has taught English at several universities in the United States and has worked as a reporter, landscaper and door-to-door salesman and at a homeless shelter and a detox center. He is the author of the story collection *We've Already Gone This Far*. His stories have been featured in *The Paris Review*, *Zoetrope: All-Story*, *Guernica*, *Bomb* magazine, *Salt Hill*, and more.